**L.T**

# The School Queens

# L.T Meade

# The School Queens

1st Edition | ISBN: 978-3-75241-307-6

Place of Publication: Frankfurt am Main, Germany

Year of Publication: 2020

Outlook Verlag GmbH, Germany.

# THE

# SCHOOL QUEENS

BY

L T. MEADE

# CHAPTER I

## THE FASCINATING MAGGIE

Cicely Cardew and her sister Merry were twins. At the time when this story opens they were between fifteen and sixteen years of age. They were bright, amiable, pretty young girls, who had never wanted for any pleasure or luxury during their lives. Their home was a happy one. Their parents were affectionate and lived solely for them. They were the only children, and were treated—as only children often are—with a considerable amount of attention. They were surrounded by all the appliances of wealth. They had ponies to ride and carriages to drive in, and each had her own luxurious and beautifully furnished bedroom.

It was Mr. Cardew's wish that his daughters should be educated at home. In consequence they were not sent to any school, but had daily masters and governesses to instruct them in the usual curriculum of knowledge. It might be truly said that for them the sun always shone, and that they were carefully guarded from the east wind. They were naturally bright and amiable. They had their share of good looks, without being quite beautiful. They had not the slightest knowledge of what the world meant, of what sorrow meant, or pain. They were brought up in such a sheltered way that it seemed to them that there were no storms in life. They were not discontented, for no one ever breathed the word in their presence. Their requests were reasonable, for they knew of no very big things to ask for. Even their books were carefully selected for them, and their amusements were of a mild and orderly character.

Such were the girls when this story opens on a bright day towards the end of a certain July. Their home was called Meredith Manor, and Merry was called after an old ancestor on their mother's side to whom the house had at one time belonged.

Mr. Cardew was a merchant-prince. Mrs. Cardew belonged to an old county family. If there was one thing in the world that Cicely and Merry thought nothing whatever about, it was money. They could understand neither poverty nor the absence of gold.

The little village near Meredith Manor was a model place, for Mr. Cardew, to whom it belonged, devoted himself absolutely to it. The houses were well drained and taken great care of. Prizes were offered for the best gardens; consequently each cottager vied with the other in producing the most lovely flowers and the most tempting fruits. The village consisted entirely of Mr. Cardew's laborers and the different servants on his estate. There were, therefore, no hardships for the girls to witness at Meredith village. They were fond of popping in and out of the cottages and talking to the young wives and mothers, and playing with the babies; and they particularly enjoyed that great annual day when Mr. Cardew threw open the grounds of Meredith to the entire neighborhood, and when games and fun and all sorts of amusements were the order of the hour.

Besides the people who lived in the village, there was, of course, the rector, who had a pretty, picturesque, old brown house, with a nice garden in one corner of the grounds. He had a good-natured, round-faced, happy wife, and a family of four stalwart sons and daughters. He was known as the Reverend William Tristram; and, as the living was in the gift of the Meredith family, he was a distant connection of Mrs. Cardew, and had been appointed by her husband to the living of Meredith at her request.

The only playfellows the girls had ever enjoyed were the young Tristrams. There were two boys and two girls. The boys were the younger, the girls the elder. The boys were not yet in their teens, but Molly and Isabel Tristram were about the same age as the young Cardews. Molly was, in fact, a year older, and was a very sympathetic, strong-minded, determined girl. She and her sister Isabel had not been educated at home, but had been sent to foreign schools both in France and Germany; and Molly, in her heart of hearts, rather looked down upon what she considered the meager attainments of the young Cardews and their want of knowledge of the world.

"It is ridiculous!" she was heard to say to Isabel on that very July morning when this story opens. "Of course they are nice girls, and would be splendid if they could do anything or knew what to do; but, as it is, they are nothing whatever but half-grown-up children, with no more idea of the world than has that baby-kitten disporting itself at the present moment on the lawn."

"Oh, they're right enough," said Isabel. "They will learn by-and-by. I don't suppose Mr. and Mrs. Cardew mean to keep them always shut up in a nutshell."

"I don't know," replied Molly. "Mr. and Mrs. Cardew are like no other people. I have heard father say that he thinks it a great pity that girls should be so terribly isolated."

"Well, as to that," replied Isabel, "I wouldn't be in their shoes for creation. I have so enjoyed my time at Hanover and in France; and now that we are to have two years at Aylmer House, in Kensington, I cannot tell you how I look forward to it."

"Yes, won't it be fine?" replied Molly. "But now we had better go up at once to Meredith Manor and ask the girls if we may bring Maggie Howland with us this afternoon. Father has sent the pony-trap to the station to meet her, and she may arrive any moment."

"All right," said Isabel; "but one of us had better stay at home to receive her. You, Molly, can run up to the Manor and ask the girls if we may bring our visitor."

"All right," replied Molly. Then she added "I wonder if Maggie is as fascinating as ever. Don't you remember, Belle, what a spell she cast over us at our school at Hanover? She was like no one else I ever met. She seems to do what she likes with people. I shall be deeply interested to know what she thinks of Cicely and Merry."

"Thinks of them!" replied Isabel. "It's my opinion she won't tolerate them for a minute; and we are bound to take her with us, for of course they will give permission."

"Well," said Molly, "I'll be off at once and secure that permission. You' look after Maggie—won't you, Isabel?—and see that her bedroom is all right." As Molly spoke she waved her hand to her sister, then departed on her errand.

She was a bright, fairly good-looking girl, with exceedingly handsome eyes and curling dark-brown hair. She was somewhat square in build and athletic in all her movements. In short, she was as great a contrast to the twin Cardew girls as could be found. Nevertheless she liked them, and was interested in them; for were not the Cardews the great people of the place? There was nothing of the snob about Molly; but it is difficult even for the most independent English girl to spend the greater part of her life in a village where one family reigns as sovereign without being more or less under its influence.

Mr. Tristram, too, was a very great friend of Mr. Cardew's; and Molly's fat, round, good-natured mother, although a little afraid of Mrs. Cardew, who was a very stately lady in her way, nevertheless held her in the greatest respect and admiration. It was one of the rules of the house of Tristram that no invitation sent to them from Meredith Manor should be refused. They must accept that invitation as though it were the command of a king.

The girls, brought up mostly at foreign schools, had in some ways wider ideas of life than had their parents. But even they were more or less influenced by the fact that the Cardews were the great people of the place.

The day was a very hot one; rather oppressive too, with thunder-clouds in the distance. But Molly was very strong, and did not feel the heat in the least. The distance from the rectory to the Manor was a little over a mile. In addition, it was all uphill. But when you passed the village—so exquisitely neat, such a model in its way—you found yourself entering a road shaded by overhanging

4

elm-trees. Here it was cool even on the hottest summer day. There were deep pine-woods at each side of the road, and the road itself had been cut right through a part of the forest, which belonged to the Meredith estate. After going uphill for nearly three-quarters of a mile you arrived at the handsome wrought-iron gates which led to the avenue that brought you to the great front door of Meredith Manor.

Molly often took this walk, but she generally did so in the company of her sister Isabel. Isabel's light chatter, her gay, infectious laughter, her merry manner, soothed the tedium of the road. To-day Molly was alone; but by no means on this account did she feel a sense of weariness; her mind was very busy. She was greatly excited at the thought of seeing Maggie Howland again. Maggie had made a remarkable impression on her. She made that impression on all her friends. Wherever she went she was a leader, and no one could quite discover where her special charm or magnetism lay; for she was decidedly plain, and not specially remarkable for cleverness—that is, she was not remarkable for what may be termed school-cleverness. She was indifferent to prizes, and was just as happy at the bottom of her form as at the top; but wherever she appeared girls clustered round her, and consulted her, and hung on her words; and to be Maggie Howland's friend was considered the greatest honor possible among the girls themselves at any school where she spent her time.

Maggie was the daughter of a widow who lived in London. Her father had died when she was a very little girl. He was a man of remarkable character. He had great strength of will and immense determination; and Maggie, his only child, took after him. She resembled him in appearance also, for he was very plain of face and rather ungainly of figure. Maggie's mother, on the other hand, was a delicate, pretty, blue-eyed woman, who could as little manage her headstrong young daughter as a lamb could manage a young lion. Mrs. Howland was intensely amiable. Maggie was very good to her mother, as she expressed it; and when she got that same mother to yield to all her wishes the mother thought that she was doing the right thing. She had a passionate love for her daughter, although she deplored her plain looks, and often told the girl to her face that she wished she had taken after her in personal appearance. Maggie used to smile when this was said, and then would go away to her own room and look at her queer, dark face, and rather small eyes, and determined mouth, and somewhat heavy jaw, and shake her head solemnly. She did not agree with her mother; she preferred being what she was. She liked best to take after her father.

It was Maggie Howland who had persuaded Mr. Tristram, during a brief visit which he had made to town at Christmas, to send his daughters to Aylmer

House. Maggie was fond of Molly and Isabel. With all her oddities, she had real affection, and one of her good qualities was that she really loved those whom she influenced.

Mr. Tristram went to see Mrs. Ward, the head-mistress of that most select establishment for young ladies at Kensington. Mrs. Ward was all that was delightful. She was a noble-minded woman of high aspirations, and her twenty young boarders were happy and bright and contented under her influence.

Maggie joined the school at Easter, and spent one term there, and was now coming on a visit to the rectory.

"I wonder what she will have to tell us! I wonder if she is as fascinating as ever!" thought Molly Tristram as she hurried her steps.

She had now reached that point in the avenue which gave a good view of the old Manor, with its castellated walls and its square towers at each end. The gardens were laid out in terraces after an old-world fashion. There was one terrace devoted to croquet, another to tennis. As Molly approached she saw Cicely and Merry playing a game of croquet rather languidly. They wore simple white frocks which just came down above their ankles, and had white washing-hats on their heads. Their thick, rather fair hair was worn in a plait down each young back, and was tied with a bunch of pale-blue ribbon at the end.

"Hello!" shouted Molly.

The girls flung down their rackets and ran joyfully to meet her.

"Oh, I am so glad you have come!" said Cicely. "It's much too hot to play tennis, and even croquet is more than we can manage. Are you going to stay and have lunch with us, Molly?"

"No," replied Molly; "I must go back immediately."

"Oh dear! I wish you would stay," continued Merry. "We could go and sit in the arbor, and you could tell us another fascinating story about that school of yours at Hanover."

"Yes, yes," said Cicely; "do stay—do, Molly! We want to hear a lot more about that remarkable girl Maggie Howland."

"I can't stay," said Molly in a semi-whisper; "but I tell you what, girls." She seized a hand of both as she spoke. "I have come with news."

"What?" "What?" asked the twins eagerly.

"There's very seldom much news going on here," said Cicely. "Not that we

6

mind—not a little bit; we're as happy as girls can be."

"Of course we are," said Merry. "We haven't a care in the world."

"All the same," said Cicely, "tell us your news, Molly, for you do look excited."

"Well," said Molly, who enjoyed the pleasure of giving her friends a piece of information which she knew would interest them intensely, "you know we are to come up here this afternoon to have tea and buns, aren't we?"

"Oh, don't talk in that way!" said Merry. "One would suppose you were school children, when you are our darling, dear friends."

"Our only friends," said Cicely. "You are the only girls in the world father allows us to be the least bit intimate with."

"Oh, well," said Molly, "of course Belle and I are very fond of you both, naturally."

"Naturally!" echoed Cicely. But then she added, "How queer you look, Molly, as though you were keeping something back!"

"Well, yes, I am," said Molly; "but I'll have it out in a minute."

"Oh, please, be quick!" said Merry. "Anything a little bit out of the common is very interesting.—Isn't it, Cicely?"

"Very," said Cicely; "more particularly in the holidays. When we are busy with our lessons things don't so much matter, you know.—But do be quick, Molly; what is it?"

"Well," said Molly, "you've asked us to spend the afternoon with you."

"Of course, and you're both coming, surely?"

"We are—certainly we are—that is, if you will allow us to bring"—

"To bring"—interrupted Cicely. "Oh Molly, do speak!"

"Well, I will; only, don't jump, you two girls. To bring Maggie Howland!"

Cicely's face grew very pink. Merry, on the contrary, turned a little pale. They were both silent for a brief space. Then Merry said excitedly, "Maggie Howland—*the* Maggie Howland?"

"Yes, *the* Maggie Howland; the one who has got the power, the charm, the fascination."

"Oh, oh!" said Cicely. "But why is she with you? How has it happened?"

"She is not absolutely with us yet; and as to how it happened I cannot exactly tell you. We had a telegram from her late last night asking if she might come to-day to spend a week or fortnight, and of course we wired back 'Yes.' We are delighted; but of course you may not like her, girls."

"Like her! like her!" said Cicely; "and after all you have said too! We shall be certain to more than like her."

"She's not a bit pretty, so don't expect it," said Molly.

"We were brought up," said Merry a little stiffly, "not to regard looks as anything at all."

"Nonsense!" replied Molly. "Looks mean a great deal. I'd give I don't know what to be beautiful; but as I am not I don't mean to fret about it. Well, Maggie's downright plain; in fact—in fact—almost ugly, I may say; and yet —and yet, she is just Maggie; and you are not five minutes in her society before you'd rather have her face than any other face in the world. But the immediate question is: may she come this afternoon, or may she not?"

"Of course—of course she may come," said Cicely; "we'll be delighted, we'll be charmed to see her. This *is* pleasant news!"

"I think, perhaps," said Merry, "we ought to go and ask mother. Don't you think so, Cis?"

"Of course we ought," said Cicely. "I forgot that. Just stay where you are, Molly, and I'll run to the house and find mother. It's only to ask her, for of course she will give leave."

Cicely ran off at once, and Merry and Molly were left alone.

"I know you'll be delighted with her," said Molly.

"It will be very delightful to see her," replied Merry.

"You must expect to be disappointed at first, all the same," continued Molly.

"Oh, looks do not matter one scrap," said Merry.

"Isabel and I are going to her school; you know that, don't you, Merry?"

"Yes," said Merry with a sigh. "What fun you do have at your different schools! Don't you, Molly?"

"Well, yes," said Molly rather gravely; "but it isn't only the fun; we see a lot of the world, and we mix with other girls and make friends."

"Mother prefers a home education for us, and so does father," remarked Merry. "Ah! here comes Cicely. She is flying down the terrace. Of course mother is delighted."

This proved to be the case. Mrs. Cardew would welcome any girl introduced to her daughters through her dear friend Mr. Tristram. She sent a further invitation for the three young people to remain to an impromptu supper, which was pleasanter than late dinner in such hot weather, and asked if Mr. and Mrs. Tristram would join them at the meal.

"Hurrah!" cried Molly. "That will be fun! I must be off now, girls. We'll be with you, all three of us, between four and five o'clock."

# CHAPTER II.

## SPOT-EAR.

Isabel took great pains arranging Maggie Rowland's bedroom. At the Castle (or Manor) there were always troops of servants for every imaginable thing; but at the rectory the servants were few, and the girls did a good many odds and ends of work themselves. They were expected to dust and keep in perfect order their exceedingly pretty bedrooms, they were further required to make their own beds, and if a young visitor arrived, they were obliged to wait on her and see to her comfort. For the Tristrams had just an income sufficient to cover their expenses, with nothing at all to put by. Mr. Tristram had his two little boys to think of as well as his two girls. His intention was to give his children the best education possible, believing that such a gift was far more valuable to them than mere money. By-and-by, when they were old enough, the girls might earn their own living if they felt so inclined, and each girl might become a specialist in her way.

Molly was exceedingly fond of music, and wished to excel in that particular. Isabel, on the contrary, was anxious to obtain a post as gymnasium teacher with the London County Council. But all these things were for the future. At present the girls were to study, were to acquire knowledge, were to be prepared for that three-fold battle which includes body, soul, and spirit, and which needs triple armor in the fight.

Mr. Tristram was a man of high religious principles. He taught his children to love the good and refuse the evil. He wanted his girls to be useful women by-and-by in the world. He put usefulness before happiness, assuring his children that if they followed the one they would secure the other.

Belle, therefore, felt quite at home now as she took out pretty mats and laid them on little tables in the neat spare room which had been arranged for the reception of Maggie Howland. She saw that all the appointments of the room were as perfect as simplicity and cleanliness could effect, and then went out into the summer garden to pick some choice, sweet-smelling flowers. She selected roses and carnations, and, bringing them in, arranged them in vases in the room.

Hearing the sound of wheels, she flew eagerly downstairs and met her friend as she stepped out of the little governess-cart.

"Well, here I am!" said Maggie. "And how is Belle? How good-natured of you all to have me, and how delightful it is to smell the delicious country air! Mother and I find town so hot and stuffy. I haven't brought a great lot of luggage, and I am not a bit smart; but you won't mind that—will you, dear old Belle?"

"You always talk about not being smart, Maggie; but you manage to look smarter than anyone else," said Isabel, her eager brown eyes devouring her friend's appearance with much curiosity. For Maggie looked, to use a proverbial phrase, as if she had stepped out of a bandbox. If she was plain of face she had an exceedingly neat figure, and there was a fashionable, trim look about her which is uncommon in a girl of her age; for Maggie was only just sixteen, and scarcely looked as much. In some ways she might almost have been a French girl, so exceedingly neat and *comme il faut* was her little person. She was built on a *petite* scale, and although her face was so plain, she had lovely hands and beautiful small feet. These feet were always shod in the most correct style, and she took care of her hands, never allowing them to get red or sunburnt.

"Where's Molly?" was her remark, as the two girls, with their arms twined round each other, entered the wide, low hall which was one of the special features of the old rectory.

"She has gone up to see the Cardews."

"Who are the Cardews?"

"Why, surely, Mags, you must have heard of them?"

"You don't mean," said Maggie with a laugh, and showing a gleam of strong white teeth, "the two little ladies who live in a bandbox?"

"Oh, you really must not laugh at them," said Isabel, immediately on the defensive for her friends; "but they do lead a somewhat exclusive life. Molly has gone up to the Castle, as we always call Meredith Manor, to announce your arrival, and to ask permission to bring you there to a tennis-party this afternoon; so you will soon see them for yourself. Now, come in and say good-morning to the mater; she is longing to see you."

"Hello, Peterkins!" called out Maggie at that moment, as a small boy with a smut across his face suddenly peeped round a door.

"I'm not Peterkins!" he said angrily.

Maggie laughed again. "I am going to call you Peterkins," she said. "Is this one of the little brothers, Belle?"

"Yes.—Come here at once, Andrew, and speak to Miss Howland."

The boy approached shyly. Then his eyes looked up into the queer face of the girl who looked down at him. The sulkiness cleared away from his brow, and he said, in an eager, hurried, half-shy, half-confidential way, "I say, do you

11

like rabbits?"

"Dote on 'em," said Maggie.

"Then I'm your man, and I don't mind being Peterkins to you; and will you—will you come and see mine? I've got Spot-ear, and Dove, and Angelus, and Clover. And Jack, he has five rabbits, but they're not near as nice as mine. You'll come and see my rabbits, won't you, Miss—Miss—"

"Oh, I am Maggie," said the girl. "I'll come and see your rabbits, Peterkins, in a minute; and I won't look at Jack's; but you must let me talk to your mother first."

"There you are, Maggie," said Belle when the boy had disappeared; "fascinating Andrew in your usual way; and Jack will be just furious, for he's the elder, you know, and he has a temper, and you mustn't set one of them against the other—promise you won't."

"Trust me," said Maggie. "Peterkins is a nice little fellow, and I'll manage Jackdaw too."

"You don't mean to say you'll call them by those names?"

"Yes, yes. I always have my own way with people, as you know."

"Indeed I do. Oh, come along, you queer creature. Here's the darling mums. Mater dearest, here is Maggie Howland."

"Delighted to see you, my dear," said Mrs. Tristram. "I hope you are not tired after your journey from town."

"Not in the least, thank you, Mrs. Tristram," said Maggie, speaking in a voice of very peculiar quality; it was sweet and rich and full of many intonations. She had the power of putting a world of meaning into the most commonplace expressions.

Mrs. Tristram had not seen Maggie before, and it was Mr. Tristram who had been completely bowled over by the young lady just at Christmas-time.

"I bid you a hearty welcome to the rectory," said the good clergyman's wife, "and I hope you will have a pleasant time with my children."

"I'll have a fascinating time," said Maggie. "I'm just too delighted to come. It was sweet of you to have me; and may I, please, give you a kiss?"

"Of course you may, dear child," said Mrs. Tristram.

Maggie bestowed the kiss, and immediately afterward was conducted to her room by the worshiping Belle.

"I do hope you'll like it," said Belle in an almost timorous voice. "I prepared it for you myself."

"Why, it's sweet," said Maggie, "and so full of the country! Oh, I say, what roses! And those carnations—Malmaisons, aren't they? I must wear a couple in this brown holland frock; they'll tone with it perfectly. What a delicious smell!"

Maggie sniffed at the roses. Belle lounged on the window-seat.

"Molly will be jealous," she said. "Think of my having you these few moments all to myself!"

"I am delighted to come, as you know quite well," replied Maggie. "It's all right about school, isn't it, Belle?"

"Yes, quite, quite right. We are to join you there in September."

"It's a perfectly splendid place," said Maggie. "I will describe it to you later on."

"But can it be nicer," said Belle, "than our darling school at Hanover?"

"Nicer!" exclaimed Maggie. "You couldn't compare the two places. I tell you it's perfect. The girls—well, they're aristocratic; they're girls of the Upper Ten. It's the most select school. You are in luck to be admitted, I can tell you. You will learn a lot about society when you are a member of Mrs. Ward's school."

"But what possible good will that do us when we are never going into it?" said Belle.

Maggie slightly narrowed her already narrow eyes, took off her hat, and combed back her crisp, dark hair from her low, full, very broad forehead. Then she said, with a smile, "You are to stay two years at Mrs. Ward's, are you not?"

"Yes, I think that is the arrangement."

"And I am to stay there for two years," said Maggie; "I mean two more. I will ask you, Isabel Tristram, what good society is worth at the end of your two years. I expect you will tell me a very different story then."

At this moment there came a hurried, nervous, excited knock at the room door.

"Aren't you coming, Miss—Miss—Maggie? Clover and Dove and Spot-ear and Angelus are all waiting. Their hutch is beautiful and clean, and I have all their lettuces waiting for them just outside, so they sha'n't begin to nibble till you come. Do, do come, please, Miss Maggie."

"Of course I will, my darling Peterkins," replied Maggie in her joyful voice. "Oh, this is—this is—this *is* fun!—Come along, Belle; come along."

"But don't let poor Jack get into a temper," said Isabel in a half-frightened whisper.

Maggie took no notice of her. She opened the bedroom door and flew downstairs, holding the dirty, hot little hand of Andrew, *alias* Peterkins, while Isabel followed in their wake.

In a far-away part of the rectory garden, on a bit of waste land at the other side of the great vegetable garden, were two hutches which stood side by side, and these hutches contained those most adorable creatures, the pets, the darlings of the Tristram boys.

The Tristram boys were aged eleven and ten years respectively. Jack was eleven, Andrew ten. They were very sturdy, healthy, fine little fellows. At present they went to a good day-school in the neighborhood, but were to be sent to a boarding-school about the same time as their sisters were to begin their education at Aylmer House in Kensington. Their passion above all things was for pets. They had tried every sort: white mice (these somehow or other were sacrificed to the reigning cat) and waltzing mice (that shared an equally luckless fate); these were followed by white rats, which got into the garden and did mischief, and were banished by order of the rector, who was a most determined master in his own house. Dogs were also forbidden, except one very intelligent Airedale, that belonged to the whole family and to no one in particular. But the boys must find vent for their passion in some way, and rabbits were allowed them. At the present moment Jack owned five, Andrew four.

In trembling triumph, Andrew brought his new friend to see his darlings. He greatly hoped that Jack would not appear on the scene just now. While Maggie was up in her bedroom taking off, her hat, he had, with herculean strength, managed to move an old wooden door and put it in such a position that Jack's hutch was completely hidden, while his hutch shone forth in all its glory, with those fascinating creatures Spot-ear, Angelus, Dove, and Clover looking through their prison-bars at the tempting meal that awaited them.

"Here they are! here they are!" said Andrew. "Beauties, all four; my own—my very own! Maggie, you may share one of them with me while you are here. He must live in his hutch, but he shall be yours and mine. Would you like Spot-ear? He is a character. He's the finest old cove you ever came across in your life. Look at him now, pretending he doesn't care anything at all for his lettuce, and he's just dying for it. Clover is the greedy one. Clover would eat till he burst if I let him. As to Angelus, she squeaks sometimes—you'll

14

hear her if you listen hard—that's why I called her Angelus; and Dove—why, she's a dear pet; but the character of all is Spot-ear. You'd like to share him with me, wouldn't you, Maggie?"

"Yes, yes; he is so ugly; he is quite interesting," said Maggie. She flung herself on the ground by the side of the hutch, and gazed in at the occupants as though her only aim in life was to worship rabbits.

"You take that leaf of lettuce and give it to Spot-ear your very own self," said Peterkins. "He'll love you ever after; he's a most affectionate old fellow."

Maggie proceeded to feed the rabbit. Peterkins hopped about in a state of excitement which he had seldom experienced before. Maggie asked innumerable questions. Belle seated herself on the fallen trunk of an old oak-tree and looked on in wonder.

Maggie was a curious girl. She seemed to have a power over every one. There was Andrew—such a shy little fellow as a rule—simply pouring out his heart to her.

Suddenly Belle rose. "It's time for lunch," she said, "and you must be hungry. Andrew, go straight to the house and wash your face and hands. No lady would sit down to lunch with such a dirty boy as you are."

"Oh, I say, am I?" said Andrew. "Do you think so, Maggie?"

"You are a most disreputable-looking little scamp," said Maggie.

"Then I won't be—I won't, most truly. I'll run off at once and get clean, and I'll get into my Sunday best if you wish it."

"Dear me, no!" said Maggie; "I don't wish it. But clean hands and face—well, they are essential to the ordinary British boy, if he's a gentleman."

"I am your gentleman—for evermore," said Andrew.

"I think you are, Peterkins."

"Then I'm off to clean up," said the small boy.

"I say, Andrew," cried his sister; "before you go take that door away from Jack's hutch. He'll be so furious at your keeping the light and air away from his rabbits."

"Not I. I can't be bothered," said Peterkins.

"Please take it away at once," said Maggie.

Andrew's brow puckered into a frown.

"But you'll see 'em, and he's got five!" he said in a most distressed voice.

"Honor bright," said Maggie, "I'll turn my back and shut my eyes. Jackdaw shall show me his rabbits himself."

Peterkins immediately removed the door, dragging it to its former place, where it leaned against a high wall. He then rushed up to Maggie.

"I've done it," he said. "Promise you won't like his bunnies."

"Can't," said Maggie, "for I'll love 'em."

"Well, at least promise you won't love him."

"Can't," said Maggie again, "for I shall."

"I'll die of raging jealousy," said Peterkins.

"No, you won't, you silly boy. Get off to the house and make yourself tidy. Come along, Belle."

"I say, Maggie," said Belle, "you mustn't set those two boys by the ears. They're fond enough of each other."

"Of course I'll do nothing of the kind," said Maggie. "That's a charming little chap, and Spot-ear is my rabbit as well as his. Jackdaw shall share two of his rabbits with me. Oh, it is such fun turning people round your little finger!"

Just then Molly, rather red in the face, ran up.

"Oh, you darling, darling Maggie!" she said. "So you've come!"

"Come!" cried Maggie. "I feel as if I'd been here for ever."

"I am delighted to see you," said Molly.

She kissed her friend rapturously. Maggie presented a cool, firm, round cheek.

"Oh, how sweet you look, Mags!"

"Don't talk nonsense, Molly; I'm not a bit sweet-looking."

"To me," said Molly with fervor, "You're the loveliest girl in all the wide world."

"I'm very ugly, and you know that perfectly well," said Maggie; "but now don't let's talk of looks."

"Whatever were you doing in this part of the garden?" inquired Molly.

"Oh, she was making love to Andrew," remarked Belle. "She calls him Peterkins, and he allows it, and he has given her one-half of Spot-ear; and she means to make love to Jack, and he's to give her a couple of his rabbits—I mean, to share them with her. She's more extraordinary than ever, more altogether out of the common."

"As if I didn't know that," said Molly. "It's all right about this afternoon, Maggie. Oh, what do you think? We're to stay to supper, and I have a special invitation for father and mother to come and join us then. Won't it be fun! I do wonder, Maggie, if you will like the Cardew girls."

"Probably not," replied Maggie in a very calm voice; "but at least I can promise you one thing: they'll both like me."

"No doubt whatever on that point," replied Belle with fervor.

They entered the house, and soon found themselves seated round the table. Mr. Tristram greeted Maggie with his usual gentle dignity. Molly delivered herself of her message from the Castle. Mr. and Mrs. Tristram said that they would be delighted to join the Cardews at supper.

The meal was proceeding cheerfully, and Maggie was entertaining her host and hostess by just those pleasant little pieces of information which an exceedingly well-bred girl can impart without apparently intending to do so, when a shy and very clean little figure glided into the room, a pair of bright-brown eyes looked fixedly at Maggie, and then glared defiance at Belle, who happened to be seated near that adorable young person.

Peterkins was making up his mind that in future that coveted seat should be his—for he and Maggie could talk in whispers during the meal about Spot-ear, Angelus, and the rest—when his father said, "Sit down, my boy; take your place at once. You are rather late."

The boy slipped into his seat.

"I am glad to see you looking so tidy, Andrew," said his mother approvingly.

Andrew looked across at Maggie. Maggie did not once glance at him. She was talking in her gentle, lady-like tone to the rector.

Presently another boy came in, bigger and broader than Andrew.

Andrew said in a raised voice, "Here's Jack, and his hands aren't a bit clean."

"Hush!" said the rector.

Jack flushed and looked defiantly at Maggie.

Maggie raised her eyes and gave him a sweet glance. "Are you really Jack?" she said. "I am so glad to know you. I have been making friends with your brother Andrew, whom I call Peterkins. I want to call you Jackdaw. May I?"

Jack felt a great lump in his throat. His face was scarlet. He felt unable to speak, but he nodded.

"I have been looking at Peterkins's rabbits," continued Maggie. "I want to see yours after lunch."

"They're beauties!" burst from Jack. "They're ever so many times better than Andrew's. I've got a cream-colored Angora. His name is Fanciful, and I've got—"

"Hush, my boy, hush!" said the rector. "Not so much talking during meals. Well, Maggie, my dear—we must, of course, call you by your Christian name—"

"Of course, Mr. Tristram; I should indeed feel strange if you didn't."

"We are delighted to see you," continued the rector, "and you must tell the girls all about your new school."

"And you too, sir," said Maggie, in her soft, rich voice. "Oh! you'll be delighted—delighted; there never was such a woman as Mrs. Ward."

"I took a very great liking to her," said the rector. "I think my girls fortunate to be placed under her care. She has been good, very good and kind, to me and mine."

"I wonder what he means by that," thought Maggie; but she made no remark aloud.

# CHAPTER III.

## LADY LYSLE.

At about a quarter to four that same afternoon three girls prepared to walk over to Meredith Manor. It was for such golden opportunities that Molly and Isabel kept their best frocks; it was for just such occasions that they arrayed themselves most neatly and becomingly. Their dress, it must be owned, was limited in quantity and also in quality; but on the present occasion, in their pretty white spotted muslins, with pale-blue sashes round their waists and white muslin hats to match, they looked as charming a young pair of English girls as could be found in the length and breadth of the land. It is true their feet were not nearly as perfectly shod as Maggie's, nor were their gloves quite so immaculate; but then they were going to play tennis, and shoes and gloves did not greatly matter in the country. Maggie thought otherwise. Her tan tennis-shoes exactly toned with her neatly fitting brown holland dress. The little hat she wore on her head was made of brown straw trimmed very simply with ribbon; it was an ugly hat, but on Maggie's head it seemed to complete her dress, to be a part of her, so that no one noticed in the least what she wore except that she looked all right.

Two boys with worshiping eyes watched the trio as they stepped down the rectory avenue and disappeared from view. Two boys fought a little afterward, but made it up again, and then lay on the grass side by side and discussed Maggie, pulling her to pieces in one sense, but adoring her all the same.

Meanwhile the girls themselves chatted as girls will when the heart is light and there is no care anywhere. It was very hot, even hotter than it had been in the morning; but when they reached the road shaded so beautifully by the elm-trees they found a delicious breeze which fanned their faces. Somehow, Maggie never seemed to suffer from weather at all. She was never too cold; she was never too hot; she was never ill; no one had ever heard her complain of ache or pain. She was always joyous, except when she was sympathizing with somebody else's sorrow, and then her sympathy was detached—that is, it did not make her personally sad, although it affected and helped the person who was the recipient of it to a most remarkable extent. One of Maggie's great attractions was her absolute health, her undiminished strength, the fact that she could endure almost any exertion without showing a trace of fatigue.

Molly and Isabel were also strong, hearty, well-made girls, and the excitement of this expedition caused them to chatter more volubly than usual. Maggie had a good deal to tell them with regard to the new school, and they had a great deal to tell her with regard to the Cardews.

19

Just as they were entering the avenue Maggie turned and faced her two companions. "May I say something?" she asked eagerly.

"Why, of course, Mags," said Molly.

"Well, it's this: from what you told me of your friends, they must be the most profoundly uninteresting girls."

"Oh no, indeed they are not!" said Isabel stanchly. "Merry has a great deal in her, and Cicely is so nice-looking! We think she will be beautiful by-and-by; but Merry undoubtedly has the most character. Then there is something dignified and aristocratic about them, and yet they are not really proud, although they might be, for they are so rich, and Meredith Manor is such a wonderful old house."

"Didn't you tell me," said Maggie, "that Meredith Manor belonged to Mrs. Cardew?"

"Did I?" said Isabel, coloring in some confusion. "I am sure I don't know; I don't remember saying it. I don't think Mrs. Cardew is the sort of woman who would call anything hers apart from her husband. She is devoted to him, and no wonder, for he is quite charming. He is nearly as charming as father, and that's saying a great deal."

"Do let's come on. We'll be late!" said Molly impatiently.

"No, not quite yet, please," said Maggie. "I want to understand the position. Mrs. Cardew was a Miss Meredith?"

"Yes, dear Maggie; but what does that matter?"

"And," continued Maggie, "she was the heiress of Meredith Manor?"

"I suppose so. Father can tell you exactly."

"Oh, I don't want to question him, but I want to get my bearings. On the mother's side, the Cardew girls belong to the country. Isn't that so?"

"Yes, yes, yes. Do come on."

"But their father," continued Maggie, "he is in trade, isn't he?"

"He's a perfect gentleman," said Isabel stoutly; "no one looks down on trade in these days."

"Of course not. I adore trade myself," said Maggie. She now proceeded to walk very slowly up the avenue. She was evidently thinking hard. After a time she said, "I mean to get those girls to come to school with you, Molly, and with you, Isabel, in September."

Both the Tristrams burst into a peal of merry laughter. "Oh Mags!" they cried, "we never did think before that you were conceited. You certainly overrate even your powers when you imagine that you will get Mr. Cardew to change his mind."

"What do you mean by his changing his mind?"

"Why, this," said Belle. "He has set his face from the very first against his girls leaving home. He wishes them to have a home education, and that alone."

"Oh, that is all right," said Maggie cheerfully. "Well, what will you bet, girls, that I have my way?"

"We don't want you to lose, Maggie; but you certainly will not get your way in this particular."

"Well, now, I am going to be generous. I am not rich; but I have got two gold bracelets at home, and I will give one to each of you for your very own if I succeed in bringing Cicely and Merry Cardew to Mrs. Ward's school."

"Oh! oh!" exclaimed both the Tristram girls.

"You'll get your bracelets," said Maggie in a most confident tone, "and I can assure you they are beauties; my darling father brought them from India years and years ago. He brought a lot of jewels for mother and me, and I will get the bracelets for you—one each—if I succeed; but you must allow me to manage things my own way."

"But you won't do anything—anything—to upset the Cardews?" said Isabel.

"Upset them!" said Maggie. "Well, yes, I do mean to upset them. I mean to alter their lives; I mean to turn things topsyturvy for them; but I'll manage it in such a fashion that neither you, nor Molly, nor your father, nor your mother, nor anyone will suspect how I have got my way, but get it I will. I thought I'd tell you, that's all. You'd like to have them at school with you, wouldn't you?"

"Oh yes, very much indeed," said Molly.

"I am not so sure," said Isabel. "It's rather fun coming back to the rectory in the holidays and telling the Cardew girls all about what we do and how we spend our time. There'll be nothing to tell them if we all go to the same school."

"Well," said Maggie, "I don't agree with you. I expect, on the contrary, you'll find a vast lot more to talk about. But come, let's hurry now; I want to be introduced to them, for I have no time to lose."

Neither Isabel nor Molly could quite make out why they felt a certain depression after Maggie Howland had explained her views. The thought of the possible possession of the bracelets did not greatly elate them. Besides, there was not the most remote chance of even such a fascinating young person as Maggie succeeding in her project. She would meet her match, if not in Mrs. Cardew, then in Mr. Cardew. There was no doubt whatever on that point. But they greatly wished she would not try. They did not want her to upset the placid existence of their young friends. The girls who lived at the Castle, the girls who pursued their sheltered, happy, refined life, were in a manner mysterious and remote to the young Tristrams, and they thought that they would not love them any more if they were brought into closer contact with them.

A turn in the avenue now brought the old manor-house into view. Some friends of Mrs. Cardew's had arrived, but there were no other young people to be seen. Cicely and Merry were standing talking to a lady of middle age who had come to pay an afternoon call, when Cicely found herself changing color and glancing eagerly at Merry.

"Oh, will you excuse me?" she said in her pretty, refined voice. "Our special friends the Tristrams, the rector's daughters, and a friend of theirs, a Miss Howland, are coming up the avenue."

"Certainly, my dear," said Lady Lysle; and Cicely and Merry were off down the avenue like arrows from the bow to meet their friends.

Lady Lysle watched the two girls, and then turned to speak to Mrs. Cardew.

"What name was that I heard Cicely say?" was her remark. "Of course I know the Tristrams, but who was the girl who was with them?"

"A special friend of theirs, a Miss Howland. She has been their school companion abroad. She is staying with them at the rectory. Why, what is the matter, Lady Lysle? Do you know anything about her?"

"I don't know her," said Lady Lysle, "but I know a little bit about her mother. I should not have supposed the Tristram girls and Miss Howland were in the same set."

"Why, what is wrong?" said Mrs. Cardew, who was exceedingly particular as regarded the people whom her daughters knew.

"Oh, nothing, nothing," said Lady Lysle. "I happen not particularly to like Mrs. Howland; but doubtless I am prejudiced."

She turned to talk to a neighbor, and by this time the five girls had met. There was an eager interchange of greetings, and then Maggie found herself walking up the avenue by Merry's side, while Cicely found a place between the two

Tristram girls.

"I am so glad you've come!" said Merry in her gentle, polite voice.

"It is kind of you to ask me," replied Maggie. "Do you know," she added, turning and fixing her curious eyes on her companion's face, "that I am one of those poor girls who have never seen a beautiful house like yours before."

"I am so glad you like our house," said Merry; "but you haven't seen it yet."

"I am looking at it now. So this is what I am accustomed to hear spoken of as one of the 'Homes of England'?"

"It certainly is a home," said Merry, "and an old one, too. Parts of the Manor have been centuries in existence, but some parts, of course, are comparatively new."

"Will you take me all over it, Miss Cardew?" asked Maggie.

"Indeed, I shall be delighted; but you must come another day for that, for we want to make up some sets of tennis without any delay. We have all our afternoon planned out. There are three or four young people who may arrive any moment, so that we shall be able to make two good sets."

"How wonderful it all is!" said Maggie, who kept on looking at the house with ever-increasing admiration, and did not seem particularly keen about tennis.

"Don't you like tennis, Miss—Miss Howland?" said Merry.

"Oh yes," replied Maggie after a pause; "but then I think," she added, after yet another pause, "that I like every nice thing in all the world."

"How delightful that must be!" said Merry, becoming more and more attracted by Maggie each moment. "And you know a lot, too, don't you? For you have seen so much of the world."

"I know very little," replied Maggie; "and as to having seen the world, that is to come. I am quite young, you know—only just sixteen."

"But Isabel and Molly told me that you knew more than any other girl of their acquaintance."

Maggie gave a cheerful laugh, and said, "You mustn't mind what they say, poor darlings! The fact is, they're fond of me, and they magnify my knowledge; but in reality it doesn't exist. Only, I must tell you, Miss Cardew, I mean to see everything, and to know everything. I mean to have a glorious future."

The enthusiasm in the charming voice was also seen, to shine through those queer, narrow eyes. Merry felt her heart beat. "I am going to tell you something in return," she said, speaking, for a wonder, without diffidence, for she was naturally very shy and retiring. "I wish with all my heart that I could live a glorious life such as you describe."

"And surely you can?" said Maggie.

"No, I must be satisfied with a very quiet life. But we won't talk of it now. I am really very happy. I should consider myself a most wicked, discontented girl were I anything else. And, please, may I take you to see mother?"

Merry brought up her new friend to introduce her to Mrs. Cardew, who for the first moment, remembering what Lady Lysle had said, was a trifle stiff to Maggie Howland, but two minutes afterward was chatting to her in a pleasant and very friendly manner. She even went the length of personally introducing Maggie to Lady Lysle, excusing herself for the act by saying that Lady Lysle knew her mother.

Maggie also succeeded in charming Lady Lysle, who said to Mrs. Cardew afterward, "I am glad you have introduced the girl to me. She is not in the least like her commonplace, affected mother. She seems a very good sort, and I like plain girls."

"But is she plain?" said Mrs. Cardew in some astonishment. "Do you know, I never noticed it."

Lady Lysle laughed. "You never noticed how remarkably plain that girl is, my dear friend?" she said.

"To be frank with you," said Mrs. Cardew, "I didn't think of her face at all. She has a pretty manner and a nice, sensible, agreeable way of talking. I do not think my girls can suffer injury from her."

"They seem to like her, at any rate," said Lady Lysle, looking significantly as she spoke at the distant part of the grounds, where Maggie, with Cicely at one side of her and Merry at the other, was talking eagerly. "Oh yes, she seems a nice child," continued the great lady, "and it would be unfair to judge a girl because her mother is not to one's taste."

"But is there anything really objectionable in the mother?" asked Mrs. Cardew.

"Nothing whatsoever, except that she is pushing, vulgar, and shallow. I am under the impression that the Howlands are exceedingly poor. Of course they are not to be blamed for that, but how the mother can manage to send the girl to expensive schools puzzles me."

"Ah, well," said Mrs. Gardew in her gentle voice, "the child is evidently very

24

different from her mother, and I must respect the mother for doing her best to get her girl well educated."

"Your girls are not going to school, are they, Sylvia?" asked Lady Lysle.

"Mine? Of course not. Their father wouldn't hear of it."

"On the whole, I think he is right," said Lady Lysle, "though there are advantages in schools. Now, that school at Kensington, Aylmer House, which my dear friend Mrs. Ward conducts with such skill and marvelous dexterity, is a place where any girl might receive advantages."

"Is it possible," said Mrs. Cardew, "that Mrs. Ward is your friend?"

"My very great friend, dear. I have known her all my life. Aylmer House is particularly select. My niece Aneta is at the school, and her mother is charmed with it."

"But that is very strange," said Mrs. Gardew after a pause. "You must talk to-night to our rector when he comes. Oh yes, of course you'll stay to supper."

"I cannot, I regret to say."

"Well, then, if you won't, there's no use in pressing you. But I have something curious to say. The rector's two little girls are going to Aylmer House in September, and that little Miss Howland whom I just introduced to you is also one of the girls under Mrs. Ward's care."

"Then she will do well," said Lady Lysle alter a pause, during which her face looked very thoughtful.

"I wonder if she knows your niece," said Mrs. Cardew.

Lady Lysle laughed. "I presume she does. The school only contains twenty boarders—never any more. I happen to know that there are two vacancies at the present moment. Really, if I were you, Sylvia, I would give your girls a couple of years there. It would do them a world of good, and they would acquire some slight knowledge of the world before they enter it."

"Impossible! quite impossible!" said Mrs. Cardew; "their father would never consent."

# CHAPTER IV.

## POWER WAS EVERYTHING TO MAGGIE.

Meanwhile the young people enjoyed themselves vastly. Maggie was very modest with regard to her tennis, but she quickly proved that she could play better than any one else at the Manor that day. The visitors walking about the grounds paused to remark on her excellent play and to inquire who she was. She took her little triumph very modestly, saying that she was rather surprised at herself, and supposed that it was the fresh and delicious air of the country which had put her into such good form.

"She is ridiculously overmodest," said Isabel Tristram to Merry, "for she always did play every sort of game better than the rest of us. She is not quite so good at her books; except, indeed, at certain things, such as recitation. I wish you could see and hear her then. She is almost a genius. She looks like one inspired."

"I think her quite delightful," said Merry; "and as to being plain—"

"I told you, didn't I?" said Belle, "that you'd never notice her looks after you had seen her for a minute or two."

By-and-by it was time for the family to go into the house for supper at Meredith Manor. The three girls from the rectory were taken upstairs, to a spacious bedroom to wash their hands and brush their hair. Molly and Isabel were both most anxious to know what Maggie thought of Cicely and Merry.

"What I think of them?" said Maggie. "Oh, they're first-rate, and not really dull at all; and the whole place is lovely, and all the people I met to-day were so nice, except, indeed, that Lady Lysle."

"Lady Lysle!" exclaimed Molly in a tone of astonishment. "Why, she is Mrs. Cardew's greatest friend. Do you mean to say you were introduced to her?"

"Yes, Mrs. Cardew was kind enough to do so, though I am sure I didn't want it at all."

"But I can't imagine why she did it," said Molly in a tone of astonishment. "Mrs. Cardew never introduces either of us to the grown-up people."

"Well, her ostensible reason," said Maggie, "was that Lady Lysle knows my mother."

"Does she, indeed?" said Isabel in a tone of great respect.

"But that doesn't make me like her any the better," said Maggie. "And now I will tell you why, girls, only you must faithfully promise you won't repeat it to any one."

"Of course not," said the girls eagerly, who were accustomed to receive secrets from their schoolfellows, though Maggie, as a rule, never gave her secrets to anyone.

"Well, I will tell you," said Maggie, the color flushing into her face and then leaving it pale again. "Aneta Lysle is one of the girls at Aylmer House. She is Lady Lysle's niece; and—well—you know I am tolerant enough, but I can't bear Aneta Lysle."

Molly and Isabel were silent for a minute.

"If *you* can't bear her," said Isabel, "then I don't suppose we'll like her either when we go to the school."

"Oh yes, you will; you'll adore her—sure to. Now promise once again that you will never repeat this."

"We certainly will not," said Molly.

Isabel nodded emphatically. "We don't tell secrets," she said. Then she added, "We had best go downstairs now, if you're quite tidy, Mags."

During supper that night Mrs. Cardew, who found herself seated near her favorite rector, began to ply him with questions with regard to Aylmer House. How had he heard of it, and why had he specially fixed on that establishment for his daughters?

The rector smiled. He had twinkling dark eyes, and they now looked down the long table until they rested for a brief moment on Maggie's young figure. She was talking to Mr. Cardew, who, stately and reserved as he was, took her remarks with good-natured tolerance.

"A nice, unaffected child," he kept saying to himself, and neither did he remark how plain she was.

"That young person yonder," said Mr. Tristram to Mrs. Cardew, "is the influence that has induced me to make arrangements for my girls at Aylmer House."

"Miss Howland! You don't mean to say that you are influenced by a schoolgirl?"

Mr. Tristram looked grave. "In this case I may as well confess at once that I have been influenced," he said. "I have heard a great deal of the child from Molly and Isabel, for they were all three at the same excellent school in Hanover. I met little Miss Howland when I was in London at Christmas.

Being such a great friend of my children's, I naturally talked to her. She told me of Mrs. Ward and of the new delightful school to which she was going. She certainly never once pressed me to send my girls there, but it occurred to me that I would visit Mrs. Ward and see if it could be arranged. My girls are quite proficient for their ages in foreign languages; but I want them now thoroughly to learn literature and English history, and also those numerous small accomplishments which are so necessary for a gentlewoman. There is also no place in the world like London, in my opinion, for hearing good music and seeing good art. I saw Mrs. Ward. A short interview with her was all-sufficient. I could not desire to put my girls in safer hands."

Mrs. Cardew listened very attentively.

"Then you think, Mr. Tristram," she said after a pause, "that school-life is really good for girls?"

"In my humble opinion, Mrs. Cardew, it is essential. A girl must find her level. She can only find it at school."

"Then what about my dear girls?" said Mrs. Cardew.

The rector bowed in a very courteous manner. "School-life may not be really necessary for them," he said; "although you know my opinion—in short you know what I would do with them did they belong to me."

Mrs. Cardew was silent for a minute or two. Then she continued the conversation by saying, "It is really a curious fact that Lady Lysle, my great friend, who was here this afternoon, spoke to me in terms of the warmest approbation with regard to Mrs. Ward and Aylmer House. She says that her own niece Aneta is a member of the school. She further said that there were two vacancies at present, and she urged me to send my girls there. But, alas I cannot do that, for their father would not hear of it."

"I do wish he would hear of it," said Mr. Tristram with some feeling. "You will never have your girls properly taught unless they go to school. It is impossible at this distance from London to command the services of the best masters and governesses. You will not have a resident governess in the house —forgive me if I speak freely, dear lady, but I love your children as though they were my own—and if you could persuade Mr. Cardew to seize this opportunity and let them go to school with Molly and Isabel I am certain you would never regret it."

"I wish I could persuade him," said Mrs. Cardew; "more particularly as that excellent music master, Mr. Bennett, has just written to say he must discontinue giving his music-lessons, as the distance from Warwick is too far for his health, and Miss Beverley, their daily governess, has also broken down. But there, I know my husband never will agree to part with the girls."

"Then the next best thing," said Mr. Tristram, speaking in a cheerful tone, "is for you to take up your abode in your London house, and give the girls the advantages of masters and mistresses straight from the Metropolis. Why, you will be bringing them out in a couple of years, Mrs. Cardew, and you would like them to have all possible advantages first."

"Something must be done, certainly," said Mrs. Cardew; "and I like that girl, Miss Howland, although Lady Lysle seemed prejudiced against her at first."

"Oh, she is a girl in a thousand," said Mr. Tristram; "so matter-of-fact and amiable and agreeable. See how she is talking to your husband at this very moment! I never saw a nicer or more modest young creature, but she is so exceedingly clever that she will push her own way anywhere. She has bowled over my two young urchins already, although she has been only a few hours at the rectory. What could Lady Lysle have to say against Maggie Howland?"

"Oh, nothing—nothing at all, and I ought not to have spoken; but it seems she does not much care for Mrs. Howland."

"I think I can explain that," said Mr. Tristram. "Mrs. Howland means well, but is a rather silly sort of woman. The girl manages her in the sweetest way. The girl herself takes after her father, poor Howland the African explorer, who lost his life in his country's cause. He had, I am told, a most remarkable personality."

When Molly and Isabel Tristram, accompanied by Maggie Howland, the rector, and his wife, walked back to the rectory that evening, Maggie was in excellent spirits. It was natural that the three young people should start on in front. Maggie talked on various subjects; but although the Tristrams were most anxious to get opinions from her with regard to the Cardews, she could not be led to talk of them until they were approaching the house.

It was now nearly eleven o'clock, and a perfect summer night. The boys, Jack and Andrew, had gone to bed, but a few lights were twinkling here and there in the dear old rectory.

"Oh, I am not a scrap sleepy", said Maggie. "This air stimulates one; it is splendid. By the way, girls," she added, suddenly turning and facing her companions, "would you like your bracelets to have rubies in them or sapphires?"

"Nonsense!" said Molly, turning crimson.

Belle laughed. "You don't suppose you are accomplishing that?" she said.

Maggie spoke rather slowly. "Mother has one dozen bracelets in her jewelry-case. Father brought them to her in the course of his travels. Some he got in India and some in Africa. They are very valuable and exceedingly quaint, and I recall now to my memory, and can-see clearly in my mind's eye one lovely gold bracelet fashioned like a snake and with eyes of ruby, and another (which I think he must have got at Colombo) that consists of a broad gold band studded here and there with sapphires. How pretty those bracelets would look on your dear little arms, Molly and Isabel; and how glad—how very, very glad—your Maggie will be to give them to you!"

"And, of course, when you do give them to us we'll be delighted to have them," said Molly and Isabel.

Then Isabel laughed and said, "But what is the good of counting your chickens before they're hatched?"

"I consider my chickens hatched," was Maggie's remark, "What fun we shall all have together next winter! Aneta won't have much chance against us. Yes, girls, of course I like your friends Cicely and Merry; but they'll be twice three times—the girls they are when they have been for a short time at Mrs. Ward's school."

"Aren't you tired, Maggie?" was Molly's remark. "Wouldn't you like to go to bed?"

"I am not a scrap tired, and I don't want to go to bed at all; but I suppose that means that you would?"

"Well, I must own to feeling a little sleepy," said Molly.

"And so am I," said Belle.

"Girls, girls, come in; your father wants to lock up," called Mrs. Tristram at that moment.

The girls all entered the house, lit their candles, and went upstairs to their rooms.

As Maggie was wishing her two dear friends good-night she said quietly, "I hope you won't mind; but Merry Cardew—or, as I ought to call her, Miss Cardew—has asked me to go over to the Manor to-morrow morning in order to show me the old house. I said I'd be there at ten o'clock, and could then get back to you in time for lunch. I do trust you don't mind."

"Of course we don't," said Molly in a hearty tone. "Now, good-night, Mags."

"But if you think, Maggie," said Isabel, "that you will succeed in that scheme of yours you will find yourself vastly mistaken."

Maggie smiled gently, and the next moment she found herself alone. She went and stood by the open window. There was a glorious full moon in the sky, and the garden, with its deep shadows and brilliant avenues of light, looked lovely. But Maggie was not thinking of the scenery. Her thoughts were busy with those ideas which were always running riot in her busy little head. She was not unamiable; she was in reality a good-hearted girl, but she was very ambitious, and she sighed, above all things for power and popularity.

When she came to visit Molly and Isabel she had not the faintest idea of inducing Cicely and Merry to join that select group who were taught by Mrs. Ward at Aylmer House. But when once the idea had entered her brain, she determined, with her accustomed quickness, to carry it into execution. She had never yet, in the whole course of her life, met with defeat. At the various schools where she had been taught she had always been popular and had won friends and never created an enemy-but at Aylmer House, extraordinary and delightful as the life was, there was one girl who excited her enmity—who, in short, roused the worst that was in her. That girl's name was Aneta Lysle. No sophistries on the part of Maggie, no clever speeches, no well-timed and courteous acts, could win the approval of Aneta; and just because she was impossible to get at, because she carried her young head high, because she had that which Maggie could never have—a stately and wonderful beauty— Maggie was jealous of her, and was determined, if she could not win Aneta over to be her friend, to use her own considerable powers against the girl. She had not for a single moment, however, thought that she could be helped by Cicely and Merry in this direction, and had intended to get them to come to the school simply because they were aristocratic and rich, in the first instance. But when she saw Lady Lysle—Lady Lysle, who hated her mother and before whom her mother trembled and shrank; Lady Lysle, who was Aneta's aunt— she knew that Cicely and Merry might be most valuable aids to her in carrying out her campaign against Aneta, and would help her to establish herself once and for all as the most powerful and important person in Mrs. Ward's school.

Power was everything to Maggie. By power she meant to rule her small school-world, and eventually by the aid of that same gift to take her position in the greater world that lies beyond school. In her heart of hearts she considered Cicely and Merry tiresome, silly, ignorant little girls; but they could be made to play into her hands. They must come to Aylmer House—oh yes! and already she felt certain she had put the thin end of the wedge beneath that opposition which she knew she must expect from Mr. Cardew. She would see him again on the morrow. Indeed, greater schemes than hers could be carried into effect within a fortnight.

Maggie was the soul of common-sense, however, and had no idea of wearing herself out thinking when she ought to be asleep. She accordingly soon turned from the window, and, getting into bed, dropped at once into healthy slumber.

When she awoke she felt remarkably light-hearted and cheerful. She got up early, and went with Andrew and Jack to see the adorable rabbits. So judicious was she on this occasion that both boys returned with her to breakfast in the highest good-humor.

"Mother, mother," cried Jackdaw, "she loves Fanciful because he's so beautiful."

"And she adores Spot-ear because he's so ugly," said Peterkins.

The boys were exceedingly happy at being allowed to sit at breakfast one on each side of Maggie, who, when she did not speak to them—for she wanted to ingratiate herself with every one present, and not with them alone—contrived to pat their hands from time to time, and so keep them in a subdued state of exceeding good-humor.

Soon after breakfast she flew up to her room, put on that strangely becoming brown hat, which would have suited no other girl but herself, and went off to the Manor. She was met at the gate by Merry, who was anxiously waiting for her appearance.

"I am so sorry that Cicely isn't here too," said Merry; "but mother wanted Cicely to drive into Warwick with her this morning. We're going for a long motor-ride this afternoon. Don't you love motors?"

"I have never been in one in my life," replied Maggie.

"Oh dear!" said Merry; "then you shall come with us, although I know I can't ask you to-day, but perhaps to-morrow we could manage."

"I must not be too much away from Molly and Isabel, for it would not be kind —would it, Miss Cardew?"

"Do call me Merry. 'Miss Cardew' sounds so stiff, and you know I feel that I have known you all my life, for Molly and Isabel have always been talking about you. Mother was so pleased when she heard that you wanted to see the old house; and, do you know, Maggie—You don't mind my saying Maggie?"

"Of course not, Merry—dear Merry."

"Well—would you believe it?—father is going to show you the manuscript-room himself. I can tell you that is an honor."

"I am so delighted!" said Maggie. "Your father is a most charming man."

"Indeed, that he is," said Merry; "but I never saw him get on so well with a young girl before."

"Oh," said Maggie in her modest way, "it was just that I wanted to listen to him; what he said was so very interesting."

The girls were now walking up the avenue.

"Please," said Merry suddenly, "tell me more about your school—I mean that new, wonderful school you are at in London."

"Aylmer House?" said Maggie.

"Yes, Aylmer House. Mother was talking about it this morning. She was quite interested in it."

"Your mother was talking about it?"

"Yes. It seems Mr. Tristram had been praising it to her like anything last night."

"Well, he can't say too much in its favor," said Maggie. "Any girl who didn't get good from it ought to be ashamed of herself."

"What is that you are saying, Miss Howland?" said the voice of Mr. Cardew at that moment.

"Oh father! I never saw you," cried Merry.

Mr. Cardew came up and shook hands with Maggie. "I was walking just behind you on the grass," he said, "and I heard your enthusiastic remarks with regard to the school that the young Tristrams are going to. I am heartily pleased; I take a great interest in the Tristrams."

"Oh sir," said Maggie suddenly, "I only wish—oh! I hardly dare to say it— but I only do wish that your girls were coming too!"

Merry turned crimson and then grew pale. "Father doesn't approve of schools," she said in a faint voice.

"As a rule, I do not," said Mr. Cardew decidedly; "but of course I am bound to say there are schools and schools. You shall tell me all about your school presently, Miss Howland. And now, I will allow my daughter to entertain you."

"But, father darling, you promised to show Maggie the manuscript-room yourself."

"Are you interested in black-letter?" said Mr. Cardew.

"I am interested in everything old," replied Maggie.

"Well, then, I will show you the manuscript-room with pleasure; but if you want to go over the Manor you have a heavy morning's work before you, and

Merry is an excellent guide. However, let me see. I will meet you in the library at a quarter to twelve. Until then, adieu."

# CHAPTER V.

## "WHAT DID YOU TALK ABOUT?"

Maggie and Merry had now reached the great porch which overshadowed the entrance to the old house. The next instant they found themselves in the hall. This, supported by graceful pillars, was open up to the roof of the house. It was a magnificent hall, and Merry began enthusiastically to explain its perfections. Maggie showed not a pretended but a real interest. She asked innumerable and sensible questions. Her queer, calm, narrow eyes grew very bright. She smiled now and then, and her face seemed the personification of intelligence. With that smile, and those gleaming white teeth, who could have thought of Maggie Howland as plain?

They went from the hall into the older part of the house, and there Merry continued her duties as guide. Never before had she been in the company of so absolutely charming a companion. Maggie was the best listener in the world. She never interrupted with tiresome or irrelevant questions. When she did speak it was with the utmost intelligence, showing clearly that she understood what she was being told.

By-and-by they found themselves in the picture-gallery. There Merry insisted on their sitting down for a time and taking a rest. She touched a bell as she spoke, and then motioned Maggie to recline in a deep arm-chair which faced the picture of a beautiful lady who was the grandmother of the present Mrs. Cardew.

"That lady's name," said Merry, "was Cicely Meredith, and she was the wife of the last Meredith but one who owned the Manor. It was little supposed in those days that my darling mother would inherit the place, and that Cardews should live at Meredith Manor after all. Ah, here comes Dixon!—Dixon, will you put our lunch on that small table? Thank you very much."

One of the servants in the Cardew livery had appeared. He was bearing a small tray of tempting drinks, fruit, and cake.

"Now, Maggie, eat; do eat," said Merry.

"I declare I am as hungry as a hawk," said Maggie, and she munched cake and ate fruit and felt that she was, as she expressed it to herself—although she would not have used the words aloud—in clover.

Nevertheless, she was not going to lose sight of that mission which she had set herself. She turned and looked thoughtfully at Merry. Merry had a pretty profile, with the short upper-lip and the graceful appearance of a very high-bred girl.

"Do you," said Maggie after a pause, "happen to know Aneta Lysle?"

"Why, of course," said Merry. "Do you mean Lady Lysle's niece?"

"Yes," replied Maggie.

"I don't know her well, but she has stayed here once or twice. Is she a friend of yours, Maggie?"

"Oh no; scarcely a friend, although we are schoolfellows."

"How stupid of me!" said Merry, speaking with some warmth. "Of course, I quite forgot that she is at Mrs. Ward's school. She is older than you, isn't she, Maggie?"

"Yes, a year older, as days are counted; but she appears even more than her age, which is just seventeen. Don't you think her very beautiful, Merry?"

"Now that I recall her, I do; but she never made a special impression on me. She never stayed here long enough."

"Nevertheless, she is a sort of cousin of yours?"

"Yes, Lady Lysle is mother's cousin; but then one doesn't love all one's relations," said Merry carelessly. "Have another piece of cake, Maggie."

"Thanks," said Maggie, helping herself. "How delicious it is!"

"And put some more cream over your raspberries. The raspberries at Meredith Manor are celebrated."

Maggie helped herself to some more cream. "I do wish" she said suddenly.

"That I would go on telling you about the pictures?" said Merry. "But you must be tired. I never knew any one take in interesting things so quickly."

"I am glad you think I do; but it so happens that I do not want to hear about the pictures this morning. I think perhaps I am, after all, a bit tired. It is the pleasure, the delight of knowing you and your sister, and of being with those sweet girls Molly and Isabel."

"Yes, aren't they darlings'?" said Merry.

"I want you to tell me a lot about yourself," said Maggie.

"We have half-an-hour yet before I am to meet your father in the manuscript-room. Begin at the beginning, and tell me just everything. You are not schoolgirls?"

"Oh, no," said Merry, speaking slowly. "We are taught at home."

"But have you a resident governess?"

"No; father objects. This is holiday-time of course; but as a rule we have a daily governess and masters."

"It must be dull," said Maggie, speaking in a low tone—so low that Merry had to strain her ears to hear it.

She replied at once, "'Tisn't nearly so interesting as school; but we—we are —quite—*quite* satisfied."

"I wonder you don't go to school," said Maggie.

"Father doesn't wish it, Maggie."

"But you'd like it, wouldn't you?"

"Like it!" said Merry, her eyes distended a little. "Like to see the world and to know other girls? Well, yes, I should like it."

"There'd be discipline, you know," said Maggie. "It wouldn't be all fun."

"Of course not," said Merry. "How could one expect education to be all fun?"

"And you would naturally like to be very well educated, wouldn't you?" said Maggie.

"Certainly; but I suppose we are—that is, after a fashion."

"Yes," said Maggie, "after a fashion, doubtless; but you will go into society by-and-by, and you'll find—well, that home education leaves out a great many points of knowledge which cannot possibly be attained except by mixing with other girls."

"I suppose so," said Merry, speaking with a slight degree of impatience; "but then Cicely and I can't help it. We have to do what father and mother wish."

"Yes, exactly, Merry; and it's so awfully sweet and amiable of you! Now, may I describe to you a little bit of school-life?"

"If you like, Maggie. Molly and Isabel have often told me of what you did in Hanover."

"Oh, Hanover?" said Maggie with a tone of slight contempt. "We don't think of Hanover now in our ideas of school-life. We had a fairly good time, for a German school; but to compare it with Mrs. Ward's house! Oh, I cannot tell you what a dream of a life I have lived during the last term! It is only to see Mrs. Ward to love her; and all the other mistresses are so nice, and the girls are so very select and lady-like. Then we take a keen interest in our lessons. You're the musical one, aren't you, Merry?"

"Yes. How ever did you find that out?"

"Well," said Maggie, "I looked at you, and I guessed it. Besides, I heard you hum an air under your breath yesterday, and I knew at once that you had a lovely voice."

"I am sure I haven't; and I'm too young to begin singing-lessons."

"Not a bit of it. That's quite an exploded idea. If, for instance—Oh, of course I know you won't be there; but if you were so lucky as to be a pupil at Mrs. Ward's you would be taught to sing, and, what is more valuable, you would hear good, wonderful, beautiful singing, and wonderful, beautiful music of all sorts. Once a week we all go to a concert at Queen's Hall. Have you ever been there?"

"No! I don't know London at all."

"Well, then, another day in the week," continued Maggie, "we go to the different museums and picture-galleries, and we get accustomed to good art, and we are taught to discern good from bad. We learn architecture at St. Paul's and the Abbey and some of the other churches. You see, Mrs. Ward's idea is to teach us everything first-hand, and during the summer term she takes us on long expeditions up the river to Kew and Hampton Court and all those dear old places. Then, in addition, she has what she calls reunions in the evenings. We all wear evening-dress, and she invites two or three friends, and we sing and play among ourselves, and we are taught the little observances essential to good society; and, besides all the things that Mrs. Ward does, we have our own private club and our own debating society, and—oh, it is a full life!—and it teaches one, it helps one."

Merry's soft brown eyes were very bright, and her cheeks had a carnation glow on them, and her pretty red lips were slightly parted. "You do all these things at school—at school?" she said.

"Why, of course; and many, many more things that you can't even imagine, for it's the whole influence of the place that is so delightful. Then you make friends—great friends—and you get to understand character, and you get to understand the value of real discipline, and you are taught also that you are not meant to live a worldly and selfish life, for Mrs. Ward is very philanthropic. Each girl in her school has to help a poor girl in East London, and the poor girl becomes in a sort of manner her property. I have got a dear little lame girl. Her name is Susie Style. I am allowed to see her once or twice a year, and I write her a letter every week, and she writes back to me, and I collect enough money to keep her in a cripples' home. I haven't enough of my own, for I am perhaps the poorest girl in the school; but that makes no difference, for Mrs. Ward doesn't allow the word money or rank to be spoken of—she lives above all that. She says that money is a great talent, and that people who are merely purse-proud are detestable. Oh, but I've told you enough, haven't I?"

"Yes, oh yes!" said Merry. "Thanks very, very much. And so Aneta is there; and as Molly and Isabel will be there, they will tell me more at Christmas. Perhaps we ought to go down now to meet father in the manuscript-room."

Maggie rose with alacrity. She followed her companion quite cheerfully. She felt assured within herself that the thin end of the wedge had been well inserted by now.

Mr. Cardew was exceedingly courteous and pleasant, and Maggie charmed him by her intelligence and her marvellous gift of assimilating knowledge. Not a word was said with regard to the London school, and at ten minutes to one Maggie bade good-bye to Mr. Cardew and Merry, and went back to the rectory in considerable spirits.

Molly and Isabel were all impatience for her return.

"Well, what did you do?" said Molly. "Who was there to meet you?"

"Only Merry. Cicely had gone with Mrs. Cardew to Warwick."

"Oh, well, Merry is the jollier of the two, although they are both perfectly sweet," said Molly. "And did she show you all the house, Maggie?"

"No," said Maggie; "I really couldn't take it all in; but she took me round the armory and into the old tower, and then we went into the picture-gallery."

"Oh, she took you into the picture-gallery! There are Romneys and Gainsboroughs and Sir Joshua Reynoldses, and all sorts of magnificent treasures there."

"Doubtless," said Maggie. "But when I tell you what we did you will laugh."

"What did you do? Do tell us, Mags."

"We sat in easy-chairs. I faced the portrait of a very beautiful lady after whom Cicely Cardew is called."

"Of course I know her well—I mean her picture," said Isabel. "That is a Gainsborough. Didn't you admire it?"

"Yes; but I want to look at it again; I'm going to do the gallery another day, and on that occasion I think I shall ask Cicely to accompany me."

"Why, what do you mean? Don't you like our sweet little Merry?"

"Like her? I quite love her," said Maggie; "but the fact is, girls, I did my duty by her this morning, and now I want to do my duty by Cicely."

"Oh Mags, you are so mysterious!" said Molly; "but come upstairs and take off your hat, for the gong will sound for lunch in a moment."

Maggie went upstairs, Molly and Isabel following her. "Come into my room, girls," she said. Then she added, dropping her voice, "I think those bracelets are pretty secure."

Molly colored. Isabel looked down.

"You will never succeed," said Molly.

Then Isabel said, "Even if you do, I don't think we ought, perhaps, to—to take them, for it would seem as though they were a sort of—sort of—bribe."

"Oh, you old goose!" said Maggie, kissing her. "How could they be a bribe when I don't ask you to do anything at all? But now, listen. We were tired when we got to the gallery; therefore that sweet little Merry of yours ordered fruit and milk and cake, and we ate and talked."

"What did you talk about?"

"School, dear."

"What was the good of your talking about school to Merry when she can't go?"

"Can't go?" said Maggie. "Why, she is going; only, it was my bounden duty to make her want to go. Well, I succeeded in doing that this morning. There's the gong, and, notwithstanding my lunch, I am quite hungry."

"Well, Andrew and Jack are perfectly mad to see you; you'll have to devote a bit of your time to them. Dear me, Mags!" said Molly, "it must be tiresome to be a sort of universal favorite, as you are."

"Tiresome!" said Maggie, glancing round with her queer, expressive eyes, "when I love it like anything? Let's get up a sort of play between ourselves this afternoon, and let the boys join in; and, oh! couldn't we—don't you think we might—get your two friends Cicely and Merry to join us, just for an impromptu thing that we could act beautifully in the hay-field? Wouldn't their father consent?"

"Why, of course he would. I'll run round the minute lunch is over and get them," said Isabel. "You are a girl for planning things, Mags! It'll be quite glorious."

"We might have tea in the hay-field too," continued Maggie. "I am sure Peterkins and Jackdaw will help us."

"Capital! capital! and we'll get David"—David was the gardener's boy—"to pick lots of fruit for the occasion."

# CHAPTER VI.

## FORBIDDEN FRUIT.

Meanwhile a little girl stood all alone on one of the terrace walks at Meredith Manor. Mrs. Cardew and Cicely would not arrive until rather late for lunch, and Merry and her father were to partake of it alone. Merry paced up and down very slowly. What a lovely day it was, and how beautiful the place looked with its long lines of stately trees, and its background of woods, and its terraces of bright flowers and green, green grass!

As far as the eye could reach the land belonged to the Cardews, and yet Merry Cardew, the joint-heiress with Cicely of all this wealth, did not feel either happy or contented at that moment. A girl had come into her life who had suddenly turned her gold to gray, her sunshine to shadow. She was a very nice girl, too—exceedingly nice. There was something about her which Merry found impossible to define, for Merry had no acquaintances just then in her sheltered life who possessed the all-important and marvelous power of charm. Merry knew quite well that Maggie Howland was neither rich nor beautiful. She was just a little schoolgirl, and yet she could not get Maggie out of her head. She sighed for the girl's companionship, and she sighed yet more for the forbidden fruit which Maggie had placed so enticingly before her mental vision: the school-life, the good life, the energetic, purposeful life. Music— oh, how passionately Merry loved the very little music she had ever heard! And art—Merry and Cicely had learned a little bit of art in their own picture-gallery; but of all there was outside they knew nothing. Then that delightful, wonderful scheme of having an East End girl for your very own to train, and help, and write to, and support; and the companionship, and all the magical things which the Tristrams had more or less enjoyed in foreign schools, but which seemed to have reached a delicacy of perfection at Aylmer House!

Yes, doubtless these were forbidden fruits; but she could not help, as she paced alone on the terrace, contrasting her mode of education with that which was put within the reach of her friends Molly and Isabel, and of Maggie herself. How dull, after all, were her lessons! The daily governess, who was always tired when she arrived, taught her out of books which even Molly and Isabel declared to be out of date; who yawned a good deal; who was always quite, quite kind, but at the same time had no enthusiasm; who said, "Yes, my dears; very nicely done," but never even punished; and who only uttered just that mild phrase which was monotonous by reason of its repetition. Where was the good of reading Racine aloud to Miss Beverley day after day, and not being able to talk French properly at all? And where was the use of struggling through German with the same instructress?

Then the drawing-master who came from Warwick: he was better than Miss Beverley; but, after all, he taught what Molly and Isabel said was now quite exploded—namely, freehand—and he only came once a week. Merry's passion was for music more than for drawing; it was Cicely who pleased Mr. Vaughan, the drawing-master, best. Then there was the music-master, Mr. Bennett; but he never would allow her to sing a note, and he taught very dull, old-fashioned pieces. How sick she was of pieces, and of playing them religiously before her father at least once a week! Her dancing was better, for she had to go to Warwick to a dancing-class, and there were other girls, and they made it exciting. But compared to school, and in especial Mrs. Ward's school, Merry's mode of instruction was very dull. After all, Molly and Isabel, although they would be quite poor girls, had a better time than she and Cicely with all their wealth.

"A penny for your thoughts, my love," said her father at that moment, and Merry turned her charming little face towards him.

"I ought not to tell them to you, dad," she said, "for they are—I'm ever so sorry—they are discontented thoughts."

"You discontented, my dear child! I did feel that I had two little girls unacquainted with the meaning of the word."

"Well, I'll just tell you, and get it over, dad. I'll be perfectly all right once I have told you."

"Then talk away my child; you know I have your very best interests at heart."

"Indeed I know that, my darling father. The fact is this," said Merry; "I"—She stopped; she glanced at her father. He was a most determined and yet a most absolutely kind man. Merry adored him; nevertheless, she was a tiny little bit in awe of him.

"What is the matter?" he said, looking round at her. "Has your companion, that nice little Miss Howland, been putting silly thoughts into your head? If so, she mustn't come here again."

"Oh father, don't say that! You'll make me quite miserable. And indeed she has not been putting silly thoughts into my head."

"Well, then, what are you so melancholy about?"

"The fact is—there, I will have it out," said Merry—"I'd give anything in the world to go to school."

"What?" said Mr. Cardew.

"Yes," said Merry, gaining courage as she spoke; "Molly and Isabel are going, and Aneta Lysle is there, and Maggie Howland is there, and I'd like to go, too, and I'm sure Cicely would; and, oh, father! I know it *can't* be; but you asked me what was the matter. Well, that's the matter. I do want most awfully to go to school!"

"Has that girl Miss Howland been telling you that you ought to go to school?"

"Indeed no, she has not breathed such a word. But I am always interested, as you know—or as perhaps you don't know—in schools; and I have always asked—and so has Cicely—Molly and Isabel to tell us all about their lives at school."

"I did not know it, my little Merry."

"Well, yes, father, Cicely and I have been curious; for, you see, the life is so very different from ours. And so to-day, when Maggie and I were in the picture-gallery, I asked her to tell me about Aylmer House, and she—she did."

"She made a glowing picture, evidently," said Mr. Cardew.

"Oh father, it must be so lovely! Think of it, father—to get the best music and the best art, and to be under the influence of a woman like Mrs. Ward. Oh, it must be good! Do you know, father, that every girl in her school has an East End girl to look after and help; so that some of the riches of the West should be felt and appreciated by those who live in the East. Oh father! I could not help feeling a little jealous."

"Yes, darling, I quite understand. And you find your life with Miss Beverley and Mr. Vaughan and Mr. Bennett a little monotonous compared to the variety which a school-life affords?"

"That is it, father darling."

"I don't blame you in the least, Merry—not in the very least; but the fact is, I have my own reasons for not approving of school-life. I prefer girls who are trained at home. If, indeed, you had to earn your living it would be a different matter. But you will be rich, dear, some day, and—Well, I am glad you've spoken to me. Don't think anything more about it. Come in to lunch now."

"I'll try not to think of it, father; and you're not really angry?"

"Angry!" said Mr. Gardew. "I'll never be angry with you, Merry, when you tell me all the thoughts of your heart."

"And you won't—you won't," said Merry in an anxious tone—"vex darling mother by talking to her about this?"

"I make no promises whatsoever You have trusted me; you must continue to trust me."

"I do; indeed I do! You are not angry with dear, nice Miss Howland, are you, father?"

"Angry with her! Why should I be? Most certainly not. Now, come in to lunch, love."

At that meal Mr. Cardew did his very utmost to be pleasant to Merry; and as there could be no man more charming when he pleased, soon the little girl was completely under his influence, and forgot that fascinating picture of school-life which Maggie had so delicately painted for her edification.

Soon after lunch Mrs. Cardew and Cicely returned; and Merry, the moment she was with her sister, felt her sudden fit of the blues departing, and ran out gaily with Cicely into the garden. They were seated comfortably in a little arbor, when Isabel's voice was heard calling them. She was hot and panting. She had come up to tell them of the proposed arrangements for the afternoon, and to beg of them both to come immediately to the rectory.

"How more than delightful!" said Merry.—"Cicely, you stay still, for you're a little tired. I'll run up to the house at once and ask father and mother if we may go."

"Yes, please do," said Isabel; "and I'll rest here for a little, for really the walk up to your house is somewhat fatiguing." She mopped her hot forehead as she spoke. "You might as well come back with me, both of you girls," she added. But she only spoke to Cicely, for Merry had already vanished.

"Father! mother!" said the young girl, bursting abruptly into their presence. "Belle Tristram has just come up to ask us to spend the afternoon at the rectory. Tea in the hay-field, and all kinds of fun! May we go?"

"Of course you may, dears," said Mrs. Cardew at once. "We intended motoring, but we can do that another day."

Mr. Cardew looked dubious for a moment. Then he said, "All right, only you must not be out too late. I'll send the pony-trap down to the rectory for you at half-past eight o'clock."

"Oh, but, father," said Merry, "we can walk home."

"No dear; I will send the little carriage. Now, go and enjoy yourself, my child."

He looked at her with great affection, and she felt herself reddening. Had she hurt that most dear father after all? Oh! no school that ever existed was worth that.

# CHAPTER VII.

## DISCONTENT.

On that special afternoon Mr. and Mrs. Cardew happened to be alone. The girls had gone down to the rectory. This was not Mrs. Cardew's At Home day, and she therefore did not expect any visitors. She was a little tired after her long drive to Warwick, and was glad when her husband suggested that they should go out and have tea all alone together under one of the wide-spreading elm-trees.

Mrs. Cardew said to herself that this was almost like the old, old times of very long ago. She and her husband had enjoyed an almost ideal married life. They had never quarreled; they had never even had a small disagreement. They were blessed abundantly with this world's good things, for when Sylvia Meredith of Meredith Manor had accepted the hand of Cyril Cardew she had also given her heart to him.

He and she were one in all particulars. Their thoughts were almost identical. She was by no means a weak-minded woman—she had plenty of character and firmness; but she deferred to the wishes of her husband, as a good wife should, and was glad! to feel that he was slightly her master. Never, under any circumstances, did he make her feel the yoke. Nevertheless, she obeyed him, and delighted in doing so.

The arrival of their little twin-daughters was the crown of their bliss. They never regretted the fact that no son was born to them to inherit the stately acres of Meredith Manor; they were the last sort of people to grumble. Mrs. Cardew inherited the Meredith property in her own right, and eventually it would be divided between her two daughters.

Meanwhile the children themselves absorbed the most loving care of their parents. Mr. Cardew was, as has already been said, a great merchant-prince. He often went to London to attend to his business affairs, but he spent most of his time in the exquisite country home. It was quite true that discontent seemed far, very far away from so lovely a spot as Meredith Manor. Nevertheless, Mr. Cardew had seen it to-day on the face of his best-loved child, his little Merry. The look had hurt him; and while he was having lunch with her, and joking with her, and talking, in his usually bright and intelligent way, her words, and still more the expression of her face and the longing look in her sweet brown eyes, returned to him again and again.

He was, therefore, more thoughtful than usual as he sat by his wife's side now under the elm-tree. He had a pile of newspapers and magazines on the grass at his feet, and his favorite fox-terrier Jim lay close to his master. Mrs. Cardew had her invariable knitting and a couple of novels waiting to occupy her attention when Mr. Cardew took up one of the newspapers. But for a time the pair were silent. Mrs. Cardew was thinking of something which she wanted to say, and Mr. Cardew was thinking of Merry. It was, as is invariably the case, the woman who first broke the silence.

"Well, Cyril," said his wife, "to find ourselves seated here all alone, without the children's voices to listen to reminds me of the old times, the good times, the beautiful times when we were first married."

"My dear," he answered, starting slightly as she spoke, "those were certainly good and beautiful times, but surely not more good and beautiful than now, when our two dear little girls are growing up and giving us such great happiness."

"That is true. Please don't misunderstand me, love; but you come even before the children."

He felt touched as she said this, and glancing at her, said to himself that he was indeed in luck to have secured so priceless a woman as his wife.

"We have had happy times together, Cyril," she said, returning his glance.

"Yes, Sylvia," he answered, and once again he thought of Merry's face.

"Nothing can alter that," she continued.

"Nothing, my love," he said.

Then he looked at her again, and saw that she was a little troubled about something; and, as was his custom, he determined to take the bull by the horns.

"You have something on your mind, Sylvia. What is it?"

"I have," she said at once; "and something of very great importance. I have a sort of fear that to talk of it with you may possibly trouble you a little. Shall we defer it, dear? The day is so peaceful, and we are so happy."

"No, no," he replied at once. "We will take the opportunity of the children being perfectly happy at the rectory to discuss the thing that worries you. But what can it be?" he continued. "That is more than I can imagine. I have never seen you worried before."

Again he thought of Merry, but it was impossible to connect his wife's trouble with his child's discontent.

"Well, I will tell you just out, Cyril," said his wife. "I urge nothing, but I feel bound to make a suggestion. I know your views with regard to the girls."

"My views, dear! What do you mean?"

"With regard to their education, Cyril."

"Yes, yes, Sylvia; we have done our very best. Have you any reason to find fault with Miss Beverley or with Vaughan or Bennett?"

"Unfortunately," said Mrs. Cardew, "Miss Beverley, who, you know, is an admirable governess, and whom we can most thoroughly trust, wrote to me yesterday morning saying that she was obliged to resign her post as daily governess to our girls. She finds the distance from Warwick too far; in fact, she has her physician's orders to take work nearer home. She regrets it immensely, but feels that she has no alternative."

"Provoking!" said Mr. Cardew; "but really, Sylvia, I wouldn't allow it to upset me if I were you. Surely there are plenty of other Miss Beverleys in the world; and"—again he thought of Merry—"we might perhaps find some one a little less old-fashioned."

"I am afraid, dear, that is impossible, for you will not allow a resident governess in the house."

"I will not," said Mr. Cardew with decision. "Such an arrangement would break in on our family life. You know my views."

"Yes, dear; and I must say I approve of them."

"You must find some one else in Warwick who is not too tired to take the train journey. Doubtless it would be quite easy," said Mr. Cardew.

"I went to Warwick this morning in order to make inquiries," said Mrs. Cardew in her gentle voice, "and I grieve to say there is no one who can in the least take the post which dear Miss Beverley has so worthily filled. But I have further bad news to give you. Mr. Bennett is leaving Warwick for a better post in London, and we shall be at our wits' end to get the girls good music-lessons for next term."

"How provoking! how annoying!" said Mr. Cardew, and his irritation was plainly shown in his face. "It does seem hard," he said after a moment's pause, "that we, with all our wealth, should be unable to give our girls the thorough education they require."

"The fact is this, dear," said Mrs. Cardew, "and I must speak out plainly even at the risk of displeasing you—Cicely and Merry are exceedingly clever girls, but at the present moment they are very far behind other girls of their age. Their knowledge of foreign languages is most deficient. I have no doubt Miss Beverley has grounded them well in English subjects; but as to accomplishments, they are not getting the advantages their rank in life and their talent demand. Dear Cyril, we ought to forget ourselves and our interests for the children."

"What has put all this into your head?" said Mr. Cardew. "As, for instance—" He paused. "It seemed impossible—"

"What, dear?" asked his wife very earnestly.

"Well, I may as well say it. Has Merry been talking to you?"

"Our little Merry!" said Mrs. Cardew in astonishment. "Of course not. What in the world do you mean?"

"I will not explain just at present, dear. You have some idea in your head, or you wouldn't speak to me as you do."

"Well, the fact is, when my cousin, Lucia Lysle, was here yesterday she spoke very strongly to me on the subject of the girls' education, and urged me to do what I knew you would never for a moment consent to."

"And what is that?" asked Mr. Gardew. "I seem to be an awful bugbear in this business."

"No, dear, no. I quite understand your scruples, and—and—respect them. But Lucia naturally wanted us to seize the opportunity of two vacancies at Aylmer House, Mrs. Ward's school."

"I shall soon begin to hate the name of Mrs. Ward," said Cardew with some asperity.

"My cousin spoke most highly of the school," continued Mrs. Cardew. "She said that two years there, or perhaps a little longer, would give the girls that knowledge of life which will be all-essential to them in the future."

"Home education is best; I know it is best," said Mr. Cardew. "I hate girls' schools."

"I gave her to understand, dear, that those were your views; but I have something else to tell you. You know how attached we both are to the dear Tristrams."

"Of course, of course," said Mr. Cardew with impatience.

"Well, at supper yesterday evening Mr. Tristram began to talk to me on the very same subject as my cousin, Lady Lysle, had spoken of earlier in the day."

"Very interfering of Tristram," replied Mr. Cardew.

"He didn't mean it in that way, I assure you, my love; nothing could be nicer than the way he spoke. I was telling him—for I had not mentioned the fact to you, and it was troubling me a little—about Miss Beverley and Mr. Bennett, and asking his advice, as I often do. He immediately urged Aylmer House as the best possible substitute for Miss Beverley and Mr. Bennett. I repeated almost the same words I had used to Lucia Lysle—namely, that you were dead-set against girls' schools."

"That was scarcely polite, my love, seeing that he sends his own daughters to school."

"Well, yes," said Mrs. Cardew; "but of course their circumstances are very different."

"I would be sorry if he should feel that difference, Sylvia. Tristram is a most excellent fellow."

"He is—indeed he is!" said Mrs. Cardew. "Feeling for him, therefore, as you do, dear, you may perhaps be more inclined to listen to an alternative which he proposed to me."

"And what is that, my dear?"

"Well, he thinks we might occupy our house in London during the school terms of each year—"

"During the school terms of each year!" echoed Mr. Cardew in a voice of dismay. "But I hate living in London."

"Yes, dearest; but you see we must think of our girls. If you and I took the children to town they could have governesses and masters—the very best— and would thus be sufficiently educated to take their place in society."

Mr. Cardew was quite silent for a full minute after his wife had made this suggestion. To tell the truth, she had done a somewhat extraordinary thing. Amongst this great lady's many rich possessions was a splendid mansion in Grosvenor Street; but, as she hated what is called London society, it had long been let to different tenants, for nothing would induce the Cardews to leave their delightful home, with its fresh air and country pursuits, for the dingy old house in town. They knew that when the girls came out—a far-distant date as yet—they would have to occupy the house in Grosvenor Street for the season; but Mrs. Cardew's suggestion that they should go there almost immediately for the sake of their daughters' education was more annoying to her husband than he could possibly endure.

"I consider the rector very officious," he said. "Nothing would induce me to live in town."

"I thought you would feel like that, dear. I was certain of it."

"You surely would not wish it yourself, Sylvia?"

"I should detest it beyond words," she replied.

"Besides, the house is occupied," said Mr. Cardew, catching at any excuse not to carry out this abominable plan, as he termed it.

"Well, dear, at the present moment it is not. I had a letter a week ago from our agent to ask if he should relet it for the winter and next season, and I have not yet replied to him."

"Nonsense, nonsense, Sylvia! We cannot go to live there."

"I don't wish it, my love."

The pair sat quite silent after Mrs. Cardew had made this last remark.

After a time her husband said, "We're really placed in a very cruel dilemma; but doubtless there are schools and schools. Now, I feel that the time has arrived when I ought to tell you about Merry."

"What about the dear child?" asked her mother. "Isn't she well?"

"Absolutely and perfectly well, but our dear little girl is consumed by the fever of discontent."

"My dear, you must be mistaken."

"I am not. Listen, and I will tell you what has happened."

Mr. Cardew then related his brief interview with Merry, and Merry's passionate desire to go to Aylmer House.

"And what did you say to her, love?" asked his wife.

"I told her it was impossible, of course."

"But it really isn't, dear, you know," said Mrs. Cardew in a low tone; "and as you cannot make up your mind to live in London, those two vacancies at Aylmer House seem providential."

At these words Mr. Cardew sprang to his feet. "Nothing will ever shake my opinion with regard to school-life," he said.

"And yet the life in town—"

"That is impossible. Look me straight in the face, Sylvia. If by any chance— don't, please, imagine that I'm giving way—but if, by any possible chance, I were to yield, could you, my darling, live without your girls?"

"With you—I could," she answered, and she held out her hand to him, which he raised to his lips and kissed.

"Well, I am upset," he said. "If only Miss Beverley and Bennett were not so silly, we should not be in this awkward fix. I'll go for a ride, if you don't mind, Sylvia, and be back with you in an hour's time."

During that ride Mr. Cardew felt as a strong man does when his most cherished wishes are opposed, and when circumstance, with its overpowering weight, bears down every objection. Beyond doubt the girls must be educated. Beyond doubt the scheme of living in London could not be entertained. Country life was essential. Meredith Manor must not be deserted for the greater part of the year. He might visit the girls whenever he went to London; but, after all, he was now more or less a sleeping partner in his great firm. There was no necessity for him to go to London more than four or five times a year. Oh! school was hateful, but little Merry had longed for it. How troublesome education was! Surely the girls knew enough.

He was riding home, his thoughts still in a most perturbed condition, when he suddenly drew up just in front of a little figure who stood by the roadside, attired as a gipsy, with a scarlet bandana handkerchief twisted round her head, a short skirt reaching not quite to her ankles made also of scarlet, and a little gay blue shawl across her shoulders. She was carrying a tambourine in one hand and in the other a great bunch of many-colored ribbons.

This little, unexpected figure was seen close to the rectory grounds, and Mr. Cardew was so startled by it, and so also was his horse, that he drew up abruptly and looked imperiously at the small suppliant for his favor.

"If you please, sir," said Maggie Howland, speaking in her most enticing voice, and knowing well that her dress magnified her charms, "will you, kind sir, allow me to cross your hand with silver and let me tell your fortune?"

Mr. Cardew now burst into a merry laugh.

"Why, Miss Howland," he said, "I beg your pardon; I did not recognize you."

Maggie dropped a low curtsy. "I'm the gipsy girl Caranina, and I should like to tell your fortune, kind and generous sir."

Just then the pretty face of Cicely was seen peeping over the rectory grounds. She was dressed as a flower-girl, and looked more lovely than he had ever seen her before.

"Why, dad, dad," she cried, "oh! you must come in and join our fun. Mustn't he, Maggie?"

"I am Caranina, the gipsy girl," said Maggie, dropping another low curtsy, and holding her little tambourine in the most beseeching attitude; "and you are Flora, queen of the flowers."

"Well, really, this is entertaining," said Mr. Cardew. "What queer little minxes you all are! And may I really come in and see the fun?"

"Indeed yóu may, dad," said the flower-girl. "Oh, and please we want you to look at Merry. Merry's a fairy, with wings. We're going to have what we call an evening revel presently, and we are all in our dress for the occasion. But Maggie—I mean Caranina—is telling our fortunes—that is, until the real fun begins."

"Do please come in, Mr. Cardew. This is the height of good luck," said Mrs. Tristram, coming forward herself at this moment. "Won't you join my husband and me under the shadow of the tent yonder? The young people are having such a good time."

"I will come for a minute or two," said Cardew, dismounting as he spoke. "Can some one hold Hector for me?"

David was quickly summoned, and Mr. Cardew walked across the hay-field to where the hastily improvised tent was placed.

"No one can enter here who doesn't submit to the will of the gipsy," remarked Caranina in her clear and beautiful voice. "This is my tent, and I tell the fortunes of all those kind ladies and gentlemen who will permit me to do so."

"Then you shall tell mine, with pleasure, little maid," said Mr. Cardew, who felt wonderfully cheered and entertained at this *al fresco* amusement.

Quick as thought Maggie had been presented with a silver coin. With this she crossed the good gentleman's palm, and murmured a few words with regard to his future. There was nothing whatever remarkable in her utterance, for Maggie knew nothing of palmistry, and was only a very pretense gipsy fortune-teller. But she was quick—quicker than most—in reading character; and as she glanced now into Mr. Cardew's face an inspiration seized her.

"He is troubled about something," thought the girl. "It's the thin end of the wedge; I'll push it in a little farther."

Her voice dropped to a low tone. "I see in your hand, kind sir," she said, "all happiness, long life, and prosperity; but I also see a little cross, just here—" she pointed with her pretty finger—"and it means self-sacrifice for the sake of a great and lasting good. Kind sir, I have nothing more to add."

Mr. Cardew left the tent and sat down beside the rector and his wife. Maggie's words were really unimportant. As one after the other the merry group of actors went to have their fortunes told he paid no attention whatever to them. Gipsy fortune-tellers always mixed a little sorrow with their joyful tidings. It was a bewitching little gipsy after all. He could not quite make out her undefined charm, but he was interested in her; and after a time, when the

52

fortune-telling had come to an end and Maggie was about to change her dress for what they called the evening revels, he crossed the field and stood near her.

"So you, Miss Howland, have been telling my daughter Merry a good many things with regard to your new school?"

She raised her queer, bright eyes, and looked him full in the face. "I have told Merry a few things," she said; "but, most of all, I have assured her that Aylmer House is the happiest place in the world."

"Happier than home? Should you say it was happier than home, Miss Howland?"

"Happier than my home," said Maggie with a little sigh, very gentle and almost imperceptible, in her voice. "Oh, I love it!" she continued with enthusiasm; "for it helps—I mean, the life there helps—to make one good."

Mr. Cardew said nothing more. After a time he bade his friends good-by and returned to Meredith Manor. In course of time the little pony-carriage was sent down to the rectory for the Cardew girls, who went back greatly elated.

How delightful their evening had been, and what a marvelous girl Maggie Howland was.'

"Why, she even manages to subdue and to rule those really tiresome boys," said Cicely.

"Yes," remarked Merry, "she is like no one else."

"You have quite fallen in love with her, haven't you, Merry?"

"Well, perhaps I have a little bit," said Merry. She looked thoughtful. She longed to say to Cicely, "How I wish beyond all things on earth that I were going to the same school!" But a certain fidelity to her father kept her silent.

She was startled, therefore, when Cicely herself, who was always supposed to be much calmer than Merry, and less vehement in her desires, clasped her sister's hand and said with emphasis, "I don't know, after all, if it is good for us to see too much of Maggie Howland."

"Why, Cissie? What do you mean?"

"I mean this," said Cicely: "she makes me—yes, I will say it—discontented."

"And me too," said Merry, uttering the words with an emphasis which astonished herself.

"We have talked of school over and over again," said Cicely, "with Molly and Belle; but notwithstanding their glowing accounts we have been quite satisfied with Miss Beverley, and dear, gray-haired Mr. Bennett, and Mr. Vaughan; but now I for one, don't feel satisfied any longer." "Nor do I," said Merry.

"Oh Merry!"

"It is true," said Merry. "I want to go to Aylmer House."

"And I am almost mad to go there," said Cicely.

"I'll tell you something, Cissie. I spoke to father about it to-day."

"Merry! you didn't dare?"

"Well, I just did. I couldn't help myself. It is hateful to be under-educated, and you know we shall never be like other girls if we don't see something of the world."

"He didn't by any chance agree with you?" said Cicely.

"Not a bit of it," said Merry. "We must bear with our present life, only perhaps we oughtn't to see too much of Maggie Howland."

"Well," said Cicely, "I've something to tell you, Merry."

"What's that?"

"You don't know just at present why mother and I went to Warwick this morning?"

"No," said Merry, who was rather uninterested. "I had a very good time with Maggie, and didn't miss you too dreadfully."

"Well, you will be interested to know why we did go, all the same," said Cicely. "It's because Miss Beverley is knocked up and can't teach us any more, and Mr. Bennett is going to London. Mother can't hear of anyone to take Miss Beverley's place, or of any music-teacher equal to Mr. Bennett; so, somehow or other, I feel that there are changes in the air. Oh Merry, Merry! suppose—"

"There's no use in it," said Merry. "Father will never change. We'll get some other dreadfully dull daily governess, and some other fearfully depressing music-master, and we'll never be like Molly and Belle and Maggie and our cousin Aneta. It does seem hard."

"We must try not to be discontented," said Cicely.

"Then we had best not ask Maggie here too often," replied Merry.

"Oh, but they're all coming up to-morrow morning, for I have asked them," said Cicely.

"Dear, dear!" replied Merry.

"We may as well have what fun we can," remarked Cicely, "for you know we shall be going to the seaside in ten days."

---

# CHAPTER VIII.

## MRS. WARD'S SCHOOL.

It is to be regretted that Mr. Cardew spent a restless night. Mrs. Cardew, on the contrary, slept with the utmost peace. She trusted so absolutely in her husband's judgment and in in his power to do the very best he could on all possible occasions for her and hers that she was never deeply troubled about anything. Her dear husband must not be forced to live in London if he did not like to do so, and some arrangement must be made for the girls' home education if he could not see his way to sending them to school.

Great, therefore, was her astonishment on the following morning when he came hastily into her room.

"My dear," he said, "I am off to London for the day."

"What for?" she asked.

"I will tell you, darling, when I return to-night."

"Cyril, may I not come with you?"

"I think not, my love. Make all the young people as happy as you can. I'm just off to the station, in the motor-car."

Mr. Cardew left his wife's room. The girls were told at breakfast that their father had gone to London; but as this frequently happened, and was invariably connected with that business which they knew nothing whatever about, they were not keenly interested. As a matter of fact, they were much more absorbed in getting things ready for the entertainment of their friends; and in this Mrs. Cardew very heartily joined them. She proposed that during Maggie Howland's visit the five girls should have as happy a time together as possible; and as the weather was perfect the invariable picnics and gipsy teas were arranged for their benefit.

"You can all make yourselves happy here to-day, my darlings," said Mrs. Cardew, addressing Cicely and Merry. "To-morrow, when your father is here, the Tristrams, he and I, and you girls will have a very pleasant picnic to the Aldersleigh woods. We will arrange it to-day, for there is nothing your father enjoys more than a whole, long, happy day in the open air. I will speak to Mrs. Fairlight, and tell her to have all things in readiness for our picnic."

"Oh mummy, how good! how good!" said Merry, clasping her mother's hand. Then she added, "Mummy, is it true that Miss Beverley is never going to teach us any more?"

"I am afraid it is only too true, Merry; but this is holiday-time, darling; we needn't talk of your education just at present."

"Only, we must be educated—mustn't we, mother?"

"Of course, dearest. Your father will see to that."

Merry ran off to join her sister, and it is not too much to say that the whole of that glorious day was one of unalloyed pleasure. The Tristram girls were always delightful to the Cardew girls, but now that they were accompanied by Maggie Howland there was a great addition to their charm. Nevertheless, Maggie, with her purpose full in view, with her heart beating a little more quickly than usual when she heard that Mr. Cardew had gone to London, religiously avoided the subject of the life at Aylmer House. She felt, somehow, that she had done her part. A great deal of her own future depended on these two girls coming to Aylmer House. She would make use of them— large use of them—at school. She was fond of Molly and Belle; but they were poor. Maggie herself was poor. She wanted to have rich friends. The Cardews were rich. By their means she would defeat her enemy, Aneta Lysle, and establish herself not only in the school but with regard to her future life. Maggie felt that she could make herself indispensable to Cicely and Merry. Oh yes, they would certainly go to Aylmer House in September. She need not worry herself any further, therefore, with regard to that matter. Little would they guess how much she had really done toward this desirable goal, and how fortunate circumstances had been in aiding her to the accomplishment of her desire. It was enough for Maggie that they were certainly going. She could, therefore, give herself up to enjoyment.

With Maggie Howland enjoyment meant a very different thing from what it does to the average English girl. She enjoyed herself with all her heart and soul, without one single reservation. To see her face at such moments was to behold pure sunshine; to hear her voice was to listen to the very essence of laughter and happiness. She had a marvelous power of telling stories, and when she was happy she told them with such verve that all people within earshot hung on her words. Then she could improvise, and dance, and take off almost any character; in short, she was the life of every party who admitted her within their circle.

Meanwhile a rather tired and rather sad man found himself, very much against his will, in London. He said to himself, "This wonderful Mrs. Ward will not be at Aylmer House now. These are the holidays, and she will be probably miles away. I will go to see her. Yes, but she won't be in; that alone will clinch the matter. But first I will pay a visit to Lucia Lysle; she said she would be in London—she told my dear wife so. But Lucia is so erratic, it is most improbable that she either will be at home."

Mr. Cardew drove first of all to Lady Lysle's house in Hans Place. He asked if she was within, and, very much to his annoyance, the servant replied in the affirmative. He entered Lady Lysle's drawing-room feeling rather silly. The first person he saw there was a tall, slim, lovely girl, whom he did not recognize at first, but who knew him and ran up to him and introduced herself as Aneta.

"Why, my dear," he said, "how are you? How you have grown!"

"How is dear Cousin Sylvia, and how are Cicely and Merry?" asked Aneta. "Oh, I am very well indeed, Mr. Cardew; I don't suppose anybody could be anything but well who was lucky enough to be at Aylmer House."

"Mrs. Ward's school?" said Mr. Cardew, feeling rather shy and almost self-conscious.

"Of course. Don't you know Mrs. Ward, Mr. Cardew?"

"No, my dear, I don't."

"It's the most marvelous school in the world," said Aneta with enthusiasm. "I do wish you would send Cicely and Merry there. They would have a good time."

"Is your aunt in?" said Mr. Cardew, a little restlessly.

"Oh yes; she'll be down in a minute."

Lady Lysle now hurried into the room.

"How do you do, Cyril?" she said. "I didn't expect to find you in town just now. Is there anything I can do for you?"

"I am rather anxious to have a chat with you," replied Mr. Cardew.

"Aneta darling, you had better leave us," said her aunt.

The girl went off with a light laugh. "Auntie," she said, "I've just been telling Mr. Cardew that he ought to send Cicely and Merry to Aylmer House." She closed the door as she made this parting shot.

"As a matter of fact, I agree with Aneta," said Lady Lysle. "A couple of years at that splendid school would do the girls no end of good."

Mr. Cardew was silent for a minute. "I may as well confess something to you, Lucia," he said then.

"What is it, Cyril?"

"I have by no means made up my mind; but we are very much annoyed at the illness of our daily governess Miss Beverley, and at the girls' music-master

Mr. Bennett removing to London. So I just thought I would ask you a question or two about this wonderful Mrs. Ward. I don't suppose for a single moment I should dream of sending the children there; and, besides, she is not in London now, is she?"

"Yes, she is," replied Lady Lysle. Mr. Cardew felt at that moment that he hated Mrs. Ward. "She came to see me only last evening. She is leaving town to-morrow; but if by any chance you would like to go and see her, and thus judge of the school for yourself—it would commit you to nothing, of course —she will, I know, be at home all this morning."

"Dear, dear!" said Mr. Cardew. "How very provoking!"

"What do you mean, Cyril?"

"Nothing, nothing, of course, Lucia. But if, as you say, the school is so popular, there will be no vacancies, for I think some one told me that Mrs. Ward only took a limited number of pupils."

"There are two vacancies at the present moment," said Lady Lysle in her calm voice, "although they are likely to be filled up immediately, for Mrs. Ward has had many applications; but then she is exceedingly particular, and will only take girls of high birth and of very distinguished character."

"Doubtless she has filled up the vacancies by this morning," said Mr. Cardew, rising with some alacrity. "Well, thank you, Lucia. As I am in town—came up on business you know—I may as well just have a look at Aylmer House and Mrs. Ward. It will satisfy my dear wife."

"Why, surely you don't for a minute really intend to send the girls there?" said Lady Lysle with a superior smile.

"I cannot tell what I may do. When a man is distracted, and when a valuable daily governess breaks down, and—and—don't question me too closely, Lucia, and keep our little interview to yourself. As I have just said, nothing will probably come of this; but I will go and see the lady just to satisfy myself."

"Aneta will be delighted if you do send the girls to Aylmer House," was Lady Lysle's last word.

She laughed as she spoke, and Mr. Cardew found himself turning rather red. He left her, called a hansom, and got into it.

"Of course the vacancies will be filled up," he said to himself as he was driving in the direction of South Kensington. He further thought, "Although that good Mrs. Ward is remaining for such an unconscionable time in town, she will very probably be out this morning. If she is out that puts an end to

59

everything; but even if she is in, she must ave filled up her vacancies. Then I shall be able to return to the Manor with a quiet mind. I'll have done my best, and the thing will be taken out of my hands. Dear little Merry! I didn't like that discontent on her sweet face. Ah, well, she can't guess what school is like. It's not home; but I suppose the educational advantages would be greater, and a man must sacrifice himself for his children. Odd what that queer little Miss Howland told me last night: that I was approaching a deed of self-sacrifice. She's a queer girl, but quite nice; and Aneta is a charming creature. I could never desire even one of my own precious girls to look nicer than Aneta does. Well, here I am. Now, then, what will Fate decide?"

Mr. Cardew sprang from the hansom, desired the man to wait, ran up some low steps, and rang the bell at the front door of a stately mansion.

A smiling, very bright-looking maid-servant opened it for him.

"Is Mrs. Ward, within?" questioned Cardew.

"Yes, sir."

"Good heavens!" murmured Cardew under his breath.

"Is she disengaged, and can she give me a few moments of her time?" continued the much-disappointed gentleman.

"Certainly, sir. Will you come into the drawing-room? What name shall I say?"

Cardew produced one of his cards.

"Have the goodness to tell your mistress that if she is particularly engaged I can "—he hesitated—"call another time."

"I will tell her, sir; but Mrs. Ward is not particularly engaged. She will see you, I am sure, directly."

The girl withdrew, and Cardew sank into a low chair.

He had to wait a few minutes, and during that time had abundant leisure to look round the beautiful room in which he found himself. It was so furnished as to resemble a fresh country room. The wall-paper was white; the pictures were all water-colors, all original, and all the works of well-known artists. They mostly represented country scenes, but there were a few admirable portraits of charming girls just in the heyday of youth and happiness. The floor was of polished oak and had a large pale-blue drugget in the center, which could be rolled up at any moment if an impromptu dance was desirable. The large windows had boxes of flowers outside, which were fresh and well kept, and had evidently been recently watered, for some sparkling drops which looked almost like summer rain still glistened on them. The room itself was also decked with flowers in every available corner, and all these flowers were fresh and beautifully arranged. They were country flowers—and of course roses, roses everywhere. There were also great bowls of mignonette and large glass vases filled with sweet peas.

The air of the room was fresh and full of delicate perfume. Mr. Cardew had to admit to himself that this was a room in which the most refined young ladies in the world might sit with pleasure and profit. There was a shelf for books running round the dado, and the books therein were good of their kind and richly and handsomely bound. There were no small tables anywhere. Mr. Cardew was glad of that—he detested small tables; but there was a harp standing close to the magnificent grand piano, and several music stands, and a violin case on a chair near by.

The furniture of the room was covered with a cool, fresh chintz. In short, it was a charming room, quite different from the rooms at Meredith Manor, which, of course, were old and magnificent and stately; but it had a refreshing, wholesome look about it which, in spite of himself, Mr. Cardew appreciated.

He had just taken in the room and its belongings when the door was opened and a lady of about thirty-five years of age entered. She was dressed very simply in a long dress made in a sort of Empire fashion. The color was pale blue, which suited her calm, fair face, her large, hazel-brown eyes, and her rich chestnut hair to perfection. She came forward swiftly.

"I am Mrs. Ward," she said, and held out her hand.

Mr. Cardew considered himself a connoisseur as regards all women, and he was immediately impressed by a certain quality in that face: a mingling of sweetness and power, of extreme gentleness and extreme determination. There was a lofty expression in the eyes, too, and round the mouth, which further appealed to him; and the hands of the lady were perfect—they were white, somewhat long, with tapering fingers and well-kept nails. There was one signet ring on the left hand, worn as a guard to the wedding-ring—that was all.

Mr. Cardew was a keen observer, and he noted these things at a glance.

"I have come to talk to you, Mrs. Ward," he said; "and, if you will forgive me, I should like to be quite frank with you."

"There is nothing I desire better," said Mrs. Ward in her exceedingly high-bred and sympathetic voice.

That voice reminded Cardew of Maggie Howland, and yet he felt at once that it was infinitely superior to hers.

"Sit down, won't you, Mr. Cardew?" said Mrs. Ward, and she set him the example by seating herself in a low chair as she spoke.

"I hope I am not taking up too much of your time," he said; "for, if so, as I said to your servant, I can call again."

"By no means," said Mrs. Ward; "I have nothing whatever to do this morning. I am, therefore, quite at your service. You will tell me what you wish?" she said in that magnetic voice of hers.

"The fact is simply this," he said. "My friend Tristram, who is rector of Meredith, in Warwickshire, is sending his two daughters to your school."

"Yes," said Mrs. Ward gently. "Molly and Isabel are coming to me next term."

"I am Tristram's near neighbor," said Mr. Cardew, "I live at Meredith Manor. At the present moment the Tristram girls have another pupil of yours staying with them—Miss Howland."

"Yes," said Mrs. Ward very quietly.

"Lady Lysle's niece Aneta is also one of your pupils."

"That is true, Mr. Cardew."

"Lady Lysle is my wife's cousin."

Mrs. Ward bowed very slightly.

"I will come to the point now, Mrs. Ward. I am the father of two little girls. They are of the same age as Molly and Isabel Tristram; that is, they are both just sixteen. They are twins. They are my only children. Some day they will be rich, for we have no son, and they will inherit considerable property." Mrs. Ward looked scarcely interested at this. "Hitherto," continued Mr. Cardew, "I have stoutly opposed school-life for my children, and in consequence they have been brought up at home, and have had the best advantages that could be obtained for them in a country life. Things went apparently all right until two or three days ago, when I discovered that my girl—her name is Meredith; we call her Merry for short—was exceedingly anxious to change her home-life for school-life. At the same time, our excellent daily governess and the music-master who taught the children have been obliged to discontinue their work. The girls are at an age when education is essential; and, although I *hate* schools, I have come here to talk over the possibility of your receiving them."

"Had you delayed coming to me, Mr. Cardew, until this evening I should have had no vacancy, for at the present moment I have twelve applications for the two vacancies which are to be filled at Aylmer House. But do you really wish me to consider the proposal of taking your girls when you hate school-life for young ladies?"

Mr. Cardew could not help smiling. "Then you are not anxious to have them?"

"Certainly not, unless you yourself and Mrs. Cardew most earnestly desire to send them to me. Suppose, before we go any further, that I take you over the house."

"Thank you," said Mr. Cardew in a tone of relief.

Mrs. Ward rose immediately, and for the next hour the head-mistress and the owner of Meredith Manor went from one dainty room to another. They visited the gymnasium; they entered the studio. All the different properties of the music-room were explained to the interested visitor. The excellent playground was also inspected.

By-and-by, when Mr. Cardew returned to the drawing-room, Mrs. Ward said, "My number of pupils is limited. You have seen for yourself that sisters are provided with a room together, and that girls who are not related have rooms to themselves. The house is well warmed in winter, and at all seasons of the year I keep it bright and cheerful with flowers and everything that a judicious expenditure of money can secure. I have my own special plan for educating my girls. I believe in personal influence. In short, Mr. Cardew, I am not at all ashamed to tell you that I believe in my own influence. I have never yet met a girl whom I could not influence."

"If by any chance my Cicely and Merry come to you," said Mr. Cardew, "you will find them—I may at least say it—perfect ladies in word and thought and deed."

Mrs. Ward bowed. "I could receive no others within this establishment," she said. "If," continued Mrs. Ward, "you decide to entrust your daughters to me, I will leave no stone unturned to do my best for them, to educate them in a three-fold capacity: to induce their minds to work as God meant them to work —without overtoil, without undue haste, and yet with intelligence and activity; to give them such exercises as will promote health to their bodies; and to teach them, above all things, to live for others, not for themselves. Please, Mr. Cardew, give me no answer now, but think it over. The vacancies at Aylmer House will remain at your disposal until four o'clock this afternoon. Will you send me before that hour a telegram saying 'Yes' or 'No'?"

"I thank you," said Mr. Cardew. He wrung Mrs. Ward's hand and left the house.

The hall was as spacious and nearly as beautiful as the drawing-room, and the pretty, bright parlor-maid smiled at the gentleman as he went out. Mrs. Ward remained for a time alone after her visitor had left.

"I should like to have those girls," she said to herself. "Any girls related to such a splendid, lofty character as Aneta could not but be welcome to me. Their poor father, he will feel parting with them; but I have no doubt that I shall receive them next September at this house."

The thought had scarcely passed through her mind before there came a brisk ring at the front door, and Lady Lysle and Aneta were announced.

"Oh, dear Mrs. Ward!" said Lady Lysle, speaking in her quick, impulsive manner, "have you seen my dear friend and cousin, Mr. Cardew?"

"And are the girls coming to the school?" asked Aneta.

"I have seen Mr. Cardew," said Mrs. Ward. "He is a very charming man. He will decide whether he will send his daughters here or not during the course of to-day."

"But," said Lady Lysle, "didn't you urge him?"

"No, dear friend; I never urge any one to put a girl in my care. I should feel myself very wrong in doing so. If Mr. Cardew thinks well of what he has seen here he may send his daughters to me, but I certainly did nothing to urge him."

"Oh dear!" said Aneta, "I should so like them to come. You can't think, Mrs. Ward, what nice people the Cardews are; and the girls—they do want school-life. Don't they, auntie darling?"

"Such a school as this would do them a world of good," said Lady Lysle.

"Well, I really hope they will come," said Mrs. Ward; "but I quite understand their father's objections. They are evidently very precious treasures, and he has the sort of objection which exists in the minds of many country gentlemen to sending his girls to school."

"Ah," said Aneta, "but there are schools and schools!"

"The girls will be exceedingly rich," said Lady Lysle. "Their mother was a Meredith and belonged to an old county family. She inherits vast wealth *and* the old family place. Their father is what may be termed a merchant-prince. By-and-by all the money of the parents will go to these girls. They are very nice children, but know nothing whatever of the world. It seems to me a cruel thing that they should be brought up with no knowledge of the great world where they must eventually live."

"I hope they will come here," said Mrs. Ward. "Great wealth means great responsibility. They can make magnificent use of their money. I should be interested to have them."

"I know you would, my dear friend," said Lady Lysle, "and they are really quite sweet girls. Now, come, Aneta; we must not keep Mrs. Ward any longer."

When her visitors had left her Mrs. Ward still remained in the pleasant drawing-room. She sank into a low chair, folded her hands in her lap, and remained very still. Although she was only thirty-five years of age, she had been a widow for over ten years. She had married when quite a young girl, and had lost her husband and child before she was five-and-twenty. It was in her generous and noble nature to love most passionately and all too well. For a time after her terrible trouble she scarcely know how to bear her grief. Then she took it to the one place where such sorrow can be borne—namely, to the foot of the throne of God; and afterwards it occurred to her to devote her life to the education of others. She was quite well-off, and did not need to work for her living. But work, to a nature such as hers, was essential. She also needed the sympathy of others, and the love of others; and so, aided by her friends, her small but most select school in South Kensington was started.

From the very first it was a success. It was unlike many other schools, for the head-mistress had broader and nobler views of life. She loved all her girls, and they all loved her; but it was impossible for her not to like some girls more than others, and of all the girls at present at her school Aneta Lysle was the one she really loved best. There was also, it is sad to relate, a girl there whom she did not love, and that girl was Maggie Howland. There was nothing whatever with regard to Maggie that her mistress could lay hold of. She was quite aware of the girl's fascination, and of her powerful influence over her schoolfellows. Nevertheless, she never thought of her without a sense of discomfort.

Maggie was one of the girls who were educated at Aylmer House for a very low fee; for Mrs. Ward was quite rich enough and generous enough to take girls who could not afford her full terms for very much less. Maggie's fees, therefore, were almost nominal, and no one knew this fact better than Maggie herself and her mother, Mrs. Howland. None of her schoolfellows knew, for she learned just what they did, and had precisely the same advantages. She was treated just like the others. No one could guess that her circumstances were different. And certainly Maggie would never tell, but none the less did she in her heart hate her position.

As a matter of fact, Molly and Isabel Tristram were also coming to the school on specially low terms; but no one would know this. Maggie, however, suspected it, and intended, if necessary, to make the fact an added power over her young friends when they all assembled at Aylmer House.

"Yes," said Mrs. Ward, half-aloud, half to herself, "I don't quite trust Maggie Howland. But I cannot possibly dismiss her from the school. I may win her round to a loftier standard of life, but at present there is no doubt she has not that high ideal in view which I think my other girls aim at."

Between three and four o'clock that day Mrs. Ward received a telegram from Mr. Cardew. It contained the following words:

"After consideration, I have made up my mind to do myself the great honor of confiding my girls to your care. Their mother and I will write to you fully in a day or two."

Mrs. Ward smiled when she received the telegram. "I will do my best for those children," she said to herself.

# CHAPTER IX.

## THE NEWS.

Mr. Cardew arrived at Meredith Manor very late that evening. The long and happy day had come to an end. The Tristram girls and Maggie Howland had returned to the rectory. Cicely and Merry were having a long, confidential chat together. They were in Merry's bedroom. They had dismissed their maid. They were talking of the pleasures of the day, and in particular were discussing the delightful fact that their beautiful cousin Aneta had wired to say she would be with them in two days' time.

They had not seen Aneta for some years, but they both remembered her vividly. Her memory shone out before them both as something specially dazzling and specially beautiful. Maggie Howland, too, had spoken of Aneta's beauty. Maggie had been told that Aneta was coming, and Maggie had expressed pleasure. Whatever Maggie's private feelings may have been, she was very careful now to express delight at Aneta's appearance at Meredith Manor.

"What a darling she is!" said Merry. "I doubt very much—I suppose it's rank heresy to say so, Cicely, but I really greatly doubt whether I shall ever prefer Aneta to Maggie. What are mere looks, after all, when one possesses such charm as Maggie has? That seems to me a much greater gift."

"We need not compare them, need we?" said Cicely.

"Oh, certainly not," said Merry; "but, Cicely darling, doesn't it seem funny that such a lot of girls who are all to meet in September at Aylmer House should be practically staying with us at the present moment?"

"Yes, indeed," said Cicely. "I feel almost as though I belonged to it, which of course is quite ridiculous, for we shall never by any chance go there."

"Of course not," said Merry, and she sighed.

After a time Cicely said, "I wonder what father went to town for to-day."

"Well, we don't know, so where's the use of troubling?" said Merry.

"I asked mother," said Cicely, "why he went to town, and she said she couldn't tell me; but she got rather red as she spoke."

"Cicely," said Merry after a long pause, "when these glorious holidays come to an end, and the Aylmer House girls have gone to Aylmer House, what shall you and I do?"

"Do," said Cicely—"do? I suppose what we've always done. A fresh governess will be found, and another music-master, and we'll work at our lessons and do the best we can."

Merry gave a deep sigh.

"We'll never talk French like Belle Tristram," she said, "and we'll never play so that any one will care to listen to us. We'll never, never know the world the way the others know it. There seems very little use in being rich when one can't get education."

It was just at that moment that there came a light tap at the girls' door. Before they could reply, it was opened and Mrs. Cardew came in. She looked as though she had been crying; nevertheless, there was a joyful sort of triumph on her face. She said quickly, "I thought, somehow, you two naughty children would not be in bed, and I told father that I'd come up on the chance of finding you. Father has come back from London, and has something important to tell you. Will you come down with me at once?"

"Oh mother! mother! what is it?" said Merry in a tone of excitement which was slightly mingled with awe.

"Your father will tell you, my darling," said Mrs. Cardew.

She put her arm round Merry's slight waist and held Cicely's hand, and they came down to the great drawing-room where Mr. Cardew was waiting for them.

He was pacing slowly up and down the room, his hands folded behind his back. His face was slightly tired, and yet he too wore that odd expression of mingled triumph and pain which Mrs. Cardew's eyes expressed.

When the mother and the girls entered the room he at once shut the door. Mr. Cardew looked first of all at Merry. He held out his hand to her. "Come to me, little girl," he said.

She flew to him and put her arms round his neck. She kissed him several times. "Oh dad! dad!" she said, "I know I was downright horrid and unkind and perfectly dreadful yesterday, and I don't—no, I *don't*—want to leave you and mother. If I was discontented then, I am not now."

Merry believed her own words at that moment, for the look on her father's face had struck to her very heart.

He disengaged her pretty arms very gently, and, still holding her hand, went up to Cicely, who was clinging to her mother. "I have just got some news for you both," he said. "You know, of course, that Miss Beverley cannot teach you any longer?"

"Poor old Beverley," said Cicely; "we are so sorry. But you'll find another good governess for us, won't you, dad?"

"I am afraid I can't," said Mr. Cardew, "So I sent for you to-night to tell you that I have broken the resolve which I always meant to keep."

"You have what?" said Merry.

"I have turned my back on a determination which I made when you were both very little girls, and to-day I went up to town and saw Mrs. Ward."

"Oh!" said Merry. She turned white and dropped her father's hand, and, clasping her own two hands tightly together, gazed at him as though she would devour his face.

"Well, it's all settled, children," said Mr. Cardew, "and: when September comes you will go with your friends Molly and Belle to Aylmer House."

This announcement was received at first in total silence. Then Merry flew to her father and kissed him a great many times, and Cicely kissed her mother.

Then Merry said, "We can't talk of it to-night; we can't quite realize it to-night; but—but—we are glad!"

Then she took Cicely's hand, and they went out of the room. Mr. and Mrs. Cardew watched them as the little figures approached the door. Merry opened it, and they both passed out.

"I wonder," said Mr. Cardew, looking at his wife, "if they are going out of our lives."

"Indeed, no," said Mrs. Cardew; "from what you have told me of Mrs. Ward, she must be a good woman—one of the best."

"She is one of the very, very best, Sylvia; and I think the very happiest thing for us both would be to run up to town to-morrow, and for you to see her for yourself."

"Very well, darling; we will do so," said Mrs. Cardew.

# CHAPTER X.

## ANETA.

So everything was settled. Cicely and Merry scarcely slept at all that night. They were too much excited; the news was too wonderful. Now that their wish was granted, there was pain mingled with their joy. It seems as though perfect joy must have its modicum of pain to make it perfect.

But when the next morning dawned the regret of the night before seemed to have vanished. In the first place, Mr. and Mrs. Cardew had gone early to London; and the mere fact that their father and mother were not present was a sort of relief to the excited girls. The picnic need not be postponed, for Mr. and Mrs. Tristram could act as chaperons on this auspicious occasion.

They were all to meet at the Manor at eleven o'clock; and, punctual to the hour, a goodly array of happy young people walked up the avenue and entered the porch of the old-house. Andrew, devoted to Maggie, was present. Jack, equally Maggie's slave, was also there. Maggie herself, looking neat and happy, was helping every one. Molly and Belle, all in white, and looking as charming as little girls could, were full of expectation of their long and delightful day.

One wagonette could hold the whole party, and as it drove round to the front door the boys fiercely took possession of the box-seat, fighting with the coachman, who said that there would be no room for Miss Howland to sit between them.

"Well then, Mags, if that is the case," said Peterkins, "you get along in at once, and take this corner close to me; then, whenever we want, we can do a bit of whispering."

"You won't whisper more than your share," said Jackdaw. "I've a frightful lot to say to Mags this morning."

"Hush, boys!" said Maggie; "if you quarrel about me I shall not speak to either of you."

This threat was so awful that the boys glanced at each other, remained silent and got quietly into their places. Then the hampers were put on the floor just under their feet.

Presently Cicely and Merry came out to join the group. They were wearing pretty pink muslins, with pink sashes to match. Merry's beautiful dark eyes were very bright. Mr. and Mrs. Tristram inquired for their host and hostess.

"Oh, I have news for you!" said Merry.

"Yes," said Cicely, "Merry will tell."

"Well, it's Just this," said Merry, almost jerking out her words in excitement: "Father and mother have been obliged to go rather unexpectedly to town."

"Why?" said Maggie; then she restrained herself, knowing that it was not her place to speak.

"They have gone to town," said Merry, scarcely looking at Maggie now, and endeavoring with all her might and main not to show undue excitement, "because a great and wonderful thing has happened; something so unexpected that—that Cicely and I can scarcely believe it."

Maggie glanced at the sweet little faces. She said to herself, "All right," and got calmly into the wagonette, where she sat close under the box-seat which contained those obstreperous young heroes Andrew and Jack. The others clustered round Merry.

"As I said, I can scarcely believe it," said Merry; "but father has done the most marvelous thing. Oh Belle! oh Molly! it is too wonderful! For after all— after all, Cicely and I are to go with you to Aylmer House in September, and —and—that is why father and mother have gone to town. Father went up yesterday and saw Mrs. Ward, and he—he settled it; and father and mother have gone up to-day—both of them—to see her, and to make final arrangements. And we're to go! we're to *go*!"

"Hurrah!" cried Molly. Immediately the boys, and Maggie and Belle, and even Mr. and Mrs. Tristram, took up the glad "Hurrah!"

"Well, children," said Mr. Tristram when the first excitement had subsided, "I must say I am heartily pleased. This is delightful! I take some credit to myself for having helped on this most excellent arrangement."

"No one thanks me for anything," thought Maggie; but she had the prudence to remain silent.

"We had better start on our picnic now," said Mr. Tristram, and immediately the whole party climbed into the wagonette. The horses started; the wheels rolled. They were off.

By-and-by Merry felt her hand taken by Maggie. Maggie just squeezed that hand, and whispered in that very, very rich and wonderfully seductive voice of hers, "Oh, I am glad! I am very, very glad!"

Merry felt her heart thrill as Maggie uttered those words. She answered back, turning her face to her young companion, "To be with you alone would be happiness enough for me."

"Is it true, Cicely," said Mrs. Tristram at the moment, "that your cousin, Aneta Lysle, is coming to stay with you?"

"Oh yes; but I had half-forgotten it in all this excitement," said Cicely. "She will arrive to-morrow.—Maggie, you'll be glad, won't you?"

"More than delighted," said Maggie.

"It is too wonderful," said Cicely. "Why, it will soon come to pass that half Mrs. Ward's school will be all together during the holidays. Fancy, we two, and you two"—she touched one of the Tristram girls—"and you, Maggie, and then dear Aneta; why, that'll make six. What a lot we shall have to talk about! Maggie, you and Aneta will be our two heroines; we shall always be applying to you for information."

The conversation was here interrupted by Jackdaw, who pinched Maggie on the arm. "You're not attending to us," he said.

"Nonsense, Jackdaw!"

"Well, stand up for a minute; I want to whisper to you."

Maggie, who never lost a chance of ingratiating herself with any one, obeyed.

"Jack dear, don't be troublesome," said his mother.

"I am not," said Jackdaw. "She loves it, the duck that she is!"

"Be quick, Jackdaw; it's very difficult for me to keep my hold standing up," said Maggie.

"How many chocolates can you eat at a pinch?" whispered Jackdaw in her ear.

"Oh, forty," replied Maggie; "but I should be rather ill afterwards."

"We've got some in our pockets. They're a little bit clammy, but you don't mind that?"

"I don't want any just now, dear boy; and I'll tell you why. I want to be really starving hungry when the picnic begins."

"That's a good notion, isn't it?" said Jackdaw.—"I say, Andrew, she wants to be starving hungry when the picnic begins!"

Maggie resumed her seat, and the boys went on whispering together, and kicking each other at intervals, and rather upsetting that very stolid personage, Mr. Charles, the Meredith Manor coachman.

The picnic was a perfect success. When people are very happy there is no room for discontent in their hearts, and all the members of that party were in the highest spirits. The Cardew girls had no time yet for that period of regret which must invariably follow a period of intense excitement. They had no time yet to realize that they must part with their father and mother for the greater portion of the year.

To children so intensely affectionate as Cicely and Merry such a parting must mean considerable pain. But even the beginning of the pain did not come to them on that auspicious day, and they returned to the house after the picnic in the highest good-humor.

Mr. and Mrs. Tristram, however, were wise in their generation; and although Cicely and Merry begged and implored the whole party to come to the Manor for supper, they very firmly declined. It is to be regretted that both Jack and Andrew turned sulky on this occasion.

As the rectory girls and Maggie and the boys and Mr. and Mrs. Tristam were all going homewards the two girls and Maggie fell behind.

"Isn't this real fun? Isn't it magnificent?" said Molly Tristram.

"It's a very good thing indeed for your friends Cicely and Merry," said Maggie. Then she added, "Didn't I tell you, girls, that you would win your bracelets?"

Belle felt herself changing color.

"We don't want them a bit—we really don't," said Molly.

"Of course we don't want them," said Isabel.

"You'll have them all the same," said Maggie. "They are my present to you. Surely you won't refuse my present?"

"But such a very rich and handsome present we ought not to accept," said Molly.

"Nonsense, girls! I shall be unhappy unless you wear them. When I return to mother—which, alas! I must do before many days are over—I shall send you the bracelets."

"I wish you wouldn't, Maggie," said Belle Tristram; "for I am certain father and mother would not like us to wear jewelry while we are so young."

"Well, then," said Maggie, "I will give them to you when we all meet at Aylmer House. You must take them; you know you promised you would. You will hurt me most frightfully if you don't."

As Molly and Isabel certainly did not wish to hurt Maggie, they remained silent, and during the rest of the walk the three girls scarcely spoke. Meanwhile Cicely and Merry entered the Manor House and waited impatiently for the return of their father and mother.

"We must get everything extra nice for them," said Cicely to her sister. "I do think it is so wonderfully splendid of them to send us to school."

The sun had already set, and twilight had come on; but it would be quite impossible for Mr. and Mrs. Cardew to arrive at the Manor until about ten o'clock. What, therefore, was the amazement of the girls when they heard carriage-wheels in the distance!

"Father and mother could not possibly have done their business and caught the early train," said Merry in some excitement. "Who can be coming now?"

The next moment their doubts were set at rest, for Aneta Lysle entered the hall.

"I came to-day after all," she said. "Auntie thought it would be more convenient. You got my telegram, didn't you?"

These words were uttered while her two cousins, in rapture and delight, were kissing her.

"No, no," said Merry, "we got no telegram; but, oh, Aneta! we are glad to see you."

"Here's the telegram on the hall-table," said Aneta, and she took up a yellow envelope. This was addressed to "Cardew, Meredith Manor." "Yes, I know this must be from me," said Aneta. "But why didn't you open it?"

"Well, the fact is," said Cicely, "father and mother were in London, and the rest of us were out on a picnic. But it doesn't matter a bit; you've come, and the sooner the better. Oh, it is nice to see you again! But how tall you are, Neta, and how grown up you look!"

"I am seventeen, remember," said Aneta. "I don't feel grown-up, but auntie says I look it."

"Oh, come into the light—do," said Merry, "and let's see you! We've heard so very much of you lately, and we want to look at your darling face again."

"And I want to look at you both," said Aneta in her affectionate manner.

The servants had conveyed Miss Lysle's luggage into the house, and now the three girls, with their arms twined round each other, entered the same big drawing-room where Mr. Cardew had given his wonderful news of the night before. There was a blaze of electric light, and this, judiciously softened with rose-colored silk, was most becoming to all those who came under its influence. But the strongest glare of light could not disfigure any one so absolutely beautiful as Aneta Lysle. Her delicate complexion, the wonderful purity and regularity of her features, her sweet, tender young mouth, her charming blue eyes, and her great luxuriance of golden hair made people who looked at her once long to study that charming face again and yet again.

There was no vanity about this young girl; her manner, her expression, were simplicity itself. There was a certain nobility about her fine forehead, and the shape of her head was classical, and showed undoubted talent. Her clear, musical voice was in itself a charm. Her young figure was the very personification of grace. Beside her, Cicely and Merry felt awkward and commonplace; not that they were so, but very few people could attain to Aneta Lysle's incomparable beauty.

"Well, girls," she said, "you do look sweet, both of you!"

"Oh Neta, what a darling you are!" said Merry, who worshipped beauty, and had never come across any one so lovely as her cousin. "It's two years since we met," she continued, "and you have altered, and not altered. You're more grown-up and more—more stately, but your face is the same. Whenever we want to think of the angels we think of you too, Neta."

"That is very sweet of you, darlings; but, indeed, I am far from being an angel. I am just a very human girl; and, please, if you don't mind, we won't discuss my looks any more."

Cicely and Merry both save their cousin a thoughtful glance. Then they said eagerly, "You must come to your room and wash your hands, and get refreshed for supper, for of course you are starving."

"I shall like to have something to eat," said Aneta. "What room am I to have, girls?"

"Oh, the white room, next to ours; we arranged it all this morning," said Cicely.

"Well, come along at once," said Aneta.

Soon the three girls found themselves in the beautiful bedroom which had been arranged for Aneta's reception. As soon as ever they got there Cicely clasped one of her cousin's arms and Merry the other.

"We have news for you—news!" they said.

"Yes?" said Aneta, looking at them with her bright, soft eyes.

"Most wonderful—most extraordinary—most—most beautiful!" said Merry, speaking almost with passion. "We're going to your school; yes, to yours—to Aylmer House, in September. Could you have believed it? Think of father consenting, and just because I felt a little discontented. Oh, isn't he an angel? Father, of all people, who until now would not hear of our leaving home! But we're going."

"Well," said Aneta, "I am not greatly surprised, for I happen to know that your father, Cousin Cyril, came to see auntie yesterday, and afterwards he went to visit Mrs. Ward, and after his visit we saw Mrs. Ward; and, although he had not quite made up his mind then whether he would send you or not, we quite thought he would do so. Yes, this is splendid. I'll he able to tell you lots about the school; but, after all, it isn't the school that matters."

"Then what matters, Aneta?"

"It's Mrs. Ward herself," said Aneta; "it's she who makes the whole thing so perfect. She guides us; she enlightens us. Sometimes I can scarcely talk of her, my love for her and my passion for her are so deep."

Cicely and Merry looked thoughtful for a minute.

"I'm ready now to come downstairs," said Aneta; and they went down, to find supper prepared for them, and the old butler waiting to attend on his young ladies.

After the meal was over the girls retired to the drawing-room, where they all three sat by one of the windows waiting for Mr. and Mrs. Cardew's return.

Merry then said, "It is so funny of you, Aneta, to speak as though the school was Mrs. Ward."

"But it is," said Aneta.

"Surely, surely," said Merry, "it's the girls too."

"You will be surprised, perhaps, Aneta, to hear," said Cicely, "that our dear, darling friends—our greatest girl-friends, except yourself perhaps, and you're a sort of sister—Molly and Isabel Tristram are also going to Aylmer House in September. They are so nice—you will like them; and then, of course, there's Maggie Howland, one of the most charming girls we have come across."

"Whom did you say?" asked Aneta.

"Maggie Howland. She is here."

"In this house?" said Aneta.

"No; she is at the rectory. She is a special friend of Molly and Isabel. She has been at school with them before in Hanover. You know her, of course? She is one of the girls at Aylmer House."

"I know her—oh yes, I know her," said Aneta.

"And you like her, you feel her charm, you—you almost worship her, don't you, Neta?"

76

Aneta was silent.

"Oh, I know she is considered plain," said Merry, "but there's something about her which prevents one even considering her features. She is the most unselfish, most fascinating girl we have ever come across. You love her, don't you, Neta?"

There had come a curious change over Aneta's face. After a brief pause she said, "I have no right to say it, but you two are my cousins"—

"Yes, yes! What does this mean?" said Cicely with great eagerness.

"Well, I know you will be faithful and not repeat it to any one; but I don't love Maggie Howland."

"Oh, Neta!"

"And," continued Aneta, "you; as my cousins, I most earnestly hope, will not make her your special friend at Aylmer House."

"But we have done so already, Neta. Oh, Neta darling! you are mistaken in her."

"I say nothing whatever against her," said Aneta, "except that personally I do not care for her. I should be very glad if I found that I had misjudged her."

"Then why don't you want us to be friends with her? We are friends with her."

"I cannot control you, darlings. When you come to school you will see a variety of girls, and most of them—indeed, all of them—nice, I think."

"Then why shouldn't we like poor Maggie?"

"You do like her, it seems, already."

"Yes; but you are so mysterious, Neta."

"I cannot say any more; you must forgive me," answered Aneta. "And I hear the sound of wheels. Your father and mother are coming."

"Yes, yes, the darlings!" said Merry, rushing into the hall to meet her parents.

Aneta and Cicely followed her example, and there was great excitement and much talk. Mrs. Cardew was now as anxious that the girls should go to Aylmer House as though she herself had always wished for such an arrangement, while Mr. Cardew could not say enough in Mrs. Ward's praise.

"You agree with me, Aneta," said Mrs. Cardew, "that the school is quite unique and above the ordinary."

"Mrs. Ward is unique and above the ordinary," was Aneta's reply.

When the girls retired to their own rooms that night, Cicely and Merry met for a brief moment.

"How funny of Aneta not to like Maggie!" said Merry.

"Well, if I were you, Merry," said Cicely, "I wouldn't talk about it. I suppose Aneta is prejudiced."

"Yes," said Merry; "but against Maggie, of all people! Well, I, for my part, will never give her up."

"I suppose," said Cicely, who was more conscientious than her sister, "that we ought to think something of Aneta's opinion."

"Oh, that's very fine," said Merry; "but we ought to think something, too, of Molly's opinion, and Belle's opinion. They have known Maggie longer than Aneta has."

"Yes," replied Cicely; "I forgot that. But isn't Aneta herself delightful? It's a pure joy to look at her."

"It certainly is," said Merry; "and of course I love her dearly and am very proud of her; but I confess I did not quite like her when she spoke in that queer way about dear little Maggie. I, at least, am absolutely determined that nothing will induce me to give Maggie up."

"Of course we won't give her up," said Cicely. But she spoke with thought.

---

# CHAPTER XI.

## TEN POUNDS.

In perfect summer weather, when the heart is brimful of happiness, and when a great desire has been unexpectedly fulfilled, what can there possibly be more delightful than an open-air life? This was what the girls who belonged to the rectory and the girls who belonged to the Manor now found. Mr. and Mrs. Cardew and Mr. and Mrs. Tristram could not do enough for their benefit. Maggie could only stay for one week longer with her friends; but Aneta had changed her mind with regard to Belgium, and was to go with the young Cardews to the seaside, and Mrs. Cardew had asked the Tristram girls to accompany them. She had also extended her invitation to Maggie, who would have given a great deal to accept it. She wrote to her mother on the subject. Mrs. Howland made a brief reply: "You know it is impossible, Maggie. You must come back to me early next week. I cannot do without you, so say no more about it."

Maggie was a girl with a really excellent temper, and, recognizing that her mother had a good reason for not giving her the desired holiday, made the best of things.

Meanwhile Cicely and Merry watched her carefully. As to Aneta, she was perfectly cordial with Maggie, not talking to her much, it is true, but never showing the slightest objection to her society. Nevertheless, there was, since the arrival of Aneta on the scene, a strange, undefinable change in the atmosphere. Merry noticed this more than Cicely. It felt to her electrical, as though there might be a storm brewing.

On the day before Maggie was to return to London to take up her abode in her mother's dull house in Shepherd's Bush, a magnificent picnic on a larger scale even than usual was the order of the hour. Some young girls of the name of Heathfield who lived a little way off were asked to Meredith Manor to spend the night, and these girls, who were exceedingly jolly and bright and lively, were a fresh source of delight to all those whom they happened to meet. Their names were Susan and Mary Heathfield. They were older than the Tristrams and the Cardews, and had, in fact, just left school. Their last year of school-life had been spent in Paris; they were highly educated, and had an enviable proficiency in the French tongue.

Mr. and Mrs. Heathfield, the parents of these girls, were also guests at the Manor, so that the picnic on this last day of Maggie's visit to the rectory was quite a large one. They drove nearly twenty miles to a beautiful place not far from Warwick. There the usual picnic arrangements were made with great satisfaction; dinner was eaten out-of-doors, and presently there was to be a gipsy-tea. This all the girls looked forward to, and Andrew and Jack were wild with delight over the prospect of making the kettle boil. This particular task was given to them, and very proud they were of the trust reposed in them.

But now, dinner being over, the older people took shelter from the fierce rays of the sun under the wide-spreading trees, and the young people moved about in groups or in couples. Merry Cardew found herself alone with Maggie Howland. Without intending to do so, she had slightly, very slightly, avoided Maggie during the last day or two; but Maggie now seized her arm and drew her down a shady glade.

"Come with me, Merry," she said; "I have a lot I want to say to you."

Merry looked at her. "Of course I will come with you, Maggie," she answered.

"I want just to get quite away from the others," continued Maggie, "for we shall not meet again until we meet in the autumn at Aylmer House. You don't know, perhaps—do you, Merry—that you owe the great joy of coming to that lovely school to me?"

"To you!" said Merry in the utmost amazement.

"Yes," replied Maggie in her calmest tone, "to me."

"Oh, dear Maggie!" replied Merry, "you surely must be mistaken."

"I don't intend to explain myself," said Maggie; "I simply state what is a fact. You owe your school-life to me. It was I who inserted the thin end of the wedge beneath your father's fixed resolution that you were to be educated at home. It was I, in short, who acted the part of the fairy princess and who pulled those silken reins which brought about the desire of your heart."

"I don't understand you, Maggie," said Merry in a distressful tone; "but I suppose," she added, "as you say so, it is the case. Only, I ought to tell you that what really and truly happened was this"—

"Oh, I know quite well what really and truly happened," interrupted Maggie. "Let me tell you. I know that there came a certain day when a little girl who calls herself Merry Cardew was very discontented, and I know also that kind Mr. Cardew discovered the discontent of his child. Well, now, who put that discontent into your mind?"

"Why, I am afraid it was you," said Merry, turning pale and then red.

Maggie laughed. "Why, of course it was," she said; "and you suppose I didn't do it on purpose?"

"But, Maggie, you didn't really mean—you couldn't for a minute mean—that I was to be miserable at home if father didn't give his consent?"

"Of course not," said Maggie lightly; "but, you see, I meant him to give his consent—I meant it all the time. I own that there were several favoring circumstances; but I want to tell you now, Merry, in the strictest confidence of course, that from the moment I arrived at the rectory I determined that you and Cicely were to come with Molly and Isabel to Aylmer House."

"It was very kind of you, Maggie," said Merry; but she felt a certain sense of distress which she could not quite account for as she spoke.

"Why do you look so melancholy?" said Maggie, turning and fixing her queer, narrow eyes on the pretty face of her young companion.

"I am not really melancholy, only I would much rather you had told me openly at the time that you wished me to come to school."

Maggie gave a faint sigh. "Had I done so, darling," she said, "you would never have come. You must leave your poor friend Maggie to manage things in her own way. But now I have something else to talk about."

They had gone far down the glade, and were completely separated from their companions.

"Sit down," said Maggie; "it's too hot to walk far even under the shade of the trees."

They both sat down.

Maggie tossed off her hat. "To-morrow," she said, "you will perhaps be having another picnic, or, at any rate, the best of good times with your friends."

"I hope so," replied Merry.

"But I shall be in hot, stifling London, in a little house, in poky lodgings; to-morrow, at this hour, I shall not be having what you call a good time."

"But, Maggie, you will be with your mother."

"Yes, poor darling mother! of course."

"Don't you love her very much?" asked Merry.

Maggie flashed round an excited glance at her companion. "Love her? Yes," she said, "I love her."

"But you must love her tremendously," said Merry—"as much as I love my mother."

"As a rule all girls love their mothers," said Maggie. "We are not talking about that now, are we?"

"What do you want to say to me in particular, Maggie?" was Merry's response.

"This. We shall meet at school on the 20th of September. There will be, as I have told you already, twenty boarders at Aylmer House. You will arrive at the school as strangers; so will Molly and Isabel arrive as strangers; but you will have two friends—Aneta Lysle and myself. You're very much taken, with your cousin Aneta, are you not?"

"Taken with her?" said Merry. "That seems to me a curious expression. She is our cousin, and she is beautiful."

"Merry, I must tell you something. At Aylmer House there are two individuals who lead the school."

"Oh," said Merry, "I thought Mrs. Ward led the school."

"Of course, of course, Mrs. Ward is just splendid; but, you see, you, poor Merry, know nothing of school-life. School-life is really controlled—I mean the inner part of it—by the girls themselves. Now, there are two girls at Aylmer House who control the school: one of them is your humble servant, Maggie Howland; the other is your cousin, Aneta Lysle. Aneta does not love me; and, to be frank with you, I hate her."

Merry found herself turning very red. She remembered Aneta's words on the night of her arrival.

"She has already told you," said Maggie, "that she doesn't like me."

Merry remained silent.

"Oh, you needn't speak. I know quite well," said Maggie.

Merry felt more and more uncomfortable.

"The petition I have to make to you is this," continued Maggie: "that at school you will, for a time at least—say for the first month or so—be *neutral*. I want you and Cicely and Molly and Isabel to belong neither to Aneta's party nor to mine; and I want you to do this because—because I have been the person who has got you to Aylmer House. Just remain neutral for a month. Will you promise me that?"

"I don't understand you. You puzzle me very much indeed," said Merry.

"You will understand fast enough when you get to Aylmer House. I wish I were not going away; I wish I hadn't to return to mother. I wish I could go with you all to Scarborough; but I am the last girl on earth to neglect my duties, and my duty is to be with poor dear mother. You will understand that what I ask is but reasonable. If four new girls came to the school, and altogether went over to Aneta's side, where should I be? What chance should I have? But I do not ask you to come to my side; I only ask you to be neutral. Merry, will you promise?"

"You distress me more than I can say," replied Merry. "I feel so completely in the dark. I don't, of course, want to take any side."

"Ah, then you will promise?" said Maggie.

"I don't know what to say."

"Let me present a picture to you," continued Maggie. "There are two girls; they are not equally equipped for the battle of life. I say nothing of injustice in the matter; I only state a fact. One of them is rich and highly born, and endowed with remarkable beauty of face. That girl is your own cousin, Aneta Lysle. Then there is the other girl, Maggie Howland, who is ugly."

"Oh no—no!" said Merry affectionately.

"Yes, darling," said Maggie, using her most magnetic voice, "really ugly."

"Not in my eyes," said Merry.

"She is ugly," repeated Maggie, speaking with great calm; "and—yes—she is poor. I will tell you as a great secret—I have never breathed it to a soul yet— that it would be impossible for this girl to be an inmate of Aylmer House if Mrs. Ward, in the kindness of her great heart, had not offered her very special terms. You will never breathe that, Merry, not even to Cicely?"

"Oh, poor Maggie!" said Merry, "are you really—really as poor as that?"

"Church mice aren't poorer," said Maggie. "But never mind; I have got something which even your Aneta hasn't got. I have talent, and I have the power—the power of charming. I want most earnestly to be your special friend, Merry. I have a very affectionate heart, and I love you and Cicely and Molly and Isabel more than I can say; but of all you four girls I love you the best. You come first in my heart; and to see you at my school turning away from me and going altogether to Aneta's side would give me agony. There, I can't help it. Forgive me. I'll be all right in a minute."

Maggie turned her face aside. She had taken out her handkerchief and was pressing it to her eyes. Real tears had filled them, for her emotions were genuine enough.

"Don't you think," she said after a pause, "that you, who are so rich in this world's goods, might be kind and loving to a poor little plain girl who loves you but who has got very little?"

"Indeed, indeed, I shall always love you, dear Maggie," said Merry.

"Then you will do what I want?"

"I don't like to make promises, and I am so much in the dark; but I can certainly say this—that, whatever happens, I shall be your friend at school. I shall look to you to help me in a hundred ways."

"Will you indeed, darling Merry?"

"Of course I shall. I always intended to, and I think Cicely will do just the same."

"I don't want you to talk to Cicely about this. She doesn't care for me as much as you do."

"Perhaps not quite," said honest Merry.

"Oh, I am sure—certain of it. Then you will be my friend as I shall be yours, and when we meet at Aylmer House you will talk of me to others as your friend?"

"Of course I shall."

"That's what I require. The thought of your friendship when I love you so passionately makes sunshine in my heart. I sha'n't be miserable at all to-morrow after what you have said. I shall think of our pleasant talk under this great oak-tree; I shall recall this lovely, perfect day. Merry, you have made me very happy!"

"But please understand," said Merry, "that, although I am your friend, I cannot give up Aneta."

"Certainly not, dear; only, don't take what you call sides. It is quite reasonable to suppose that girls who have only just come to school would prefer to be there at first quite free and untrammeled; and to belong to a certain set immediately trammels you."

"Well, I, for one, will promise—at any rate at first—that I won't belong to any set," said Merry. "Now, are you satisfied, Maggie?"

"Oh, truly I am! Do let me kiss you, darling."

The girls kissed very affectionately.

Then Maggie said, "Now I am quite happy." After a pause, she continued as though it were an after-thought, "Of course you won't speak of this to any one?"

"Unless, perhaps, to Cicely," said Merry.

"No, not even to Cicely; for if you found it hard to understand, she would find it impossible."

"But," said Merry, "I never had a secret from her in my life. She is my twin, you know."

"Please, please," said Maggie, "keep this little secret all to yourself for my sake. Oh, do think how important it is to me, and how much more you have to be thankful for than I have!"

"If you feel it like that, poor Maggie," said Merry, "I will keep it as my own secret."

"Then I have nothing further to say." Maggie sprang to her feet. "There are the boys running to meet us," she said. "I know they'll want my help in preparing the fire for the gipsy-kettle."

"And I will join the others. There's Susan Heathfield; she is all alone," said Merry. "But one moment first, please, Maggie. Are you going to make Molly and Isabel bind themselves by the same promise?"

"Dear me, no!" said Maggie. "They will naturally be my friends without any effort; but you are the one I want, for you are the one I truly love."

"Hallo! there you are," called Andrew's voice, "hobnobbing, as usual, with Merry Cardew."

"I say, Merry," cried Jack, "it is unfair of you to take our Maggie away on her last day."

The two boys now rushed up.

"I am going to cry bottles-full to-morrow," said Andrew; "and, although I am a boy, about to be a man, I'm not a bit ashamed of it."

"I'll beat you at that," said Jackdaw, "for I'll cry basins-full."

"Dear me, boys, how horrid of you!" said Maggie. "What on earth good will crying do to me? And you'll both be so horribly limp and damp after it."

"Well, come now," said Jackdaw, pulling her by one arm while Peterkin secured the other.—"You've had your share of her, Merry, and it's our turn."

Maggie and her devoted satellites went off in the direction where the bonfire was to be made; and Merry, walking slowly, joined Susan Heathfield.

Susan was more than two years older than Merry, and on that account the younger girls looked up to her with a great deal of respect. Up to the present, however, they had had no confidential talk.

Susan now said, "So you are to be a schoolgirl after all?"

"Yes. Isn't it jolly?" said Merry.

"Oh, it has its pros and cons," replied Susan. "In one sense, there is no place like school; but in the best sense of all there is no place like home."

"Were you long at school, Susan?"

"Of course; Mary and I went to a school in Devonshire when we were quite little girls. I was eleven and Mary ten. Afterwards we were at a London school, and then we went to Paris. We had an excellent time at all our schools; but I think the best fun of all was the thought of the holidays and coming home again."

"That must be delightful," said Merry. "Did you make many friends at school?"

"Well, of course," said Susan. "But now let me give you a word of advice, Merry. You are going to a most delightful school, which, alas! we were not lucky enough to get admitted to, although mother tried very hard. It may be different at Aylmer House from what it is in the ordinary school, but I would strongly advise you and Cicely not to join any clique at school."

"Oh dear, how very queer!" said Merry, and she reddened deeply.

"Why do you look like that?" said Susan.

"Nothing, nothing," said Merry.

Susan was silent for a minute or two. Then she said, "That's a curious-looking girl."

"What girl?" said Merry indignantly.

"I think you said her name was Howland—Miss Howland."

"She is one of the most delightful girls I know," replied Merry at once.

"Well, I don't know her, you see, so I can't say. Aneta tells me that she is a member of your school."

"Yes; and I am so delighted!" said Merry.

Again Susan Heathfield was silent, feeling a little puzzled; but Merry quickly changed the conversation, for she did not want to have any more talk with regard to Maggie Howland. Merry, however, had a very transparent face. Her conversation with her friend had left traces of anxiety and even slight apprehension on her sweet, open face. Merry Cardew was oppressed by the first secret of her life, and it is perhaps to be regretted, or perhaps the reverse, that she found it almost impossible to keep a secret.

"Well," Cicely said to her as they were hurrying from the shady woods in the direction of the picnic-tea, "what is wrong with you, Merry? Have you a headache?"

"Oh no; I am perfectly all right," said Merry, brightening up. "It's only—well, to say the truth, I am sorry that Maggie is going to-morrow."

"You are very fond of her, aren't you?" said Cicely.

"Well, yes; that is it, I am," said Merry.

"We'll see plenty of her at school, anyway," said Cicely.

"I wish she were rich," said Merry. "I hate to think of her as poor."

"Is she poor?" asked Cicely.

"Oh yes; she was just telling me, poor darling!"

"I don't understand what it means to be poor," said Cicely. "People say it is very bad, but somehow I can't take it in."

"Maggie takes it in, at any rate," said Merry. "Think of us to-morrow, Cicely, having more fun, being out again in the open air, having pleasant companions all round us, and our beautiful home to go back to, and our parents, whom we love so dearly; and then, next week, of the house by the sea, and Aneta and Molly and Isabel our companions."

"Well, of course," said Cicely.

"And then think of poor Maggie," continued Merry. "She'll be shut up in a musty, fusty London lodging. I can't think how she endures it."

"I don't know what a musty, fusty lodging is," said Cicely; "but she could have come with us, because mother invited her."

"She can't, because her own mother wants her. Oh dear! I wish we could have her and her mother too."

"Come on now, Merry, I don't think we ought to ask father and mother to invite Mrs. Howland."

"Of course not. I quite understand that," replied Merry. "Nevertheless, I am a little sad about dear Maggie."

Merry's sadness took a practical form. She thought a great deal about her friend during the rest of that day, although Maggie rather avoided her. She thought, in particular, of Maggie's poverty, and wondered what poverty really meant. The poor people—those who were called poor at Meredith—did not really suffer at all, for it was the bounden duty of the squire of the Manor to see to all their wants, to provide them with comfortable houses and nice gardens, and if they were ill to give them the advice of a good doctor, also to send them nourishing food from the Manor. But poor people of that sort were quite different from the Maggie Howland sort. Merry could not imagine any lord of the manor taking Maggie and Mrs. Howland in hand and providing them with all the good things of life.

But all of a sudden it darted through her eager, affectionate little heart that she herself might be lord of the manor to Maggie, and might help Maggie out of her own abundance. If it were impossible to get Maggie Howland and her mother both invited to Scarborough, why should not she, Merry, provide Maggie with means to take her mother from the fusty, dusty lodgings to another seaside resort?

Merry thought over this for some time, and the more she thought over it the more enamored she was of the idea. She and Cicely had, of course, no special means of their own, nor could they have until they came of age. Nevertheless, they were allowed as pocket-money ten pounds every quarter. Now, Merry's ten pounds would be due in a week. She really did not want it. When she got it she spent it mostly on presents for her friends and little gifts for the villagers; but on this occasion she might give it all in one lump sum to Maggie Howland. Surely her father would let her have it? She might give it to Maggie early to-morrow morning. Maggie would not be too proud to accept it just as a tiny present.

Merry had as little idea how far ten pounds would go toward the expenses of a visit to the seaside as she had of what real poverty meant. But it occurred to her as a delightful way of assuring Maggie of her friendship to present Maggie with her quarter's pocket-money.

On their way home that evening, therefore, she was only too glad to find herself by her father's side.

"Well, little girl," he said, "so you're forsaking all your young companions and wish to sit close to the old dad?"

The old dad, it may be mentioned, was driving home in a mail-phaeton from the picnic, and Merry found herself perched high up beside him as he held the reins and guided a pair of thoroughbred horses.

"Well, what is it, little girl?" he said.

"I wonder, father, if you'd be most frightfully kind?"

"What!" he answered, just glancing at her; "that means that you are discontented again. What more can I do for you, Merry?"

"If I might only have my pocket-money to-night."

"You extravagant child! Your pocket-money! It isn't due for a week."

"But I do want it very specially. Will you advance it to me just this once, dad?"

"I am not to know why you want it?"

"No, dad darling, you are not to know."

Mr. Cardew considered for a minute.

"I hope you are not going to be a really extravagant woman, Merry," he said. "To tell the truth, I hate extravagance, although I equally hate stinginess. You will have no lack of money, child, but money is a great and wonderful gift and ought to be used to the best of best advantages. It ought never to be wasted, for there are so many people who haven't half enough, and those who are rich, my child, ought to help those who are not rich."

"Yes, darling father," said Merry; "and that is what I should so awfully like to do."

"Well, I think you have the root of the matter in you," said Mr. Cardew, "and I, for one, am the last person to pry on my child. Does Cicely also want her money in advance?"

"Oh no, no! I want it for a very special reason."

"Very well, my little girl. Come to me in the study to-night before you go to bed, and you shall have your money."

"In sovereigns, please, father?"

"Yes, child, in sovereigns."

"Thank you ever so much, darling."

During the rest of the drive there was no girl happier than Merry Cardew. Mr. Cardew looked at her once or twice, and wondered what all this meant. But he was not going to question her.

When they got home he took her away to his study, and, opening a drawer, took out ten sovereigns.

"I may as well tell you," he said as he put them into her hand, "that when you go to school I shall raise your pocket-money allowance to fifteen pounds a quarter. That is quite as large a sum as a girl of your age ought to have in the year. I do this because I well understand that at Mrs. Ward's school there will be special opportunities for you to act in a philanthropic manner."

"Oh, thank you, thank you, father!" said Merry.

# HAPTER XII.

## SHEPHERD'S BUSH.

While Merry was in a state of high rejoicing at this simple means of helping her friend, Maggie Howland herself was not having quite such a good time. She had been much relieved by her conversation with Merry, but shortly after the picnic-tea Aneta had come up to her.

"Would you like to walk with me," said Aneta, "as far as the giant oak? It isn't a great distance from here, and I'll not keep you long."

"Certainly I will come with you, Aneta," said Maggie; but she felt uncomfortable, and wondered what it meant.

The two girls set off together. They made a contrast which must have been discernible to the eyes of all those who saw them: Aneta the very essence of elegance; Maggie spotlessly neat, but, compared to her companion, downright plain. Aneta was tall and slim; Maggie was short. Nevertheless, her figure was her good point, and she made the most of it by having perfectly fitting clothes. This very fact, however, took somewhat from her appearance, and gave her the look of a grown-up girl, whereas she was still only a child.

As soon as ever the girls got out of earshot, Aneta turned to Maggie and said gravely, "My cousins the Cardews are to join us all at Aylmer House in September."

Maggie longed to say, "Thank you for nothing," but she never dared to show rudeness to Aneta. No one had ever been rude to the stately young lady.

"Yes," she said. Then she added, "I am so glad! Aren't you?"

"For some reasons I am very glad," said Aneta.

"But surely for all, aren't you?"

"Not for all," replied Aneta.

How Maggie longed to give her companion a fierce push, or otherwise show how she detested her!

"I will tell you why I regret it," said Aneta, turning her calm, beautiful eyes upon Maggie's face.

"Thank you," said Maggie.

"I regret it, Maggie Howland, because you are at the school."

"How very polite!" said Maggie, turning crimson.

"It is not polite," said Aneta, "and I am sorry that I have to speak as I do; but it is necessary. We needn't go into particulars; but I have something to say to you, and please understand that what I say I mean. You know that when first you came to the school I was as anxious as any one else to be kind to you, to help you, to be good to you. You know the reason why I changed my mind. You know what you did. You know that were Mrs. Ward to have the slightest inkling of what really occurred you would not remain another hour at Aylmer House. I haven't told any one what I know; but if you, Maggie, tamper with Cicely and Merry Cardew, who are my cousins and dear friends—if you win them over to what you are pleased to call your side of the school—I shall consider it my duty to tell Mrs. Ward what I have hitherto kept back from her."

Maggie was trembling very violently.

"You could not be so cruel," she said after a pause.

"I have long thought," continued Aneta, speaking in her calm, gentle voice, "that I did wrong at the time to keep silent; but you got my promise, and I kept it."

"Yes, yes," said Maggie, "I got your promise; you wouldn't dare to break it?"

"You are mistaken," said Aneta. "If the circumstances to which I have just alluded should arise I would break that promise. Now you understand?"

"I think you are the meanest, the cruellest—I think you are—There, I hate you!" said Maggie.

"You have no reason to. I will not interfere with you if you, on your part, leave those I love alone. Cicely and Merry are coming to the school because I am there, because my aunt recommends the school, because it is a good school. Leave off doing wrong, and join us, Maggie, in what is noble and high; but continue your present course at your peril. You would do anything for power; you go too far. You have influenced one or two girls adversely already. I am convinced that Mrs. Ward does not trust you. If you interfere with Cicely or Merry, Mrs. Ward will have good reason to dislike you, for I myself shall open her eyes."

"You will be an informer, a tell-tale?"

"You can call me any names you like, Maggie; I shall simply do what I consider my duty."

"Oh, but—I hate you!" said Maggie again.

"I am sorry you hate me, for it isn't necessary; and if I saw you in the least like others I should do all in my power to help you. Now, will you give me your promise that you won't interfere with Cicely and Merry?"

"But does this mean—does this mean," said Maggie, who was almost choking with rage, "that I am to have nothing to do with the Cardews?"

"You are on no account to draw the Cardews into the circle of your friends, who are, I am thankful to say, limited. If you do, you know the consequences, and I am not the sort of girl to go back when I have firmly made up my mind on a certain point."

Maggie suddenly clutched hold of her companion's arm.

"I am miserable enough already," she said, "and you make my life unendurable! You don't know what it is to have a mother like mine, and to be starvingly poor."

"I am very sorry you are poor, Maggie, and I am very sorry for you with regard to your mother, although I do not think you ought to speak unkindly of her. But your father was a very good man, and you might live up to his memory. I saw you and Merry together to-day. Beware how you try to influence her."

"Oh, I can't stand you!" said Maggie.

"I have said my say. Shall we return to the others?" said Aneta in her calm voice.

"If she would only get into a rage and we might have a hand-to-hand fight I should feel better," thought Maggie. But she was seriously alarmed, for she well remembered something which had happened at school, which Aneta had discovered, and which, if known, would force Mrs. Ward to dismiss her from the establishment. Such a course would spell ruin. Maggie had strong feelings, but she had also self-control; and by the time the two joined the others her face looked much as usual.

On the following morning early a little girl ran swiftly from the Manor to the rectory. Maggie was to leave by the eleven o'clock train. Merry appeared on the scene soon after nine.

"I want you, Maggie, all quite by yourself," said Merry, speaking with such excitement that Molly and Belle looked at her in unbounded amazement.

"You can't keep her long," said Peterkins and Jackdaw, "for it is our very last day, and Spot-ear and Fanciful want to say good-bye to her. You can't have the darling more than three minutes at the most."

"I am going to keep Maggie for ten minutes, and no longer.—Come along at once, Maggie," said Merry Cardew.

They went out into the grounds, and Merry, putting her hand into her pocket, took out a little brown leather bag. She thrust it into her companion's hand.

"What is it?" said Maggie.

"It is for you—for you, darling," said Merry. "Take it, as a loan, if you like—only take it. It is only ten pounds. I am afraid you will think it nothing at all; but do take it, just as a mere loan. It is my pocket-money for the next quarter. Perhaps you could go from the musty, fusty lodgings to some fresher place with this to help you. Do—do take it, Maggie! I shall so love you if you do."

Maggie's narrow eyes grew wide. Maggie's sallow face flushed. There came a wild commotion in her heart—a real, genuine sense of downright love for the girl who had done this thing for her. And ten pounds, which meant so very little to Merry Cardew, held untold possibilities for Maggie.

"You will hurt me frightfully if you refuse," said Merry.

Maggie trembled from head to foot. Suppose, by any chance, it got to Aneta's ears that she had taken this money from Merry; suppose it got abroad in the school! Oh, she dared not take it! she must not!

"What is it, Maggie? Why don't you speak?" said Merry, looking at her in astonishment.

"I love you with all my heart and soul," said Maggie; "but I just can't take the money."

"Oh Maggie! but why?"

"I can't, dear; I can't. It—it would not be right. You mustn't lower me in my own estimation. I should feel low down if I took your money. I know well I am poor, and so is dear mother, and the lodgings are fusty and musty, but we are neither of us so poor as that. I'll never forget that you brought it to me, and I'll love you just more than I have ever done; but I can't take it."

"Do come on, Maggie!" shouted Jackdaw. "Fanciful is dying for his breakfast; and as to Peterkins, he has got Spot-ear out of his cage. Peterkins is crying like anything, and his tears are dropping on Spot-ear, and Spot-ear doesn't like it. Do come on!"

"Yes, yes; I am coming," said Maggie—"Good-bye, darling Merry. My best thanks and best love."

That evening, or in the course of the afternoon, Maggie appeared at Shepherd's Bush. She had been obliged to travel third-class, and the journey was hot and dusty.

She lay back against the cushions with a tired feeling all over her. For a time she had been able to forget her poverty. Now it had fully returned to her, and she was not in the mood to be good-natured. There was no need to show any charm or any kindliness to her neighbors, who, in their turn, thought her a disagreeable, plain girl, not worth any special notice.

It was, therefore, by no means a prepossessing-looking girl who ran up the high flight of steps which belonged to that lodging-house in Shepherd's Bush where Mrs. Howland was staying. Maggie knew the lodgings well, although she had never spent much time there. As a rule, she contrived to spend almost all her holidays with friends; but on this occasion her mother had sent for her in a very summary manner; and, although Maggie had no real love for her mother, she was afraid to disobey her.

Mrs. Howland occupied the drawing-room floor of the said lodgings. They were kept by a Mrs. Ross, an untidy and by no means too clean-looking woman. Mrs. Ross kept one small "general," and the general's name was Tildy. Tildy had bright-red hair and a great many freckles on her round face. She was squat in figure, and had a perpetual smut either on her cheek or forehead. In the morning she was nothing better than a slavey, but in the afternoon she generally managed to put on a cap with long white streamers and an apron with a bib. Tildy thought herself very fine in this attire, and she had donned it now in honor of Miss Howland's arrival. She had no particular respect for Mrs. Howland, but she had a secret and consuming admiration for Maggie.

Maggie had been kind to Tildy once or twice, and had even given the general a cast-off dress of her own. Maggie was plain, and yet people liked her and listened to her words.

"Oh miss," said Tildy when she opened the front door, "it's me that's glad to see you! Your ma is upstairs; she's took with a headache, but you'll find her lyin' down on the sofy in the drawin'-room."

"Then I'll run up at once, Matilda," said Maggie. "And how are you?" she added good-naturedly. "Oh, you've got your usual smut."

"Indicate the spot, miss, and it shall be moved instancious," said Tildy. "Seems to me as if never could get rid of smuts, what with the kitchen-range, and missus bein' so exacsheous, and Tildy here, Tildy there; Tildy do this, Tildy do t'other, soundin' in my hears all day long."

"You are a very good girl," said Maggie, "and if I were in your place I'd have a hundred smuts, not one. But take it off now, do; it's on the very center of your forehead. And bring me some tea to the drawing-room, for I'm ever so thirsty."

"You've been in a blessed wondrous castle since, haven't you, missie?" said Matilda in a voice of suppressed awe.

"I know some young ladies who live in a castle; but I myself have been at a rectory," said Maggie. "Now, don't keep me. Oh, here's a shilling for the cabman; give it to him, and get my box taken upstairs."

Maggie flew up the steep, badly carpeted stairs to the hideous drawing-room. Her spirits had been very low; but, somehow, Tildy had managed to revive them. Tildy was plain, and very much lower than Maggie in the social scale; but Tildy admired her, and because of that admiration made her life more or less endurable in the fusty, musty lodgings. She had always cultivated Tildy's good will, and she thought of the girl now with a strange sense of pity.

"Compared to her, I suppose I am well off," thought Maggie. "I have only five weeks at the most to endure this misery; then there will be Aylmer House."

She opened the drawing-room door and entered. Mrs. Howland was lying on a sofa, which was covered with faded rep and had a broken spring. She had a handkerchief wrung out of aromatic vinegar over her forehead. Her eyes were shut, and her exceedingly thin face was very pale. When her daughter entered the room she opened a pair of faded eyes and looked at her, but no sense of pleasure crossed Mrs. Howland's shallow face. On the contrary, she looked much worried, and said, in a cross tone, "I wish you would not be so noisy, Maggie. Didn't Tildy tell you that I had an acute headache?"

"Yes, mother; and I didn't know I was noisy," replied Maggie. "I came upstairs as softly as possible. That door"—she pointed to the door by which she had entered—"creaks horribly. That is not my fault."

"Excusing yourself, as usual," said Mrs. Howland.

"Well, mother," said Maggie after a pause, "may I kiss you now that I have come back against my will?"

"I knew you'd be horribly discontented," said Mrs. Howland; "but of course you may kiss me."

Maggie bent down and touched her mother's cheek with her young lips.

"I was having a beautiful time," she said, "and you don't seem glad now that I have come back. What is the matter?"

"I have something to communicate to you," said Mrs. Howland. "I did not think I could write it; therefore I was obliged to have you with me. But we won't talk of it for a little. Have you ordered tea?"

"Yes, mother. Tildy is bringing it."

"That's right," said Mrs. Howland. "What a hot day it is!" she continued.

"This room is stifling," replied Maggie. "Do you mind if I pull down the Venetian blinds? That will keep some of the sun out."

"The blinds are all broken," said Mrs. Howland. "I have spoken to that woman Ross till I am tired, but she never will see to my wishes in any way."

"I can't imagine why we stay here, mother."

"Oh! don't begin your grumbles now," said Mrs. Howland. "I have news for you when tea is over."

Just then the drawing-room door was opened by means of a kick and a bump, and Tildy entered, weighed down by an enormous tea-tray. Maggie ran to prepare a table for its reception, and Tildy looked at her with eyes of fresh admiration. Mrs. Howland raised herself and also looked at the girl.

"Have you kept the cakes downstairs, and the muffins that I ordered, and the gooseberries?"

"No, um," said Tildy. "I brought them up for Miss Maggie's tea."

"I told you they were not to be touched till Mr. Martin came."

"Yes, um," said Tildy; "but me and Mrs. Ross thought as Miss Maggie 'u'd want 'em."

Mrs. Howland glanced at her daughter. Then all of a sudden, and quite unexpectedly, her faded face grew red. She perceived an expression of inquiry in Maggie's eyes which rather frightened her.

"It's all right," she said. "Now that you've brought the things up, Tildy, leave them here, and go. When Mr. Martin comes, show him up. Now leave us, and be quick about it."

Tildy departed, slamming the door behind her.

"How noisy that girl is!" said Mrs. Howland. "Well, I am better now; I'll just go into our bedroom and get tidy. I'll be back in a few minutes. I mustn't be seen looking this fright when Mr. Martin comes."

"But who is Mr. Martin?" said Maggie.

"You will know presently," said Mrs. Howland. "It's about him that I have news."

Maggie felt her heart thumping in a very uncomfortable manner. The bedroom which she and her mother shared together—that is, when Maggie was with her mother—was at the back of the drawing-room. Mrs. Howland remained there for about five minutes, and during that time Maggie helped herself to a cup of tea, for she was feverishly hot and thirsty.

Her mother returned at the end of five minutes, looking wonderfully better, and in fact quite rejuvenated. Her dress was fairly neat. She had a slight color in her pale cheeks which considerably brightened her light-blue eyes. Her faded hair was arranged with some neatness, and she had put on a white blouse and a blue alpaca skirt.

"Oh mother," said Maggie, hailing this change with great relief, "how much better you look now! I am a comfort to you, am I not, mums? I sha'n't mind coming back and giving up all my fun if I am a real comfort to you."

"I wouldn't have sent for you but for Mr. Martin," said Mrs. Howland. "It was he who wished it. Yes, I am much better now, though I cannot honestly say that you are the cause. It's the thought of seeing Mr. Martin that cheers me up; I must be tidy for him. Yes, you may pour out a cup of tea for me; only see that you keep some really strong tea in the teapot for Mr. Martin, for he cannot bear it weak. He calls weak tea wish-wash."

"But whoever is this mysterious person?" said Maggie.

"I will tell you in a minute or two. You may give me one of those little cakes. No, I couldn't stand muffins; I hate them in hot weather. Besides, my digestion isn't what it was; but I shall be all right by-and-by; so will you too, my dear. And what I do, I do for you."

"Well, I wish you would tell me what you are doing for me, and get it over," said Maggie. "You were always very peculiar, mums, always—even when dear father was alive—and you're not less so now."

"That's a very unkind way for a child to speak of her parent," said Mrs. Howland; "but I can assure you, Maggie, that Mr. Martin won't allow it in the future."

Maggie now sprang to her feet.

"Good gracious, mother! What has Mr. Martin to do with me? Is he—is he— it cannot be, mother!"

"Yes, I can," said Mrs. Howland. "I may as well have it out first as last. I am going to marry Mr. Martin."

"Mother!"

There was a wailing cry in Maggie's voice. No girl can stand with equanimity her mother marrying a second time; and as Maggie, with all her dreams of her own future, had never for an instant contemplated this fact, she was simply staggered for a minute or two.

"You will have to take it in the right spirit, my dear," said her mother. "I can't stand this life any longer. I want money, and comforts, and devotion, and the love of a faithful husband, and Mr. Martin will give me all these things. He is willing to adopt you too. He said so. He has no children of his own. I mean, when I say that, that his first family are all settled in life, and he says that he wouldn't object at all to a pleasant, lively girl in the house. He wants you to leave school."

"Leave Aylmer House!" said Maggie. "Oh no, mother!"

"I knew you'd make a fuss about it," said Mrs. Howland. "He has a great dislike to what he calls fine folks. He speaks of them as daisies, and he hates daisies."

"But, mother—mother dear—before he comes, tell me something about him. Where did you meet him? Who is he? A clergyman—a barrister? What is he, mother?"

Mrs. Howland remained silent for a minute. Then she pressed her hand to her heart. Then she gave way to a burst of hysterical laughter.

"Just consider for a minute, Maggie," she said, "what utter nonsense you are talking. Where should I be likely to meet a clergyman or a barrister? Do clergymen or barristers or people in any profession come to houses like this? Do talk sense when you're about it."

"Well, tell me what he is, at least."

"He is in—I am by no means ashamed of it—in *trade*."

Now, it so happened that it had been duly impressed upon Maggie's mind that Mr. Cardew of Meredith Manor was also, so to speak, in trade; that is, he was the sleeping partner in one of the largest and wealthiest businesses in London. Maggie therefore, for a minute, had a glittering vision of a great country-house equal in splendor to Meredith Manor, where she and her mother could live together. But the next minute Mrs. Howland killed these glowing hopes even in the moment of their birth.

"I want to conceal nothing from you," she said. "Mr. Martin keeps the grocer's shop at the corner. I may as well say that I met him when I went to that shop to get the small articles of grocery which I required for my own consumption. He has served me often across the counter. Then one day I was taken rather weak and ill in the shop, and he took me into his back-parlor, a very comfortable room, and gave me a glass of excellent old port; and since then, somehow, we have been friends. He is a widower, I a widow. His children have gone into the world, and each one of them is doing well. My child is seldom or never with her mother. It is about a week ago since he asked me if I would accept him and plenty, instead of staying as I am—a genteel widow with so little money that I am half-starved. His only objection to our marriage is the thought of you, Maggie; for he said that I was bringing you up as a fine lady, with no provision whatever for the future. He hates fine ladies, as he calls them; in fact, he is dead nuts against the aristocracy."

"Oh mother!" wailed poor Maggie; "and my father was a gentleman!"

"Mr. Martin has quite a gentlemanly heart," said Mrs. Howland. "I don't pretend for a moment that he is in the same position as my late lamented husband; but he is ten times better off, and we shall live in a nice little house in Clapham, and I can have two servants of my own; he is having the house refurnished and repapered for me—in his own taste, it is true, for he will not hear of what he calls Liberty rubbish. But it is going to be very comfortable, and I look forward to my change of surroundings with great satisfaction."

"Yes, mother," said Maggie, "you always did think of yourself first. But what about me?"

"You had better not talk to me in that strain before Mr. Martin. He is very deeply devoted to me," said Mrs. Howland; "and do not imagine that we have not given you careful consideration. He is willing to adopt you, but insists on your leaving Aylmer House and coming to Laburnum Villa at Clapham. From what he says, you are quite sufficiently educated, and your duty now is to look after your mother and your new father, to be pleasant to me all day long, and to be bright and cheerful with him when he comes back from business in the evening. If you play your cards well, Maggie, he will leave you well provided for, as he is quite rich—of course, not rich like those people you are staying near, but rich for his class. I am very much pleased myself at the engagement. Our banns were called last Sunday in church, and we are to be married in a fortnight. After that, you had best stay on here until we desire you to join us at Laburnum Villa."

"I can't, mother," said Maggie. "I can't—and I won't."

"Oh, come, I hear a step on the stairs," said Mrs. Howland. "That is Mr. Martin. Now, you will restrain yourself for my sake."

There *was* a step on the stairs—firm, solid, heavy. The drawing-room door was opened about an inch, but no one came in.

Mrs. Howland said in a low whisper to her daughter, "He doesn't know you have returned; he is very playful. Just stay quiet. He really is a most amusing person."

"Bo-peep!" said a voice at the door; and a round, shining, bald head was popped in and then disappeared.

"Bo-peep!" said Mrs. Howland in response.

She stood up, and there came over her faded face a waggish expression. She held up her finger and shook it playfully. The bald head appeared again, followed immediately by a very round body. The playful finger continued to waggle.

"Ducksie dear!" said Mr. Martin, and he clasped Mrs. Howland in his arms.

Maggie gave a smothered groan.

"It's the child," said Mrs. Howland in a whisper. "She is a bit upset; but when she knows you, James, she'll love you as much as I do."

"Hope so," said Mr. Martin. "I'm a duckle, Little-sing; ain't I, Victoria?" Here he chuckled the good lady under the chin. "Ah, and so this is Maggie?—How do, my dear? How do, Popsy-wopsy?"

"How do you do?" said Maggie.

"Come, come," said Mr. Martin. "No flights and vapors, no fine airs, no affected, mincing ways. A little girl should love her new parent. A little girl should kiss her new parent."

"I won't kiss you, Mr. Martin," said Maggie.

"Oh, come, come—shy, is she? Let me tell you, Popsy-wopsy, that every man wouldn't want to kiss you.—She is not a bit like you, my dear Victoria. Wherever did she get that queer little face? She is no beauty, and that I will say.—Now, your mother, Popsy, is a most elegant woman; any one can see that she is a born aristocrat; but I hate 'em, my dear—hate 'em! I am one of those who vote for the abolition of the House of Lords. Give me the Commons; no bloated Lords for me. Well, you're a bit took aback, ain't you? Your mother and me—we settled things up very tidy while you were sporting in the country. I like you all the better, my dear, for being plain. I don't want no beauties except my beloved Victoria. She's the woman for me.—Ain't you, my Little-sing? Eh dear! Eh dear! It's we three who'll have the fun.—I'll take you right into my heart, Popsy-wopsy, and snug and comfortable you'll find yourself there."

Poor Maggie! The overwhelming contrast between this scene and the scenes of yesterday! The awful fact that her mother was going to marry such a being as Mr. Martin overpowered her with such a sense of horror that for the time she felt quite dumb and stupid.

Mr. Martin, however, was in a radiant humor. "Now then, Little-sing," he said, addressing Mrs. Howland, "where's the tea! Poor Bo-peep wants his tea.

He's hungry and he's thirsty, is Bo-peep. Little-sing will pour out Bo-peep's tea with her own pretty, elegant hands, and butter his muffins for him, and Cross-patch in the corner can keep herself quiet."

"May I go into our bedroom, mother?" said Maggie at that juncture.

"No, miss, you may not," said Martin, suddenly rousing himself from a very comfortable position in the only easy-chair the room afforded. "I have something to say to you, and when I have said it you may do what you please."

"Stay quiet, dear Maggie, for the present," said Mrs. Howland.

The poor woman felt a queer sense of shame. Bo-peep and Little-sing had quite an agreeable time together when they were alone. She did not mind the boisterous attentions of her present swain; but with Maggie by there seemed to be a difference. Maggie made her ashamed of herself.

Maggie walked to the window, and, taking a low chair, sat down. Her heart was beating heavily. There was such a misery within her that she could scarcely contain herself. Could anything be done to rescue her mother from such a marriage? She was a very clever girl; but, clever as she was, she could see no way out.

Meanwhile Mr. Martin drank his tea with huge gulps, ate a quantity of muffins, pooh-poohed the gooseberries as not worth his attention, and then said, "Now, Victoria, my dearest dear, I am ready to propound my scheme to your offspring.—Come forward, Popsy-wopsy, and listen to what new pa intends to do for you."

Maggie rose, feeling that her limbs were turned to ice. She crossed the room and stood before Mr. Martin.

"Well?" she said.

"None of those airs, Popsy."

"I want to know what you mean to do," said Maggie, struggling hard to keep her temper.

"Well, missie miss, poor Bo-peep means to marry your good ma, and he wants a nice 'ittle dirl to come and live with ma and pa at Clapham; pretty house, solid furniture, garden stocked with fruit-trees, a swing for good 'ittle dirl, a nice room for dear Popsy to sleep in, no more lessons, no more fuss, no more POVERTY! That's what new pa proposes to ma's 'ittle dirl. What does 'ittle dirl say?"

There was a dead silence in the room. Mrs. Howland looked with wild apprehension at her daughter. Mr. Martin had, however, still a jovial and smiling face.

"Down on its knees ought Popsy-wopsy to go," he said. "Tears might come in Popsy-wopsy's eyes, and the 'ittle dirl might say, 'Dearest pa that is to be, I love you with all my heart, and I am glad that you're going to marry ma and to take me from horrid school.'"

But there was no sign on the part of Maggie Howland of fulfilling these expectations on the part of the new pa. On the contrary, she stood upright, and then said in a low voice, "This has been a very great shock to me."

"Shock!" cried Martin. "What do you mean by that, miss?"

"I must speak," said Maggie. "You must let me, sir; and, mother, you must let me. It is for the last time. Quite the last time. I will never be here to offend you any more."

"'Pon my word!" said Martin, springing to his feet, and his red, good-humored face growing crimson. "There's gratitude for you! There's manners for you!—Ma, how ever did you bring her up?"

"Let me speak," said Maggie. "I am sorry to hurt your feelings, sir. You are engaged to my mother."

"Ra-*ther!*" said Mr. Martin. "My pretty birdling hopped, so to speak, into my arms. No difficulties with her; no drawing back on the part of Little-sing. She wanted her Bo-peep, and she—well, her Bo-peep wanted her."

"Yes, sir," said Maggie. "I am exceedingly sorry—bitterly sorry—that my mother is going to marry again; but as she cares for you"—

"Which I *do!*" said Mrs. Howland, who was now reduced to tears.

"I have nothing more to say," continued Maggie, "except that I hope she will be happy. But I, sir, am my father's daughter as well as my mother's, and I cannot for a single moment accept your offer. It is impossible. I must go on with my own education as best I can."

"Then you *re-fuse,*" said Martin, "to join your mother and me?"

"Yes," said Maggie, "I refuse."

"Has she anything to live on, ma?" asked Mr. Martin.

"Oh, dear James," said Mrs. Howland, "don't take all the poor child says in earnest now! She'll be down on her knees to you to-morrow. I know she will. Leave her to me, James dear, and I'll manage her."

"You can manage most things, Little-sing," said Mr. Martin; "but I don't know that I want that insolent piece. She is very different from you. If she is to be about our pleasant, cheerful home snubbing me and putting on airs—why, I'll have none of it. Let her go, Victoria, I say—let her go if she wants to; but if she comes to me she must come in a cheerful spirit, and joke with me, and take my fun, and be as agreeable as you are yourself, Little-sing."

"Well, at least," said Mrs. Howland, "give us till to-morrow. The child is surprised; she will be different to-morrow."

"I hope so," said Mr. Martin; "but if there's any philandering, or falling back, or if there's any *on*-gratitude, I'll have naught to do with her. I only take her to oblige you, Victoria."

"You had best leave us now, dear," said Mrs. Howland. "I will talk to Maggie, and let you know."

Mr. Martin sat quite still for a minute. Then he rose, took not the slightest notice of Maggie, but, motioning Mrs. Howland to follow him, performed a sort of cake-walk out of the room.

When he reached the door and had said good-bye, he opened it again and said, "Bo-peep!" pushing a little bit of his bald head in, and then withdrawing it, while Mrs. Howland pretended to admire his antics.

At last he was gone; but by this time Maggie had vanished into the bedroom. She had flung herself on her knees by the bed, and pushed her handkerchief against her mouth to stifle the sound of her sobs. Mrs. Howland gently opened the door, looked at her daughter, and then shut it again. She felt thoroughly afraid of Maggie.

An hour or two later a pale, subdued-looking girl came out of the bedroom and sat down by her mother.

"Well," said Mrs. Howland, "he is very pleasant and cheerful, isn't he?"

"Mother, he is horrible!"

"Maggie, you have no right to say those things to me. I want a good husband to take care of me. I am very lonely, and no one appreciates me."

"Oh mother!" said poor Maggie—"my father!"

"He was a very good man," said Mrs. Howland restlessly; "but he was above me, somehow, and I never, never could reach up to his heights."

"And you really tell me, his child, that you prefer that person?"

"I think I shall be quite happy with him," said Mrs. Howland. "I really do. He is awfully kind, and his funny little ways amuse me."

"Oh mother!"

"You will be good about it, Maggie; won't you?" said Mrs. Howland. "You won't destroy your poor mother's happiness? I have had such lonely years, and such a struggle to keep my head above water; and now that good man comes along and offers me a home and every comfort. I am not young, dear; I am five-and-forty; and there is nothing before me if I refuse Mr. Martin but an old age of great poverty and terrible loneliness. You won't stand in my way, Maggie?"

"I can't, mother; though it gives me agony to think of your marrying him."

"But you'll get quite accustomed to it after a little; and he is really very funny, I can assure you; he puts me into fits of laughter. You will get accustomed to him, darling; you will come and live with your new father and me at Laburnum Villa?"

"Mother, you must know that I never will."

"But what are you to do, Maggie? You've got no money at all."

"Oh mother!" said poor Maggie, "it costs very little to keep me at Aylmer House; you know that quite, quite well. Please do let me go on with my education. Afterwards I can earn my living as a teacher or in some profession, for I have plenty of talent. I take after father in that."

"Oh yes, I know I always was a fool," said Mrs. Howland; "but I have a way with people for all that."

"Mother, you have a great deal that is quite sweet about you, and you're throwing yourself away on that awful man! Can't we go on as we did for a year or two, you living here, and I coming to you in the holidays? Then, as soon as ever I get a good post I shall be able to help you splendidly. Can't you do it, mother? This whole thing seems so dreadful to me."

"No, I can't, and won't," said Mrs. Howland in a decided voice. "I am exceedingly fond of my Bo-peep—as I call him—and greatly enjoy the prospect of being his wife. Oh Maggie, you have not returned to be a thorn in our sides? You will submit?"

"Never, never, never!" said Maggie.

"Then I don't know what you are to do; for your new father insists on my keeping the very little money I have for my own personal use, and if you refuse to conform to his wishes he will not allow me to spend a farthing of it on you. You can't live on nothing at all."

"I can't," said Maggie. "I don't know quite what to do. Are you going to be so very cruel as to take away the little money you have hitherto spent on me?"

"I must, dear; in fact, it is done already. Mr. Martin has invested it in the grocery business. He already provides for all my wants, and we are to be married in a fortnight. I have nothing whatever to spend on you."

"Well, mother, we'll say no more to-night. I have a headache, but I'll sleep on the sofa here; it's less hot than the bedroom."

"Won't you sleep with your poor old mother?"

"No, I can't, really. Oh, how dreadfully hot this place is!"

"You are spoilt by your fine life, Maggie; but I grant that these lodgings are hot. The house at Clapham, however, is very cool and fresh. Oh Maggie! My dear Bo-peep is getting such a sweet little bedroom ready for you. I could cry when I think of your cross obstinacy."

But even the thought of the sweet little bedroom didn't move Maggie Howland. Tildy presently brought up a meagre supper, of which the mother and daughter partook almost in silence. Then Mrs. Howland went to her room, where she fell fast asleep, and Maggie had the drawing-room to herself. She had arranged a sort of extempore bed on the hard sofa, and was about to lie down, when Tildy opened the door.

"I say," said Tildy, "ain't he cunnin'?"

"What do you mean, Matilda?" said Maggie.

"Oh my," said Tildy, "wot a 'arsh word! Does you know, missie, that he's arsked me to go down to Clap'am presently to 'elp wait on your ma? If you're there, miss, it'll be the 'eight of 'appiness to me."

"I may as well say at once, Matilda, that I shall not be there."

"You don't like 'im, then?" said Tildy, backing a step. "And 'e is so enticin'— the prettiest ways 'e 'ave—at least, that's wot me and Mrs. Ross thinks. We always listen on the stairs for 'im to greet your ma. We like 'im, that we do."

"I have an old dress in my trunk, Tildy, which I will give you. You can manage to make it look quite nice for your new post as parlor-maid at Laburnum Villa. But now go, please; for I must be alone to think."

Tildy went. She crept downstairs to the kitchen regions. There she met Mrs. Ross.

"The blessed young lady's full of ructions," said Tildy.

"And no wonder," replied Mrs. Ross. "She's a step above Martin, and Martin knows it."

"I 'ope as she won't refuse to jine us at Laburnum Villa," said Tildy.

"There's no sayin' wot a spirited gel like that'll do," said Mrs. Ross; "but ef she do go down, Martin 'll be a match for 'er."

"I don't know about that," replied Tildy. "She 'ave a strong, determined w'y about 'er, has our Miss Maggie."

If Mrs. Howland slept profoundly, poor Maggie could not close her eyes. She suddenly found herself surrounded by calamity. The comparatively small trials which she had thought big enough in connection with Aylmer House and Cicely and Merry Cardew completely disappeared before this great trouble which now faced her. Her mother's income amounted to a hundred and fifty pounds a year, and out of that meagre sum the pair had contrived to live, and, owing to Mrs. Ward's generosity, Maggie had been educated. But now that dreadful Mr. Martin had secured Mrs. Howland's little property, and the only condition on which it could be spent on Maggie was that she should accept a home with her future stepfather. This nothing whatever would induce her to do. But what was to be done?

She had no compunction whatever in leaving her mother. They had never been really friends, for the girl took after her father, whom her mother had never even pretended to understand. Mrs. Howland, when she became Mrs. Martin, would be absolutely happy without Maggie, and Maggie knew well that she would be equally miserable with her. On the other hand, how was Maggie to live?

Suddenly it flashed across her mind that there was a way out, or at least a way of providing sufficient funds for the coming term at Aylmer House. Her mother had, after all, some sort of affection for her, and if Maggie made her request she was certain it would not be refused. She meant to get her mother to give her all that famous collection of jewels which her father had collected in different parts of the world. In especial, the bracelets flashed before her memory. These could be sold, and would produce a sum which might keep Maggie at Aylmer House, perhaps for a year—certainly for the approaching term.

# HAPTER XIII.

## BREAKFAST WITH BO-PEEP.

After Maggie's restless night she got up early. The day promised to be even hotter than the one before; but as the drawing-room faced west it was comparatively cool at this hour.

Tildy brought her favorite young lady a cup of tea, and suggested that she should go for an outing while Tildy herself freshened up the room. Maggie thought that a good idea, and when she found herself in the street her spirits rose a trifle.

A curious sort of fascination drew her in the direction of Martin's shop. It was a very large corner shop, had several entrances, and at this early hour the young shopmen and shopwomen were busy dressing the windows; they were putting appetizing sweetmeats and cakes and biscuits and all kinds of delectable things in the different windows to tempt the passers-by.

Maggie felt a hot sense of burning shame rising to her cheeks as she passed the shop. She was about to turn back, when whom should she see standing in the doorway but the prosperous owner himself! He recognized her immediately, and called out to her in his full, pompous voice, "Come along here, Wopsy!"

The young shop-people turned to gaze in some wonder as the refined-looking girl approached the fat, loud-mannered man.

"I'm in a hurry back to breakfast with my mother," said Maggie in her coldest voice.

"Well, then, I will come along with you, my dear; I am just in the mood. Little-sing, she will give me breakfast this morning. I'll be back again in the shop soon after nine. It's a fine shop, ain't it, Popsy?"

"It does seem large," said Maggie.

"It's the sort of shop," responded Martin, "that takes a deal of getting. It's not done in a day, nor a month, nor a year. It takes a lifetime to build up premises like these. It means riches, my dear—riches." He rolled out the words luxuriously.

"I am sure it does," said Maggie, who felt that for her own sake she must humor him.

"You think so, do you?" said Martin, giving her a keen glance.

"Of course I do," replied Maggie.

Martin gazed at her from head to foot. She was plain. He rather liked her for that. He admired her, too, for, as he expressed it, standing up to him. His dear Little-sing would never stand up to him. But this girl was not the least like her mother. She had a lot of character; Little-sing had none.

"You'd make an admirable accountant, Popsy," he said. "How would you like to take that post by-and-by in my shop?"

Maggie was about to reply that nothing would induce her to accept such a position, when a quick thought darted through her mind. She could scarcely hope to make anything of her mother, for, alack and alas! Mrs. Howland was one of those weak characters who slip away from you even as you try to grasp them. But Martin, with his terrible vulgarity and awful pleasantry, was at least fairly strong.

"Mr. Martin," said Maggie then, "instead of going in to breakfast with mother, will you take me to some restaurant and give me a good meal, and let me talk to you?"

"Well, now," said Martin, chuckling, "you *are* a girl! You have cheek! I am not a man to waste my money, and breakfast with Little-sing won't cost me anything."

"But under the circumstances you will waste a little money in order to oblige me?" said Maggie.

"There now, I admire your cheek. So be it. You don't deserve anything from me, for a ruder 'ittle dirl than you were yesterday to poor Bo-peep could not have been found in the length and breadth of England."

"You could scarcely expect me to be pleased, sir. The news was broken to me very suddenly, and I was tired after my long journey, too."

"Yes; and you vented your spite on me, on poor old Bo-peep, who has the kindest heart in Christendom."

"I may have said some things that I regret," said Maggie; "but, at any rate, I had the night to think matters over, and if you give me some breakfast I can talk to you."

"I will take you to Harrison's for breakfast," said Martin. "You'll get a topper there, I can tell you—eggs, bacon, kidneys, liver, game-pie, cocoa, coffee, tea, chocolate; anything and everything you fancy, and the best marmalade in London."

Maggie felt rather hungry, and when the pair entered Harrison's she was not displeased at the liberal supply of food which her future stepfather ordered.

He pretended to hate the aristocracy, as he called them, and poor Maggie could certainly never claim this distinction in her own little person. Nevertheless, she was entirely superior to Martin, and he felt a sort of pride in her as she walked up the long restaurant by his side.

"Now, waiter," he said to the man who approached to take orders, "you look slippy. This young 'oman and me, we want a real comfortable, all-round, filling meal. You give us the best the house contains; and look slippy, I say."

The waiter did look "slippy," whatever that word might imply, and Martin proceeded to treat Maggie to really excellent viands and to satisfy himself to his heart's content. Maggie ate with a certain amount of relish, for, as has been said, she was really hungry.

"Like it, don't you?" said Martin as he watched her consuming her eggs and bacon.

"Oh yes, very much indeed," said Maggie.

"I'm fond of a good table myself," said Martin. "This is the sort of thing you'll have on all occasions and at every meal at Laburnum Villa. We'll soon fill your poor mother's thin cheeks out, and get her rosy and plump, and then she'll be a more charming Little-sing to her own Bo-peep than ever."

Maggie was silent.

"Come, come," said Martin, patting her hand; "it's all right about Laburnum Villa, ain't it, my girl?"

"No, Mr. Martin," said Maggie then.

She withdrew her hand and turned and looked at him fixedly. "I want to tell you all about myself," she said. "I was really rude to you yesterday, and I am sorry; but I couldn't go to live with you and mother at Laburnum Villa. I will tell you the principal reason why I couldn't go."

"Oh, come, come, you're only a child; you must do what you are told. Your mother has no money to give you, and you can't live on air, you know. Air is all very well, but it don't keep folks alive. You'll have to come to me whether you like it or not."

"Before you come to that determination, Mr. Martin, may I tell you something about myself?"

"Oh dear! I hope it isn't a long story."

"It's very important, and not very long. I am not the least like mother"—

"My good girl, any one can see that. Your mother's a remarkably pretty and elegant woman, and you're the plainest young person I ever came across."

"I am plain," said Maggie; "and, in addition, I am by no means good-natured."

"Oh, you admit that? For shame!"

"I was born that way," said Maggie. "I'm a very high-spirited girl, and I have got ideas with regard to my future. You said just now that perhaps some day you might make me accountant in your shop. That was kind of you, and I might be a good accountant; but, of course, all that is for the future. I shouldn't mind that—I mean, not particularly. But if you were to follow out your plan, and take me to live with you and mother at Laburnum Villa, you would never have a happy moment; for, you see, I am much stronger in character than mother, and I couldn't help making your life miserable; whereas you and mother would be awfully happy without me. Mother says that she loves you, and wishes to be your wife"—

"Now, what are you driving at, Popsy? For if you have nothing hanging on your hands I have a vast lot hanging on mine, and time is precious."

"I will tell you quite frankly what I want you to do, Mr. Martin. You are taking mother."

"I am willing to take you too. I can't do any more."

"But then, you see, I don't want to be taken. Until you came forward and proposed to mother to be your wife she spent a little of her money on my education. She tells me that she has put it now into your business."

"Poor thing!" said Martin. "She was making ducks and drakes of it; but it is safe enough now."

"Yes," said Maggie in a determined voice; "but I think, somehow, that a part of it does lawfully belong to me."

"Oh, come! tut, tut!"

"I think so," said Maggie in a resolute tone; "for, you see, it was father's money; and though he left it absolutely to mother, it was to go to me at her death, and it was meant, little as it was, to help to educate me. I could ask a lawyer all about the rights, of course."

For some extraordinary reason Martin looked rather frightened.

"You can go to any lawyer you please," he said; "but what for? let me ask. If I take you, and do for you, and provide for you, what has a lawyer to say in the matter?"

"Well, that is just it—that's just what I have to inquire into; because, you see, Mr. Martin, I don't want you to provide for me at all."

"I think now we are coming to the point," said Martin. "Stick to it, Popsy, for time's precious."

"I think you ought to allow me to be educated out of mother's money."

"Highty-tighty! I'm sure you know enough."

"I don't really know enough. Mrs. Ward, of Aylmer House, has taken me as an inmate of her school for forty pounds a year. Her terms for most girls are a great deal more."

Martin looked with great earnestness at Maggie.

"I want to go on being Mrs. Ward's pupil, and I want you to allow me forty pounds a year for the purpose, and twenty over for my clothes and small expenses—that is, sixty pounds a year altogether. I shall be thoroughly educated then, and it seems only fair that, out of mother's hundred and fifty a year, sixty pounds of the money should be spent on me. There's no use talking to mother, for she gets so easily puzzled about money; but you have a very good business head. You see, Mr. Martin, I am only just sixteen, and if I get two more years' education, I shall be worth something in the world, whereas now I am worth nothing. I hope you will think it over, Mr. Martin, and do what I wish."

Martin was quite silent for a minute. The waiter came along and was paid his bill, with a very substantial tip for himself thrown in. Still Martin lingered at the breakfast-table with his eyes lowered.

"There's one thing—and one thing only—I like about this, Popsy-wopsy," he said.

"And what is that?" asked Maggie.

"That you came to me on the matter instead of going to your mother; that you recognized the strength and force of my character."

"Oh, any one can see that," said Maggie.

"You put it straight, too, with regard to your own disagreeable nature."

"Yes, I put it straight," said Maggie.

"Well, all I can say at present is this: I will think it over. You go home to your mother now, and tell her that her Bo-peep will be in as usual to tea; and you, little girl, may as well make yourself scarce at that hour. Here's a sovereign for you. Go and have a jolly time somewhere."

"Oh, Mr. Martin, I"—began Maggie, her face crimson.

"You had best not put on airs," said Martin; and Maggie slipped the sovereign into her pocket.

When she reached her mother's lodgings she felt well assured that she had done the right thing. Hitherto she had been too stunned and miserable to use any of her power—that strange power which she possessed—on Mr. Martin. But she felt well assured that she could do so in the future. She had gauged his character correctly. He was hopelessly vulgar, but an absolutely good-natured and straight person.

"He will do what I wish," she thought. Her uneasiness vanished as soon as the first shock of her mother's disclosure was over. She entered the house.

"Why, missie?" said Tildy, "w'erehever 'ave you been? The breakfast's stony cold upstairs, and Mrs. 'Owland's cryin' like nothin' at all."

"Thank you, Tildy; I'll see mother immediately," said Maggie. "And I don't want any breakfast, for I've had it already."

"With the haristocracy?" asked Tildy in a low, awed kind of voice. "You always was one o' they, Miss Maggie."

"No, not with the aristocracy," said Maggie, trying to suppress her feelings. "Tildy, your smut is on your left cheek this morning. You can remove the breakfast-things, and I'll go up to mother."

Maggie ran upstairs. Mrs. Howland had eaten a little, very indifferent breakfast, and was looking weepy and washed-out as she sat in her faded dressing-gown near the open window.

"Really, Maggie," she said when her daughter entered, "your ways frighten me most terribly! I do wish poor Mr. Martin would insist on your coming to live with us. I shall never have an easy moment with your queer pranks and goings-on."

"I am sure you won't, dear mother," said Maggie. "But come, don't be cross with me. Here's Matilda; she'll clear away the breakfast-things in no time, and then I have something I want to say to you."

"Oh dear! my head is so weak this morning," said Mrs. Howland.

"If I were you, Miss Maggie," said Tildy as she swept the cups and saucers with noisy vehemence on to a tray, "I wouldn't worrit the poor mistress, and she just on the eve of a matrimonial venture. It's tryin' to the nerves, it is; so Mrs. Ross tells me. Says she, 'When I married Tom,' says she, 'I was on the twitter for a good month.' It's awful to think as your poor ma's so near the brink—for that's 'ow Mrs. Ross speaks o' matrimony."

"Please be quick, Tildy, and go," said Maggie in a determined voice.

Matilda cleared the table, but before she would take her departure she required definite instructions with regard to dinner, tea, and supper.

Mrs. Howland raised a distracted face. "Really, I can't think," she said, "my head is so weak."

"Well, mum," said Matilda, "s'pose as missus and me does the 'ousekeepin' for you to-day. You ain't fit, mum; it's but to look at you to know that. It's lyin' down you ought to be, with haromatic vinegar on your 'ead."

"You're quite right, Matilda. Well, you see to the things to-day. Have them choice, but not too choice; fairly expensive, but not too expensive, you understand."

"Yus, 'um," said Tildy, and left the room.

Maggie found herself alone with her mother. "Mother," she said eagerly, "now I will tell you why I was not home for breakfast this morning."

"Oh, it doesn't matter, Maggie," said Mrs. Howland; "I am too weak to be worried, and that's a fact."

"It won't worry you, mother. I breakfasted with Mr. Martin."

"What—what!" said Mrs. Howland, astonishment in her voice, and with eyebrows raised almost to meet her hair.

"And an excellent breakfast we had," said Maggie. "He isn't a bad sort at all, mother."

"Well, I am glad you've found that out. Do you suppose your mother would marry a man who was not most estimable in character?"

"He is quite estimable, mother; the only unfortunate thing against him is that he is not in your rank in life."

"A woman who lives in these rooms," said Mrs. Howland, "has no rank in life."

"Well, dear mother, I cannot agree with you. However, as I said, I breakfasted with him."

"Then you're coming round?" said Mrs. Howland. "You're going to be good, and a comfort to us both?"

"No, mother, I haven't come round a bit. When I was breakfasting with Mr. Martin I fully explained to him what a fearful trial I should be to him; how, day by day and hour by hour, I'd annoy him."

"You did that! Oh you wicked child!"

"I thought it best to be frank, mother. I made an impression on him. I did what I did as much for your sake as for mine."

"Then he'll break off the engagement—of course he will!" said Mrs. Howland. She took a moist handkerchief from her pocket and pressed it to her eyes.

"Not he. He is just devoted to you, mother; you need have no such apprehension."

"What else did you say to him?"

"Well, mother darling, I said what I thought right."

"Oh, of course you won't confide in me."

"I think not. I will let him do that. He is coming to tea this afternoon, and he has given me a sovereign"—how Maggie felt inclined to kick that sovereign! —"to go and have some pleasure somewhere. So I mean to take the train to Richmond, and perhaps get a boatman to take me out on the river for a little."

"He is certainly more playful and amusing when you are not here," said Mrs. Howland, a faint smile dawning on her face.

"I am certain of that," said Maggie; "and what's more, he is very fond of good living. I mean to go out presently and get some excellent things for his tea."

"Will you, Maggie? Will you, my child? Why, that will be quite sweet of you."

"I will do it with pleasure, mother. But now I want you to do something for me."

"Ah," said Mrs. Howland, "I thought you were coming to that."

"Well, it is this," said Maggie. "When he talks to you about me, don't oppose him. He will most probably propound a scheme to you, as his own perhaps; and you are to be quite certain to let him think that it is his own scheme. And you might make out to him, mother, that I am really very disagreeable, and that nothing in all the world would make me anything else. And if you are a very wise little mother you will tell him that you are happier alone with him."

"Which I am—I am," said Mrs. Howland. "He is a dear, quite a dear; and so comical and amusing!"

"Then it's all right," said Maggie. "You know I told you yesterday that nothing would induce me to live at Laburnum Villa; but I will certainly come to you, mums, in the holidays, if you wish it."

"But, dear child, there is no money to keep you at that expensive school.

There isn't a penny."

"Oh, well, well, mother, perhaps that can be managed. But now we needn't talk any more about my future until after Mr. Martin has had tea with you to-day. If you have any news for me when I return from Richmond you can let me know."

"You are a very independent girl to go to Richmond by yourself."

"Oh, that'll be all right," said Maggie in a cheerful tone.

"Have you anything else to say to me?"

"Yes. You know all that beautiful jewellery that my dear father brought back with him from those different countries where he spent his life."

Mrs. Howland looked mysterious and frightened.

"It was meant for me eventually, was it not?" said Maggie.

"Oh, well, I suppose so; only, somehow, I have a life-interest in it."

"You won't want for jewellery when you are Mr. Martin's wife."

"Indeed no; why, he has given me a diamond ornament for my hair already. He means to take me out a great deal, he says."

"Out!—oh mother—in his set!"

"Well, dear child, I shall get accustomed to that."

"Don't you think you might give me father's jewellery?" said Maggie.

"Is it worth a great deal?" said Mrs. Howland. "I never could bear to look at it —that is, since he died."

"You haven't given it to Mr. Martin, have you, mother?"

"No, nor said a word about it to him either."

"Well, suppose, now that we have a quiet time, we look at the jewellery?" said Maggie.

"Very well," said Mrs. Howland. Then she added, "I was half-tempted to sell some of it; but your father was so queer, and the things seemed so very ugly and unlike what is worn, that I never had the heart to part with them. I don't suppose they'd fetch a great deal."

"Let's look at them," said Maggie.

Mrs. Howland half-rose from her chair, then sank back again.

"No," she said, "I am afraid of them. Your father told me so many stories about each and all. He courted death to get some of them, and others came into his hands through such extraordinary adventures that I shudder at night when I recall what he said. I want to forget them. Mr. Martin would never admire them at all. I want to forget all my past life absolutely. You're like your father, and perhaps you admire that sort of thing; but they are not to my taste. Here's the key of my wardrobe. You will find the tin boxes which hold the jewels. You can take them; only never let out a word to your stepfather. He doesn't know I posses them—no one does."

"Thank you, mother," said Maggie in a low voice. "Will you lie down on the sofa, mums? Oh, here's a nice new novel for you to read. I bought it coming up in the train yesterday. You read and rest and feel quite contented, and let me go to the bedroom to look at the jewels."

"Very well," said Mrs. Howland; "you can have them. I consider them of little or no importance; only don't tell your stepfather."

"He is not that yet, mums."

"Well, well," said Mrs. Howland, "what does a fortnight matter? He'll be your stepfather in a fortnight. Yes, take the key and go. I shall be glad to rest on the sofa. You're in a much more reasonable frame of mind to-day."

"Thank you, dear mother," said Maggie.

She entered the bedroom and closed the door softly behind her. She held her mother's bunch of keys in her hand. First of all she unlocked the wardrobe, and then, removing the tin boxes, laid them on the table which stood at the foot of the bed. She took the precaution first, however, to lock the bedroom door. Having done this, she seated herself at the table, and, selecting the proper keys, unlocked the two tin boxes. One of them contained the twelve famous bracelets which Maggie had described to Molly and Isabel Tristram. She would keep her word: she would give a bracelet to each girl. She recognized at once the two which she considered suitable for the girls, and then examined the others with minute care.

Her mother could not admire what was strange in pattern and dimmed by neglect; but Maggie, with her wider knowledge, knew well that she possessed great treasures, which, if possible, she would keep, but which, if necessary, she could sell for sums of money which would enable her to start in life according to her own ideas.

She put the twelve bracelets back into their case, and then, opening the second tin box, took from it many quaint curios, the value of which she had no means of ascertaining. There was a great deal of gold and silver, and queer beaten-work in brass, and there were pendants and long chains and brooches and queer ornaments of all kinds.

"Poor father!" thought the girl. She felt a lump in her throat—a choking sensation, which seemed to make her mother's present conduct all the more intolerable. How was she to live in the future with the knowledge that her father's memory was, as she felt, profaned? But at least she had got his treasures.

She relocked the two tin boxes, and, stowing them carefully away in her own trunk, transferred the keys from her mother's bunch to her own, and brought her mother's keys back to Mrs. Howland.

"Have you looked at them? Are they worth anything, Maggie?"

"Memories mostly," said Maggie evasively.

"Oh, then," said Mrs. Howland, "I am glad you have them; for I hate memories."

"Mother," said Maggie, and she went on her knees to her parent, "you have really given them to me?"

"Well, of course, child. Didn't I say so? I don't want them. I haven't looked at the things for years."

"I wonder, mums, if you would write something on a piece of paper for me."

"Oh dear! oh dear!" said Mrs. Howland. "Mr. Martin doesn't approve of what he calls documents."

"Darling mother, you're not Mr. Martin's wife yet. I want you to put on paper that you have given me father's curios. He always meant them for me, didn't he?"

"He did! he did!" said Mrs. Howland. "One of the very last things he said—in his letter, I mean, for you know he died in Africa—was: 'The treasures I am sending home will be appreciated by my little girl.'"

"Oh mother! yes, and they are. Please, mother, write something on this bit of paper."

"My head is so weak. I haven't an idea what to say."

"I'll dictate it to you, if I may."

"Very well, child; I suppose I can't prevent you."

Maggie brought paper, blotting-pad, and pen, and Mrs. Howland presently wrote: "I have given, on the eve of my marriage to Mr. Martin, her father's treasures to my daughter, Margaret Howland."

"Thank you, mother," said Maggie.

The date was affixed. Mrs. Howland added the name she was so soon to resign, and Maggie almost skipped into the bedroom.

"It's all right now," she said to herself.

She unlocked her trunk, also unlocking one of the tin boxes. In the box which contained the twelve bracelets she put the piece of paper in her mother's handwriting. She then relocked the box, relocked the trunk, and came back to her mother, restored to perfect good-humor.

Maggie was in her element when she was planning things. Yesterday was a day of despair, but to-day was a day of hope. She sat down by her mother's desk and wrote a long letter to Molly Tristram, in which she told Molly that her mother was about to be married again to a very rich man. She mentioned the coming marriage in a few brief words, and then went on to speak of herself, and of how delightful it would be to welcome Molly and Isabel when they arrived at Aylmer House. Not by the faintest suggestion did she give her friend to understand the step down in the social scale which Mrs. Howland's marriage with Mr. Martin meant.

Having finished her letter, she thought for a minute, then wrote a careful line to Merry Cardew. She did not tell Merry about her mother's approaching marriage, but said that Molly would have news for her. In other respects her letter to Merry was very much more confidential than her letter to Molly. She assured Merry of her deep love, and begged of her friend to regard this letter as quite private. "If you feel you must show it to people, tear it up rather than do so," said Maggie, "for I cannot bear that our great and sacred love each for the other should be commented on."

When Merry received the letter she neither showed it to any one else nor tore it up. She could not forget Maggie's face as she parted from her, and the fact that she had refused to accept the ten pounds which the little girl had wanted to give her in order to remove her from musty, fusty lodgings had raised Maggie considerably in her friend's estimation.

Meanwhile Maggie Howland, having finished her letters, went out and posted them. She then changed her sovereign, and bought some excellent and appetizing fruit and cakes for her mother's and Mr. Martin's tea. She consulted with Tildy as to how these dainties were to be arranged, and Tildy entered into the spirit of the thing with effusion, and declared that they were perfect crowns of beauty, and that most assuredly they would melt in Mr. Martin's mouth.

On hearing this Maggie hastened to change the conversation; but when she had impressed upon Tildy the all-importance of a snowy cloth being placed upon the ugly tray, and further begged of her to polish up the teapot and spoons, Tildy thought that Miss Maggie was more wonderful than ever.

"With them as is about to step into the life-matrimonial, pains should be took," thought Tildy, and she mentioned her sentiments to Mrs. Ross, who shook her head sadly, and replied that one ought to do the best one could for the poor things.

At three o'clock Maggie put on her hat, drew her gloves on, and, taking up a parasol, went out.

"Good-bye, darling," she said to her mother.

After all, she did not go to Richmond; it was too far off, and she was feeling a little tired. Besides, the thought of her father's wonderful treasures filled her mind. She determined to go to South Kensington and look at similar jewels and ornaments which she believed she could find there. It occurred to her, too, that it might be possible some day to consult the manager of the jewel department with regard to the worth of the things which her dear father had sent home; but this she would not do to-day.

Her visit to the South Kensington Museum made her feel positively assured that she had articles of great value in the tin boxes.

Meanwhile Mrs. Howland waited impatiently for Mr. Martin. She was puzzled about Maggie, and yet relieved. She wondered much what Maggie could have said to Mr. Martin that day when she breakfasted with him. She was not really alarmed. But had she been able to look into Mr. Martin's mind she would have felt a considerable amount of surprise. The worthy grocer, although an excellent man of business, knew little or nothing about law. Maggie's words had made him distinctly uncomfortable. Suppose, after all, the girl could claim a right in her father's beggarly hundred and fifty pounds a year? Perhaps the child of the man who had settled that little income on his wife must have some sort of right to it? It would be horrible to consult lawyers; they were so terribly expensive, too.

There was a man in the shop, however, of the name of Howard. He was the principal shopwalker, and Mr. Martin had a great respect for him. Without mentioning names, he put the case before him—as he himself expressed it—in a nutshell.

Howard thought for a few minutes, then said slowly that he had not the slightest doubt that a certain portion of the money should be spent on the child—in fact, that the child had a right to it.

Martin did not like this. A heavy frown came between his brows. The girl was a smart and clever girl, not a bit like Little-sing, and she could make herself very disagreeable. Her modest request for sixty pounds a year did not seem unreasonable. He thought and thought, and the more he thought the more inclined he felt to give Maggie her way.

When he arrived at Mrs. Ross's house he did not look quite as cheerful as usual. He went upstairs, as Tildy expressed it, "heavy-like"; and although both she and Mrs. Ross watched for that delightful scene when he was "Bo-peep" to "Little-sing," Martin entered the drawing-room without making any exhibition of himself. The room looked quite clean and inviting, for Maggie had dusted it with her own hands, and there was a very nice tea on the board, and Mrs. Howland was dressed very prettily indeed. Martin gave a long whistle.

"I say, Little-sing," he remarked, "whoever has been and done it?"

"What do you mean, James?" said Mrs. Howland.

"Why, the place," said Martin; "it looks sort of different."

"Oh, it's Maggie," said Mrs. Howland. "She went out and bought all those cakes for you herself."

"Bless me, now, did she?" said Martin. "She's a smart girl—a *ver*-ry smart girl."

"She's a very clever girl, James."

"Yes, that's how I put it—very clever. She has a way about her."

"She has, James. Every one thinks so."

"Well, Little-sing, give me a good meal, and then we'll talk."

Mrs. Howland lifted the teapot and was preparing to pour out a cup of tea for Mr. Martin, when he looked at her, noticed her extreme elegance and grace, and made a spring toward her.

"You haven't give Bo-peep one kiss yet, you naughty Little-sing."

Mrs. Howland colored as she kissed him. Of course she liked him very much; but somehow Maggie had brought a new atmosphere into the house. Even Mrs. Howland felt it.

"Let's eat, let's eat," said Martin. "I never deny myself the good things of life. That girl knows a thing or two. She's a ver-ry clever girl."

"She is, James; she is."

"Now, what on earth do you call me James for? Ain't I Bo-peep—ain't I?"

"Yes, Bo-peep, of course you are."

"And you are Little-sing. You're a wonderfully elegant-looking woman for your years, Victoria."

---

# CHAPTER XIV.

## IN THE PARK.

Mrs. Howland did not like to have her years mentioned. Mr. Martin had been careful never to do so until Maggie appeared on the scene. On the contrary, he had dropped hints that his birdling, his Little-sing, his Victoria, was in the early bloom of youth. But now he said that she was a wonderful woman for her years.

Mrs. Howland bridled slightly. "I am not old, James," she said.

"Come, come," said the good-natured grocer; "no 'Jamesing' of me. I'm your Bo-peep. What does it matter whether you are old or young, Victoria, if you suit me and I suit you? This is a first-rate tea, and that girl's clever— uncommon clever. By the way, how old may she happen to be?"

"Sixteen her last birthday," said Mrs. Howland. "I was very, very young, a mere child, when I married, James."

"There you are with your 'James' again! Strikes me, you're a bit huffy to-day, Little-sing."

"No, I am not; only I've been worried since Maggie came back. She was so rude to you yesterday. I felt it terribly."

"Did you now? Well, that was very sensible of you. We'll finish our tea before we begin our talk. Come, Little-sing, eat your cake and drink your tea, and make yourself agreeable to your Bo-peep."

Mrs. Howland felt cheered. She did enjoy her meal; and, if she liked it, Mr. Martin liked it immensely also.

"What a useful girl that would be!" he said. "We could make her housekeeper at Laburnum Villa in no time. She has a head on her shoulders."

Mrs. Howland was silent. She was dreading inexpressibly the little scene which she felt must be endured between her and her intended.

"We'll ring the bell now," said Martin, wiping a few crumbs from his mouth and dusting his trousers with his pocket-handkerchief. "We'll get Tildy to remove all these things, and then what do you say to my taking you for a drive to the Park?"

"Oh, I should like that!" said Mrs. Howland in surprise,

"Thought so. Never say that Bo-peep isn't thoughtful.—Ah, here you be, Tildy. You clear away—smart, my girl, and then whistle for a 'ansom. Do you hear me? A 'ansom, not a four-wheeler. Look as sharp as you can, my girl, and I'll give you sixpence."

"Thank you, sir," said Tildy. She looked with admiring eyes at the pair who were so close to the matrimonial venture, and quickly removed all traces of the meal.

"Now then, Little-sing, go into your room and get dressed for your drive."

Mrs. Howland did so. She put on an elegant sort of bonnet-hat which had been presented to her by Martin, a lace fichu over her shoulders, and a pair of long white gloves. She had also been presented with a white parasol by Martin. He thought that no one could look more beautiful than his ladylove when she reappeared in the drawing-room.

"The 'ansom's at the door," he said. "We'll go now and start on our drive."

Mrs. Howland rose, and Tildy agreed with Martin as to Mrs. Howland's appearance when she stepped into that hansom. Tildy said she looked bride-like. Mrs. Ross remarked that as elegant women before now had become widows in no time. Tildy shuddered, and said that Mrs. Ross should not say things of that sort. Mrs. Ross replied that she invariably spoke the truth, and then returned to her dismal kitchen.

Meanwhile Martin and Mrs. Howland were driven swiftly in the direction of Hyde Park. London society people were fast going out of town, for it was very nearly the end of July; but still there were a few carriages about, and some fine horses, and some gaily dressed ladies and several smart-looking men. Martin provided a couple of chairs for himself and his future wife, and they sat for some little time enjoying the fresh air and looking on at the gay scene.

"It is wonderful," said Martin, "what a sight of money is wasted in this sort of thing."

"But they enjoy it, don't they?" said Mrs. Howland.

"Yes, my pet," he replied, "but not as you and me will enjoy Laburnum Villa. And now, Little-sing, can you attend to business?"

"I have a very weak head for business, Bo-peep," was the reply.

"Don't I know it, my pet; and I am the last person on earth to allow you to be worried; but I tell you what it is, Victory, if your head is weak as regards money matters, your girl has a topping good brain in that direction. Now, I have a notion in my head about her."

"You can't do anything with her," said Mrs. Howland; "she is quite impossible. I never thought she would treat you as she did. I could weep when

I think of it. I shouldn't be surprised if, on account of her rudeness and ingratitude, we broke off the engagement. I shouldn't really, James."

"What do you take me for?" said James. "It isn't the girl I want to marry! it's you."

"Oh dear!" said Mrs. Howland; "of course, I know."

"She ain't a patch on you, Little-sing—that is, I mean as regards looks. But now, don't you fret. If you have been turning things over in your mind, so have I been turning things over in my mind, and the sum and substance of it all is that I believe that girl's right after all."

"Right after all! But dear, dear James, the child can't live on nothing!"

"Who said she was to live on nothing?" said Martin. "Don't tremble, Little-sing; it's more than I can stand. I have been thinking that a sharp young miss like that wants a bit more training. She wants breaking in. Now, I've no mind to the job. I can manage my shop-people—not one of them can come round me, I can tell you—but a miss like your daughter, brought up altogether, I will say, above her station, is beyond me. What I have been turning over in my mind is this, that a year or two's training longer will do her no sort of harm."

"Oh!" said Mrs. Howland. She was trembling exceedingly.

"I think, too," continued Martin, "that Laburnum Villa might not be agreeable to her at present; and if it ain't agreeable to her she'll put on the sulks, and that's more than I *can* abide. Cheerfulness I must have. My joke I must be allowed to make. My fun in my own way I must enjoy. You and me—we'll hit it off splendid, and let the girl go for the present."

"But she must go somewhere," said Mrs. Howland.

"Good gracious, my lady! do you suppose I'd allow the girl to be destitute? No; I'm ready to do the generous; and now, I'll tell you something. You mustn't blame her too much. She repented of her ill-natured manner last night, and came to me as pretty as you please this morning, and asked me to breakfast with her. I was taken aback, but she came round me, and we went to Harrison's and had a topping meal. Then she spoke to me very sensible, and explained that she wanted more 'parlez-vooing' and more 'pi-annofortying,' and all the rest of the so-called ladies' accomplishments. She consulted me very pretty and very proper indeed; and the long and the short of it is that I am willing to allow her forty pounds a year for her education at that blessed Aylmer House where all the swells go, and to keep her there for two years certain; and I am willing, further, to give her twenty pounds a year to spend on dress. Of course she takes her holidays with us. Then, if at the end of that time she turns out what I hope she will, I will make her an accountant in the shop; it will be a first-rate post for her, and I am sure, from the way she talks, she has a splendid head for business. Now, what do you say to that, Littlesing?"

"I say there never was your like, Bo-peep."

Mr. Martin rubbed his hands. "Thought you'd be pleased," he said. "The girl spoke very proper indeed this morning, and she is a good girl—plain and sensible, and I couldn't but take notice of her words. Now then, s'pose we take a fresh 'ansom, and hurry home; and I'll take you out and give you a right good bit of dinner, and afterwards we'll go to the play."

"Oh dear!" said Mrs. Howland, "you are good to me, Bo-peep."

# CHAPTER XV.

## TWO SIDES.

Mrs. Ward's school reopened on the 20th of September. For two or three days beforehand the immaculate and beautiful house was being made, if possible, still more immaculate and still more lovely. The window-boxes were refilled with flowers; the dainty little bedrooms were supplied with fresh curtains to the windows and fresh drapery for the beds.

Mrs. Ward herself arrived at the school about a week before her pupils made their appearance. She had much to sette during this week. She had, in short, to prepare her plan of campaign for the ensuing term: to interview her different masters and mistresses, to consult with her resident English governess (a charming girl of the name of Talbot), to talk over matters with Fräulein Beck, and to reassure Mademoiselle Laplage, who was very lively, very conscientious, but at the same time very nervous with regard to her own powers. *"Les jeunes filles Anglaises sont bien capables et bien distinguées mais—ma foi! comme elles me fatiguent les nerfs!"* Mademoiselle Laplage would say; and, although she had been at Aylmer House for three terms, she always doubted her powers, and made the same speech over and over again at the beginning of each term. In addition to Miss Talbot, there was a very cheery, bright girl of the name of Johnson, who looked after the girls' wardrobes and helped them, if necessary, with their work, saw that they were punctual at meals, and occasionally took an English class. She was a great favorite with all the girls at Mrs. Ward's school. They called her Lucy, instead of Miss Johnson. She was quite young—not more than twenty years of age.

These four ladies resided at Aylmer House; but masters and mistresses for various accomplishments came daily to instruct the girls. Mrs. Ward loved her teachers almost as much as she loved her girls, and they each and all adored her.

Miss Talbot was an exceedingly clever woman, close on thirty years of age. She had taken very high honors at Cambridge, and was a person of great penetration of character, with a genius for imparting knowledge.

Unlike most head-mistresses, Mrs. Ward seldom changed her staff of teachers. She had the gift of selection to a marvellous degree, and never was known to make a mistake with regard to the choice of those women who helped her in her great work of education.

Summer was, of course, over when the girls assembled at Aylmer House. Nevertheless, there was a sort of afterglow of summer, which was further intensified by the beautiful flowers in the window-boxes and by the fresh, clean, fragrant atmosphere of the house itself.

The two Cardews and the two Tristrams came up to Aylmer House by an early train. Mr. Tristram brought them to school, Mr. and Mrs. Cardew at the last moment feeling unequal to the task of parting with their darlings in the presence of their companions. The real parting had taken place the previous night; and that pain which Merry had felt at intervals during the end of the summer vacation was sharp enough to cause her to cry when she lay down to sleep on the night before going to school. But Merry was brave, and so was Cicely; and, although Merry did hate beyond words the thought of not seeing her beloved father and her dear mother until Christmas, she thought also that very good times were before her, and she was resolved to make the best of them.

Molly and Isabel, who were quite accustomed to going to school, had no pangs of heart at all when they bade their mother good-bye. As to Peterkins and Jackdaw, as they were also going to school on the following day, they scarcely observed the departure of their sisters, only saying, when Belle hugged one and Molly the other, "What a fuss you girls do make! Now, if Spot-ear and Fanciful were to fret about us there'd be some reason in it. But mother's going to look after them; and mother's a brick, I can tell you." The girls laughed very merrily, and asked what message her two adorers would like to send to Maggie.

The two adorers only vouchsafed the remark, "Don't bother; we're going to be with boys now, and boys are worth all the girls in creation put together."

The journey to town was taken without any special adventure, and at about three o'clock in the afternoon an omnibus containing the four girls, accompanied by Mr. Tristram, with their luggage piled on the roof, stopped at Aylmer House.

Aneta had already arrived; and as the girls entered with a new feeling of timidity through the wide-open doors they caught a glimpse of Maggie in the distance. There were other girls, absolute strangers to them, who peeped for a minute over the balusters and then retired from view. But, whatever the four strangers might have felt with regard to these interesting occurrences, every other feeling was brought into subjection by the appearance of Mrs. Ward on the scene.

Mrs. Ward looked quite as stately as Mrs. Cardew, with her beautiful face still quite young; with her most kind, most gentle, most protective manner; with the glance of the eye and the pressure of the hand which spoke untold volumes of meaning. Merry felt her loving heart rise in sudden adoration.

Cicely gave her a quick, adoring glance. As to Molly and Isabel, they were speechless with pleasure.

"You have come, dears," said Mrs. Ward. "Welcome, all four!—These are your girls, Mr. Tristram"—she singled out Molly and Isabel without being introduced to them. "I know them," she said with a smile, "from their likeness to you. And these are the Cardews. Now, which is Cicely and which Merry? Ah, I think I can tell. This is Merry, is she not?" and she laid her hand on the pretty girl's shoulder.

"Yes, I am Merry," replied Meredith Cardew in a voice which almost choked her.

"And you, of course, are Cicely," said Mrs. Ward. "In this house all the girls speak to each other by their Christian names; and you will be Cicely and Merry to me, as Molly and Isabel Tristram will be Molly and Isabel to me. You know Aneta, of course. She is hovering near, anxious to take possession of you. Go with her, dears. I think all my girls have now come.—Is it not so, Miss Talbot?"

"Yes, Mrs. Ward," replied Miss Talbot.

"Miss Talbot, may I introduce my four new pupils to you, Cicely and Merry Cardew, and Molly and Isabel Tristram?—You will have a good deal to do with Miss Talbot, girls, for she is our English teacher, and my very great friend."

Miss Talbot blushed slightly from pleasure. She said a gentle word to each girl, and a minute afterwards they had, so to speak, crossed the Rubicon, and were in the heart of Aylmer House; for Aneta had seized Merry's hand, and Cicely followed immediately afterwards, while Molly and Belle found themselves one at each side of Maggie Howland.

"Oh, this is delightful!" said Maggie. "We have all met at last. Isn't the day glorious? Isn't the place perfect? Aren't you in love with Mrs. Ward?"

"She seems very nice," said Molly in an almost timid voice.

"How nice Merry and Cicely look!" continued Maggie.

"You look nice, yourself, Maggie. Everything is wonderful," said Molly; "not a bit like the school in Hanover."

"Of course not. Who could compare it?" said Maggie.

Meanwhile Aneta, Cicely, and Merry had gone on in front. But as they were ascending the broad, low stairs, Merry turned and glanced at Maggie and smiled at her, and Maggie smiled back at Merry. Oh, that smile of Merry's, how it caused her heart to leap! Aneta, try as she would, could not take Merry

Cardew quite away from her.

Cicely and Merry had a bedroom together. Two little white beds stood side by side. The drugget on the floor was pale blue. The room was a study in pale blue and white. It was all exquisitely neat, fresh, airy, and the smell of the flowers in the window-boxes came in through the open windows.

"Why," said Cicely with a gasp, "we might almost be in the country!"

"This is one of the nicest rooms in the whole house," said Aneta. "But why should I say that," she continued, "when every room is, so to speak, perfect? I never saw Mrs. Ward, however, more particular than she was about your bedroom, girls. I think she is very much pleased at your coming to Aylmer House."

Cicely ran to the window and looked out.

"It is so nice to be in London," she said; "but somehow, I thought it would be much more noisy."

Aneta laughed.

"Aylmer House," she said, "stands in the midst of a great square. We don't have huge traffic in the squares; and, really, at night it is as quiet as the country itself."

"But hark! hark!" said Merry, "there is a funny sound after all."

"What do you take it for?" asked Aneta.

"I don't know," said Merry. "I could almost imagine that we were by the seaside, and that the sound was the roar of the breakers on the beach."

"It is the roar of human breakers," said Aneta. "One always hears that kind of sound even in the quietest parts of London. It is the great traffic in the thoroughfares not far away."

"It is delightful! wonderful!" said Merry. "Oh, I long to know all the girls! You will introduce us, won't you, Aneta?"

"Of course; and you must be very quick remembering names. Let me see. You two, and Molly and Isabel, and Maggie Howland, and I make six. There are twenty girls in the house altogether, so you have to make the acquaintance of fourteen others."

"I never can possibly remember their names," said Merry.

"You will have to try. That's the first thing expected of a schoolgirl—to know the names of her schoolfellows."

"Well, I will do my best."

"You had better do your best; it will be a good occupation for you during this first evening. Now, are you ready? And shall we go down? We have tea in the refectory at four o'clock. Mademoiselle Laplage presides over the tea-table this week."

"Oh, but does she talk English?"

"Of course not—French. How can you learn French if you don't talk it?"

"I shall never understand," said poor Merry.

"Well, I've no doubt she will let you off very easily during the first few days," said Aneta. "But afterwards she is just as particular as woman can be."

The girls went downstairs, where a group of other girls—most of them wearing pretty white dresses, for they were all still in full summer attire—met in the wide, pleasant hall. Aneta performed the ceremony of introduction.

"Henrietta and Mary Gibson, may I introduce my special friends and cousins, Cicely and Meredith—otherwise Merry—Cardew?"

Two tall, fair, lady-like girls responded to this introduction with a hearty shake of the hand and a hearty welcome to the new-comers.

"Here is Rosamond Dacre," continued Aneta, as a very dark, somewhat plain girl appeared in view.—"Rosamond, my friends and cousins, Cicely and Merry Cardew."

Rosamond shook hands, but stiffly and without any smile. The next minute a laughing, merry, handsome little girl, with dark-blue eyes, very dark curling eyelashes, and quantities of curling black hair, tumbled rather than walked into view.

"Ah Kathleen—Kitty, you're just as incorrigible as ever!" cried Aneta:
—"Girls, this is our Irish romp, as we always call her. Her name is Kathleen O'Donnell.—Now then, Kathleen, you must be good, you know, and not too terribly Irish. I have the honor to present to you, Kathleen, my cousins Cicely and Merry Cardew."

Kathleen did more than smile. She laughed outright. "I am delighted you have come," she said. "How are you? Isn't school glorious? I do love it! I have come straight from Glengariff—the most beautiful part of the whole of Ireland. Do you know Ireland? Have you ever seen Bantry Bay? Oh, there is no country in all the world like it, and there is no scenery so magnificent."

"Come, Kitty, not quite so much chatter," said Aneta.—"Ah, there's the tea-gong."

The girls now followed Aneta into a pleasant room which looked out on to a small garden. The garden, compared to the great, sweeping lawns and lovely parterres of Meredith Manor, was insignificant. Nevertheless, with the French windows of the refectory wide open, and the beds full of hardy flowers—gay geraniums, late roses, innumerable asters, fuchsias, etc.—it appeared as a fresh surprise to the country girls.

"It isn't like London," thought Merry.

At tea she found herself, greatly to her relief, at Maggie's side. There was also another piece of good fortune—at least so it seemed to the Cardews, whose conversational French was still almost *nil*—Mademoiselle Laplage was unexpectedly absent, the good lady being forced to remain in her room with a sudden, overpowering headache, and pleasant, good-natured Lucy—otherwise Miss Johnson—took her place.

"Perfect freedom to-day, girls," said Miss Johnson.

"Ah, good Lucy! thank you, Lucy!" exclaimed Kathleen.

"That's right, Lucy! Hurrah for Lucy!" cried several other voices.

"No discipline at all to-day," continued Lucy. "School doesn't begin until to-morrow."

Cicely was seated near Aneta, with Kathleen O'Donnell at her other side. Just for a minute Aneta's eyes traveled across the table and fixed themselves on Maggie's face. Maggie found herself coloring, and a resentful feeling awoke in her heart. She could not dare to oppose Aneta; and yet—and yet—she was determined at any cost to keep the love of Merry Cardew for herself.

Meanwhile Merry, who was equally delighted to find herself by Maggie's side, began to talk to her in a low tone.

"You don't look very well, Mags," she said—"not nearly as robust as when I saw you last; and you never wrote to me after that first letter."

"I have a great deal I want to tell you," said Maggie in a low tone. "Lucy is quite right; there are no lessons of any sort this evening. Mrs. Ward always gives us the first evening to settle and to get perfectly at home in, so we shall be able to chatter to our heart's content. This is going to be a glorious night, and we can walk about in the garden."

"But won't there be a lot of other people in the garden?" asked Merry.

"Why, of course," said Maggie in a surprised tone. "I suppose we'll all be there."

"We can't talk any secrets, if that is what you mean," said Merry, "for the garden is so very small."

Maggie laughed. "That's because you are accustomed to Meredith Manor," she said. "Anyhow," she continued, dropping her voice, "I must talk to you. I have a great, great deal to say, and you'll have to listen."

"Of course I will listen, dear," said Merry.

Rosamond Dacre now joined in, and the conversation became general. Henrietta and Mary Gibson had a very agreeable way of describing things. Maggie felt herself reinstated in the life she loved; Merry, the girl she cared for best, was by her side, and she would not have had a single thorn in the flesh but for the presence of Aneta.

It has been said that in this school there were two girls who held considerable sway over their companions. One of them was Aneta Lysle, the other Maggie Howland. Aneta had, of course, far and away the greater number of girls under her spell, if such a word could describe her high and noble influence over them. But Maggie had her own friends, among whom were Rosamond Dacre, Kathleen O'Donnell, Matty and Clara Roache, and Janet Burns. All these girls were fairly nice, but not so high-bred and not so noble in tone as the girls who devoted themselves to Aneta. Kathleen was, indeed, altogether charming; she was the romp of the school and the darting of every one. But Rosamond Dacre was decidedly morose and sulky. She was clever, and on this account her mistresses liked her; but she was a truly difficult girl to deal with, being more or less shut up within herself, and disinclined to true friendship with any one. She liked Kathleen O'Donnell, however, and Kathleen adored Maggie. Rosamond was, therefore, considered to be on Maggie's side of the school. Matty and Clara Roache were quite ordinary, everyday sort of girls, neither very good-looking nor the reverse, neither specially clever nor specially stupid. Their greatest friend was Janet Burns, a handsome little girl with a very lofty brow, calm, clear gray eyes, and a passionate adoration for Maggie Howland. Matty and Clara would follow Janet to the world's end, and, as Janet adhered to Maggie, they were also on Maggie's side.

Maggie naturally expected to add to the numbers of her special adherents her own two friends, the Tristrams. She felt she could easily have won Merry also to join, the ranks of adorers; but then it suddenly occurred to her that her friendship for Merry should be even more subtle than the ordinary friendship that an ordinary girl who is queen at school gives to her fellows. She did not dare to defy Aneta. Merry must outwardly belong to Aneta, but if her heart was Maggie's what else mattered?

When tea was over several of the girls drifted into the garden, where they walked in twos, discussing their holidays, their old friends, and the time which was just coming. There was not a trace of unhappiness in any face. The whole atmosphere of the place seemed to breathe peace and goodwill.

Aneta and Cicely, with some of Aneta's own friends, two girls of the name of Armitage—Anne and Jessie—and a very graceful girl called Sylvia St. John, walked up and down talking quietly together for some little time.

Then Cicely looked eagerly round her. "I can't see Merry anywhere," she remarked.

"She is all right, dear, I am sure," said Aneta. But Aneta in her inmost heart did not think so. She was, however, far too prudent to say a word to make her cousin Cicely uneasy.

Meanwhile Maggie and Merry had found a cosy corner for themselves in one of the conservatories. They sat side by side in two little garden-chairs.

"Well, you've come!" said Maggie. "I have carried out my design. My heart's desire is satisfied."

"Oh, how sweet you are, Maggie!" said Merry. "I have missed you so much!" she added. "I have so often wished for you!"

"Do you really love me?" asked Maggie, looking at Merry in her queer, abrupt manner.

"You know I do," said Merry.

"Well," said Maggie, "there are a great many girls in the school who love me very dearly."

"It is easy to perceive that," said Merry. "Why, Maggie, at tea-time that handsome little Irish girl—Kathleen you call her—couldn't take her eyes off you."

"Oh, Kitty," said Maggie. "Yes, she is on my side."

"What do you mean by your side?"

"Well, of course I have told you—haven't I?—that there are two of us in this school who are more looked up to than the others. It seems very conceited for me to say that I happen to be one. Of course I am not a patch on Aneta; I know that perfectly well."

"Aneta is a darling," said Merry; "and she is my own cousin; but"—she dropped her voice—"Maggie, somehow, I can't help loving you best."

"Oh," said Maggie with a start, "is that true?"

"It is! it is!"

Maggie was silent for a minute. At the end of that time she said very gently,

"You won't be hurt at something I want to tell you?"

"Hurt! No," said Merry; "why should I be?"

"Well, it is just this: Aneta is frightfully jealous of me."

"Oh! I don't believe it," said Merry indignantly. "It isn't in her nature to be jealous. It's very low-minded to be jealous."

"There is no school," said Maggie, "where jealousy does not abound. There is no life into which jealousy does not enter. The world itself is made up of jealous people. Aneta is jealous of me, and I—I am jealous of her."

"Oh, Maggie dear, you must not, and you ought not to be jealous of Aneta! She thinks so kindly, so sweetly of every one."

"She loves you," said Maggie. "You just go and tell her how much you care for me, that you love me better than you love her, and see how she will take it."

"But I wouldn't tell her that," said little Merry, "for it would hurt her."

"There!" said Maggie with a laugh; "and yet you pretend that you don't think her jealous."

"She will never be jealous of me, for I'll never give her cause—dear Aneta!" said Merry.

Maggie was again silent and thoughtful for a few minutes. "Listen to me, Merry," she said. "In this school the girls follow the queens. If I wanted to make Aneta Lysle really mad with jealousy I'd get you over to me; but— don't speak for a minute—I won't get you over to me. You shall stay at school and be on Aneta's side."

"I suppose—I suppose I ought," said Merry in a faint voice.

"You must—you must be on Aneta's side of the school, and so must Cicely; but you can, all the same, love me best."

"Can I?" said Merry, brightening up. "Then, if I can, I sha'n't mind a bit."

Maggie patted her hand very gently. "You can, Merry; and you can help me. You will always take my part, won't you?"

"Indeed—indeed I will! But it won't be necessary."

"It may be," said Maggie very earnestly. "Promise that, if the time comes, you will take my part."

"I promise, of course. What can be the matter with you, Maggie? You don't look a bit yourself."

Maggie did not at once reply. "I shall have a great deal to do this term," she said after a pause; "and my party in the school won't be so weak after all. There'll be Rosamond Dacre—"

"I didn't very much like Rosamond," said Merry, speaking in a low voice.

"Oh, she is excellent fun when you know her," said Maggie; "but as she won't be on your side, nor in your form, you are not likely to have much to do with her. Then Matty and Clara are first-rate, and they're mine too; and Kathleen O'Donnell is a perfect brick; and Janet Burns, she's as strong as they make 'em. Of course the Tristrams will belong to me. Let me see: Tristrams, two; Rosamond, three; Kathleen, four; Matty and Clara, six; Janet, seven. Ah, well, I am quite in the minority. Aneta carries off eleven girls as her share."

"Don't be sad about it, Maggie. Surely we might all be one in the school! Why should there be parties?" said Merry.

"Little you know, Merry, how impossible school-life would be without parties, and great friends, and medium friends, and favorites, and enemies. Why, Merry, school is a little world, and the world is made up of elements such as these."

"Tell me," said Merry after a pause, "what you did after you left us."

Maggie colored. "Oh, stayed for a time in that horrid Shepherd's Bush."

"In those fusty, musty lodgings?" said Merry.

"Yes, and they were fusty, musty."

"Oh dear! I am sorry for you. We had such a glorious time!"

"I know it, dear; but glorious times don't come to girls like me."

"Why, are you so very, very sad, Maggie? Oh, now I know—of course I know. I didn't like to write to you about it, for it seemed to me quite—you will forgive me, won't you?—quite dreadful that your mother should have married again. Is she married yet, Maggie?"

Maggie nodded.

"Oh, I can sympathize with you, dear Maggie! It must be so fearful to have a stepfather!"

"It is," said Maggie.

"Is he a nice man, Maggie? Or would you rather I didn't speak of him?"

"No; you may speak of him if you like. He is a rich man—he is very rich."

"I am glad of that at any rate," said Merry. "You will never be in fusty, musty lodgings any more."

"Oh no, never! My mother's husband—I cannot speak of him as my stepfather—will see to that."

"What is his name?"

Maggie hesitated. Not for the world would she have let any of her schoolfellows know the real position; but she could not very well conceal her stepfather's name.

"Martin," she said.

"Spelt with a 'y'? We know some awfully nice Martyns. They live about twenty miles away from Meredith Manor. I wonder if your Mr. Martyn is related to them."

"Oh, very likely," said Maggie.

"Then perhaps you will go to stay with them—your mother, and your—your mother's husband, and you too; and we'll all meet. They live at a place-called The Meadows. It isn't as old or as beautiful as our Manor, but it's a sweet place, and the girls are so nice you'll be sure to like them."

"Yes, I dare say I shall," said Maggie, who didn't care to contradict Merry's innocent ideas with regard to her mother's marriage.

"Well, I am glad," said Merry, "that your dear mother has married a rich gentleman. Has he a country place of his own?"

"Of course he has," said Maggie, who felt that she could at least utter these words with truth.

"And is it far, far from London, or quite in the country?"

"It is," said Maggie, "in—in the Norwood direction."

This remark made no impression whatever on Merry, who had not the least idea where the Norwood direction was. But by-and-by, when she parted from Maggie and joined her sister and Aneta, she said, "I have a piece of rather good news to tell about dear Maggie Howland. She won't be poor any more."

"That is a word we never discuss at school," said Aneta.

"Well, we needn't after to-night," said Merry with a slight touch of irritation in her manner. "But although I haven't the faintest idea what poverty means, I think poor Maggie knows a good deal about it. Well, she won't have anything to do with it in future, for her mother has just married again."

"Oh!" said Aneta, with a show of interest.

"Yes; and a very nice gentleman he must be. He is a cousin of the Martyns of The Meadows. You know how you liked them when we spent a day there during these holidays—didn't you, Aneta?"

"Yes," said Aneta, "most charming people. I felt quite sorry that the Martyn girls were too old for school. I wonder they didn't mention the fact of their cousin being about to marry Mrs. Howland; for you know we were talking of Maggie to them, or at least you were, Merry."

"Of course I was," said Merry in a determined voice. "I am very, very fond of Maggie Howland."

"Perhaps we had better go to bed now," said Aneta. "I may as well tell you, girls, that we have to get up at half-past six. Lucy comes to us and wakes us at that hour, and we are expected to be downstairs at seven. Lucy will tell you, too, girls, that it is expected of us all that we shall keep our rooms in perfect order. Now, shall we say good-night?"

The Cardews kissed their cousin and went to their own pleasant room.

As soon as they were there Merry said, "Cicely, I am glad about poor Maggie."

"And so am I," said Cicely.

"When we write home we must be sure to mention to mother about Mr. Martyn. I don't think dear Maggie knew anything about The Meadows; so perhaps, after all, he is a somewhat distant cousin; but it is such a comfort to know that he is rich and a gentleman."

"Yes," said Cicely. Then she added, "I don't think Aneta wants you to make too great a friend of Maggie Howland."

"Oh, nonsense!" said Merry, coloring slightly. "I am never going to give Maggie up, for I love her dearly."

"Of course," said Cicely, "it would be very mean to give her up; but you and I, as Aneta's cousins, must be on her side in the school. What I am afraid of is that Maggie will try to induce you to join her set."

"That shows how little you know her," said Merry, roused to the defensive. "She explained everything to me this afternoon, and said that I certainly must belong to Aneta."

"Did she? Well, I call that splendid," said Cicely.

137

# CHAPTER XVI.

## BO-PEEP.

When Aneta found herself alone that evening she stayed for a short time thinking very deeply. She felt a queer sense of responsibility with regard to the Cardews. If Maggie imagined that it was through her influence they had come to Aylmer House, Aneta was positive that they would never have entered the school but for her and her aunt, Lady Lysle. Besides, they were her very own cousins, and she loved them both dearly. She was not especially anxious about Cicely, who was a more ordinary and less enthusiastic girl than Merry; but about Merry she had some qualms. There was no doubt whatever that the girl was attracted by Maggie; and, in Aneta's opinion, Maggie Howland was in no sense of the word a proper companion for her.

Aneta, as she sat calmly by her open window—for it was not necessary to hurry to bed to-night—thought much over the future which spread itself immediately in front of her and her companions. She was naturally a very reserved girl. She was born with that exclusiveness and reserve which a distinguished class bestows upon those who belong to it. But she had in her heart very wide sympathies; and, like many another girl in her position, she could be kind to the poor, philanthropic to the last degree to those in real distress, denying herself for the sake of those who wanted bread. Towards girls, however, who were only a trifle below her in the social scale she could be arbitrary, haughty, and strangely wanting in sympathy. Maggie Howland was exactly the sort of girl who repelled Aneta. Nevertheless, she was a member of the school; and not only was she a member of the school, but a very special member. Had she even been Janet Burns (who was so clever, and as far as learning was concerned carried all before her), or had she been as brilliant and witty as Kathleen O'Donnell, Aneta would not have troubled herself much over her. But Maggie was possessed of a curious sense of *power* which was hers by heritage, which her father had possessed before her, and which caused him—one of the least prepossessing and yet one of the most distinguished men of his day—to be worshipped wherever he went. This power was greater than beauty, greater than birth, greater than genius. Maggie had it, and used it to such effect that she and Aneta divided the school between them. Aneta was never quite certain whether some of her special friends would not leave her and go over to Maggie's side; but she felt that she did not greatly care about this, provided she could keep Merry and Cicely altogether to herself.

After thinking for a little time she sprang to her feet, and going to the electric bell, sounded it. After a short delay a servant appeared.

"Mary," said Aneta, "will you have the goodness to ask Miss Lucy if I may speak to her for a minute?"

"Yes, miss," replied Mary, closing the door behind her in her usual noiseless fashion.

In a very few minutes Miss Johnson entered Aneta's room.

"I was just thinking of going to bed, dear," said that good-natured young woman. "Can I do anything for you?"

"I only want to say something to you, Lucy."

"What is it, my love? I do not like to see that our dear Aneta looks worried, but your face almost wears that expression."

"Well," said Aneta, "it is just this: I am a trifle worried about a matter which I hope I may set right. It is against the rules for girls to leave their rooms after they have gone to them for the night, and it would never do for me to be the first to break a rule at Aylmer House. Nevertheless, I do want to break it. May I, Miss Lucy?"

"Well, Aneta, I do not think that there'll be the slightest difficulty, for we don't really begin school till to-morrow. What do you wish to do, dear?"

"I want to go and visit one of my schoolmates, and stay with her for a time."

"Of course you may go, Aneta. I give you permission; but don't remain too long, for we get up early to-morrow, as to-morrow school really begins."

"I won't remain a minute longer than I can help. Thank you, Lucy," said Aneta.

Miss Johnson kissed her pupil and left the room.

A minute later Aneta Lysle was running down the corridor in the direction of the bedroom occupied by Maggie Howland. It was some distance from her own room. She knocked at the door. She guessed somehow that Maggie would be still up.

Maggie said, "Come in," and Aneta entered.

Maggie was in a white dressing-gown, with her thick, handsome hair falling below her waist. Her hair was her strongest point, and she looked for the time being almost pretty.

"What do you want, Aneta?" she said.

"To speak to you, Maggie."

"But it's against the rules," said Maggie, drawling out her words a little, and giving Aneta a defiant glance.

"No," said Aneta. "I asked for permission to come and see you, and I have obtained it."

"Well, sit down, won't you?" said Maggie.

Aneta availed herself of the invitation, and took a chair.

Maggie remained standing.

"Won't you sit too, Maggie?" said Aneta.

"I don't particularly want to, but I will if you insist on it. To tell the truth, I am a little sleepy. You won't keep me long, will you?"

"That depends on yourself."

Maggie opened her narrow eyes. Then she contracted them and looked fixedly at her companion. "Have you come here to talk about Merry Cardew?"

"Yes, about her, and other matters."

"Don't you trust me at all, Aneta?"

Aneta looked full up at the girl. "No, Maggie," she said.

"Do you think when you say so that you speak kindly?"

"I am afraid I don't, but I can't help myself," said Aneta.

Maggie gave a faint yawn. She was, in reality, far too interested to be really sleepy. Suddenly she dropped into a sitting position on the floor. "You have me," she said, "in the hollow of your hand. Do you mean to crush me? What have I done that you should hate me so much?"

"I never said I hated you," said Aneta. "I don't hate you, but I am exceedingly anxious that you should not have any influence over my two young cousins who came here to-day."

"I thought we discussed that when you were staying at Meredith Manor," said Maggie. "You made me unhappy enough then, but I gave you my promise."

"I was sorry to make you unhappy, Maggie; and you did give me your promise; but I have come here to-day to know why you have broken it."

"Broken it!" said Maggie. "Broken it!"

"Don't you understand me?" said Aneta. "You and Merry were together the greater part of the evening, and even Cicely wondered where her sister was.

Why did you do it?"

"Merry is my friend," said Maggie.

"I don't wish her to be your friend."

"I am afraid you can't help it," said Maggie. She looked a little insolent, and round her mouth there came a dogged expression. After a minute she said, "I did want to talk to Merry to-night; but, at the same time, I most undoubtedly did not forget my promise to you. I explained to Merry what I think she already knew: that there were two girls in the school who greatly influence their fellows; in short, that you and I are the two queens of the school. But I said that, compared to you, I had a comparatively small number of subjects. Merry was interested, and asked questions, and then I most particularly explained to her that, although I knew well she cared for me, and I cared for her, she was to be on your side in the school. If you don't believe me, you have but to ask Merry herself."

"I have no reason not to believe you, Maggie," said Aneta, "and I am relieved that you have spoken as you did to Merry. But now I want to say something else. I have thought of it a good deal during the holidays, and I am firmly convinced that this taking sides, or rather making parties, in a school is pernicious, especially in such a small school as ours. I am willing to give up my queendom, if you, on your part, will give yours up. I want us all to be in unity—every one of us—all striving for the good of the school and for the happiness and welfare each of the other. If you will agree to this I will myself speak to Mrs. Ward to-morrow."

"Mrs. Ward!" said Maggie. "What has she to do with it?"

"I want to consult with her, so that *she* may be the queen of the school—not one girl or two girls. She is so clever, so young, so resourceful, that she will more than make up to us for the little we lose in this matter. But, of course, there is no manner of use in my resigning my queendom if you won't resign yours."

"I will never do it," said Maggie—"never! Two queens in the school means little or nothing at all. All it does mean is that I have special friends whom I can influence, and whom I love to influence, and you have special friends whom you love to influence. Well, go on influencing them as hard as ever you can, and I will do the same with my friends. Your cousins will belong to you. I could, I believe, have won Merry Cardew to my side, but I am not going to do so."

"It would be very unwise of you," said Aneta in a low tone. "Very well, Maggie," she added after a pause, "if you won't give up being queen in the minds of a certain number of girls, I must, of course, continue my influence on the other side. It's a great pity, for we might all work together."

"We never could work together," said Maggie with passion. "It is but to talk to you, Aneta, to know how you despise and hate me."

"I neither despise nor hate you, Maggie."

"Well, I despise and hate you, so I suppose it comes to the same thing."

"I am very, very sorry, Maggie. Some day, perhaps, you will know me as I really am."

"I know you now as you really are—eaten up with pride of birth, and with no sympathy at all for girls a trifle poorer than yourself."

"You speak with cruelty, and I am sorry."

To Aneta's astonishment, Maggie's face underwent a queer change. It puckered up in an alarming manner, and the next moment the girl burst into tears.

The sight of Maggie's tears immediately changed Aneta Lysle's attitude. Those tears were genuine. Whether they were caused by anger or by sorrow she did not stop to discriminate. The next minute she was down on her knees by the other girl and had swept her young arms round Maggie's neck.

"Maggie, Maggie, what is it? Oh, if you would only understand me!"

"Don't!—don't touch me!" said Maggie. "I am a miserable girl!"

"And I have hurt you, poor Maggie!" said Aneta. "Oh, I am terribly sorry! Sit here now, and let me comfort you."

"Oh! I can't, Aneta. You don't understand me—not a bit."

"Better than you think, perhaps; and I am terribly sorry you are troubled. Oh, perhaps I know. I was told to-night that your mother had married again. You are unhappy about that?"

Maggie immediately dried her fast-falling tears. She felt that she was in danger. If Aneta found out, or if Mrs. Ward found out, who Maggie's stepfather was, she would certainly not be allowed to stay at Aylmer House. This was her dread of all dreads, and she had so managed matters with her mother that Mrs. Ward knew nothing at all of Mrs. Howland's change of name.

"Yes, my mother is married again," said Maggie. "She is a rich woman now; but the fact is, I dearly loved my own father, and—it hurt me very much to see another put into his place."

"Of course it did," said Aneta, with deep sympathy; "it would have driven me nearly wild. Does Mrs. Ward know that your mother is married again, Maggie?"

"Well, I haven't told her; and, please, Aneta, will you promise me not to do so?"

"But is there any occasion to keep it a secret, dear?"

"I would so much rather she did not know. She received me here as Maggie Howland. I am Maggie Howland still; my mother having changed her name makes no difference, except, indeed, that she is very well off, whereas she was poor."

"Well, that of course is a comfort to you," said Aneta. "Perhaps by-and-by you will learn to be glad that your mother has secured the care of a good husband. I am told that she has married one of those very nice Martyns who live in Warwickshire. Is that true?"

Maggie nodded. She hated herself after she had given that inclination of her head; but she had done it now, and must abide by it. To own Martin the grocer as a stepfather was beyond her power.

Aneta did not think it specially necessary to worry about Maggie's mother and her new husband. She said that the whole thing was Maggie's own affair; and, after trying to comfort the girl for a little longer, she kissed Maggie, and went to her own room. When there, she went at once to bed and fell fast asleep.

But Maggie sat for a long time by her open window. "What an awful and ridiculous position I have put myself in!" she thought. "The Martyns of The Meadows and Bo-peep of Laburnum Villa to be connected! I could almost scream with laughter if I were not also inclined to scream with terror. What an awful idea to get into people's heads, and now I have, confirmed it! Of course I shall be found out, and things will be worse than ever."

Before Maggie went to bed she sat down and wrote a brief note to her mother. She addressed it when written to Mrs. Martyn (spelt with a "y"), Laburnum Villa, Clapham. Maggie had seen Laburnum Villa, and regarded it as one of the most poky suburban residences she had ever had the pleasure of entering. The whole house was odiously cheap and common, and in her heart poor Maggie preferred Tildy and Mrs. Ross, and the fusty, musty lodgings at Shepherd's Bush.

Her note to her mother was very brief:

"I am back at school, and quite happy. Tell Mr. Martin, if he should happen to write to me, to spell his name with a 'y,' and please spell your name with a 'y.' Please tell Mr. Martin that I will explain the reason of this when we meet. He is so good to me, I don't know how to thank him enough."

Maggie managed the next day to post this letter unknown to her fellows, and in course of time a remarkable post-card arrived for her. It was dated from Laburnum Villa, Clapham, and was written in a sprawly but business-like hand:

"No 'y's' for me, thank you.—Bo-PEEP."

Very fortunately, Maggie received her card when none of her schoolfellows were present; but it was certainly the reverse of reassuring.

# CHAPTER XVII.

## THE LEISURE HOURS.

School-life began in real earnest, and school-life at Aylmer House was so stimulating, so earnest, so invigorating, that all that was best in each girl was brought to the fore. There was an admirable time-table, which allowed the girls periods for play as well as the most suitable hours for work. In addition, each day there were what were called the "leisure hours." These were from five to seven o'clock each evening. The leisure hours began immediately after tea, and lasted until the period when the girls went to their rooms to dress for dinner. During these two hours they were allowed to do precisely what they pleased.

Mrs. Ward was most particular that no teacher should interfere with her girls during the leisure hours. From the very first she had insisted on this period of rest and absolute relaxation from all work. Work was strictly forbidden in the school from five to seven, and it was during that period that the queens of the school generally exercised their power. Aneta then usually found herself surrounded by her satellites in one corner of the girls' own special sitting-room, and Maggie was in a similar position at the farther end. Aneta's satellites were always quiet, sober, and well-behaved; Maggie's, it is sad to relate, were a trifle rowdy. There is something else also painful to relate—namely, that Merry Cardew cast longing eyes from time to time in the direction of that portion of the room where Maggie and her friends clustered.

The girls had been about a fortnight at school, and work was in full swing, when Kathleen, springing from her seat, said abruptly, "Queen, I want to propose something."

"Well, what is it?" asked Maggie, who was lying back against a pile of cushions and supplying herself daintily from a box of chocolates which her adorers had purchased for her.

"I want us all," said Kathleen, "to give a party to the other queen and her subjects; and I want it to be about the very jolliest entertainment that can be found. We must, of course, ask Mrs. Ward's leave; but she is certain to give it."

"I don't know that she is," said Maggie.

"Oh, she is—certain sure," said Kathleen. "May I go and ask her now?"

"Do you dare?" said Rosamond Dacre, looking at Kitty's radiant face with some astonishment.

"Dare!" cried Irish Kitty. "I don't know the meaning of anything that I don't dare. I am off. I'll bring you word in a few minutes, girls." She rushed out of the room.

Janet Burns looked after her, slightly raising her brows. Rosamond Dacre and the two Roaches began to sound her praises. "She is sweet, isn't she?"

"Yes," said Clara; "and I do so love her pretty Irish brogue."

"Mother tells me," said Janet, who was Scotch, "that Irish characters are not much good—they're not reliable, I mean."

"Oh, what a shame!" said Matty Roache.

"I don't think we need discuss characters," said Maggie. "I don't know a great deal about the Irish, but I do know that Kitty is a darling."

"Yes, so she is—one of the sweetest girls in the whole school," said Molly Tristram, who was quite as excited as Kathleen herself with regard to the party scheme.

Meantime Kitty found herself tapping at Mrs. Ward's private door. Mrs. Ward said, "Come in," and the pretty girl, with her great dark-blue eyes and wild-rose complexion, entered abruptly.

"Well, Kathleen?" said Mrs. Ward in her pleasant tone.

"Oh, please, Mrs. Ward, I've come with such a lovely scheme."

"And you want me to help you?"

"Oh yes, please, do say you will before I let you into the secret!"

"I can't do that, dear; you must just tell me what is in your mind, and be satisfied with my decision. The only thing that I can assure you beforehand is that if it is a workable scheme, and likely to give you great pleasure, I will do my best to entertain it."

"Then we're certain to have it—certain," said Kathleen.

"It was I who thought of it. You will forgive me if I speak out just as plainly as possible?"

"Of course, Kathleen dear."

"Well, you know you are the head-mistress."

"That is scarcely news to me, my child."

"And people, as a rule," continued Kathleen, "respect their head-mistress."

"Dear me," said Mrs. Ward with a smile, "have you come here, Kathleen, to say that you don't respect me?"

"Respect you!" said Kathleen. "We do a jolly lot more than that. We adore you! We love you! You're—you're a sort of—of mother to us."

"That is what I want to be," said Mrs. Ward with fervor, and she took the girl's hand and smoothed it gently.

"I often want to hug you, and that's a fact," said Kathleen.

"You may kiss me now if you like, Kitty."

"Oh, Mrs. Ward!" Kitty bent down and bestowed a reverent kiss on that sweet face.

"I have permitted you to kiss me, Kitty," said Mrs. Ward, "in order to show you that I sympathize with you, as I do with all my dear girls. But now, what is the matter?"

"Well, the fact is this. We want, during the 'leisure hours' to give a party."

"Is that all? Do you all want to give a party?"

"Our side wants to give a party, and we want to invite the other side to it."

"But what do you mean by 'our side' and 'the other side'?"

"Oh, Mrs. Ward! you know—of course you know—that Aneta and Maggie divide the school."

"I know," said Mrs. Ward after a pause, "that Aneta has considerable influence, and that Maggie also has influence."

"Those two girls divide the school," said Kathleen, "the rest of us follow them. As a matter of fact, we only follow our leaders in the leisure hours; but as they come every day a good deal can be done in that time, can't it?"

"Yes," said Mrs. Ward, and her tone was not exactly cheerful. "On which side are you, Kitty?"

"Oh, dear Mrs. Ward, of course, on Maggie's! Do you think that a girl like me, with all my spirit and that irresistible sort of fun always bubbling up in me, could stand the stuck-ups?"

"Kitty, you have no right to speak of any girls in the school by such an offensive term."

"I am sorry," said Kitty. "I ought not to have said it to you. But they are stuck-ups; they really are."

"And what do you call yourself?"

"Oh, the live-and-let-live—that's our title. But it's only quite among ourselves, and perhaps I ought not to have said it."

"I will never repeat what you have told me in confidence, dear. But now for your request?"

"Well, we of Maggie's set want to invite the Aneta set to a sort of general party. We should like it to be on the half-holiday, if possible. We want to give them a right royal entertainment in order to knock some of their stuck-upness out of them. We wish for your leave in the matter."

"You must describe your entertainment a little more fully."

"I can't; for we haven't really and truly planned it all out yet. But I tell you what we'll do. If you give us leave to have the party, we will ask Queen Aneta and her satellites if possible this very evening, and then we'll submit our programme to you. Now, may we do this, or may we not?"

"Who sent you to me, Kathleen?"

"I came of my own very self, but of course the others approved. We have no intention of doing shabby things in the dark, as they do in some schools. That would be unfair to you."

Mrs. Ward thought a little longer. "I will give you the required permission," she said, "on one condition."

"Oh, Mrs. Ward, darling! what is that?"

"You can have your party on Saturday week, and I will give you from early in the afternoon until bedtime to enjoy it."

"Oh, Mrs. Ward, you are too angelic!"

"Stop a minute. You may not care for it so much when I have finished what I have got to say."

"What is it, dear Mrs. Ward?"

"It is this: that you ask me too as one of your guests."

"Oh! oh!" said Kathleen. Her expressive face changed from red to white and then to red again. Her eyes brimmed over with laughter, and then as suddenly filled with tears. "But would you—would you like it?"

"Yes, and I don't want to destroy your pleasure; but I presume you will have a sort of supper or an entertainment which will include refreshments. Let me assist you with the expense of your supper, and may I be present at it as one of your guests? I will promise to leave soon after supper, and not to appear until supper. How will that do?"

148

"Oh, it would be just, heavenly! It will give such distinction. I know the girls will love it."

"I think I can make myself pleasant to you all," said Mrs. Ward, "and I should like to be there."

"But as to paying anything, Mrs. Ward, you will come as our guest, and you know we have most of us plenty of money. Please, please, let us do the entertaining."

"Very well, dear, I will not press that point. I hope I have made you happy, Kathleen."

"Oh! you have—very, very happy indeed. And Saturday week is to be the day?"

"Yes, Kathleen."

Kathleen bent down, took one of Mrs. Ward's hands, and kissed it. Then she skipped out of the room and flew back to her companions. They were waiting for her in a state of suppressed eagerness.

"Well, Kathleen—Kitty—Kit, what's the news?" asked Maggie.

Room was made for Kathleen in the center of the group.

"We have won! We may do it!" she said, speaking in a low tone. "Oh, she's— she's like no one else! I don't know how you will take it, girls; but if you're not just delighted you ought, to be. Why, what *do* you think? She wants to come herself."

"Mrs. Ward!" said Maggie in amazement.

"Yes, just to supper. She says she will come—she wishes to come—that we're to invite her; in fact, she makes it a *sine quâ non*. She will go away again after supper, and we're to have the whole glorious day, next Saturday week, from two in the afternoon until bedtime. Oh, sha'n't we have fun!"

"Yes, of course," said Maggie. "It's much better even than I thought. I will write the letters of invitation immediately."

"But why should you write a whole lot of letters?" said Kathleen. "You are one queen. Write to the other queen and mention that Mrs. Ward is coming."

There was nothing like the present time for making arrangements; and Maggie wrote on a sheet of headed note-paper provided for her by her satellites the following words:

"Queen Maggie presents her compliments to Queen Aneta, and begs for the pleasure of her company with all her subjects on Saturday the

15th of October, to an entertainment from three to nine o'clock. She hopes that the whole school will be present, and writes in the names of her own subjects as well as of herself.

"*P.S.*—Mrs. Ward has most kindly promised to attend."

This letter was subjected to the approval of the group of girls who surrounded Maggie. It was then addressed to "Queen Aneta," and Kathleen crossed the room with it and dropped it, there and then, into Aneta Lysle's lap.

It caused very deep amazement in the hearts of all the girls who belonged to Aneta's party, and it is highly probable that they might have refused to accept the invitation but for that magical postscript, "Mrs. Ward has most kindly promised to attend." But there was no withstanding that patent fact, as Mrs. Ward knew very well when she made the proposal to Kathleen.

After a lapse of about twenty minutes, Cicely Cardew crossed the room and laid the answer to Maggie's note in her lap:

"Queen Aneta and her subjects have much pleasure in accepting Queen Maggie's invitation for the 15th inst."

"Hip, hip, hurrah!" cried Kathleen. "The thing's arranged, and we'll have about the jolliest flare-up and the most enticing time that girls ever had at any school." She sprang from her seat, and began tossing a book which had lain in her lap into the air, catching it again. In short, the subjects of the two queens broke up on the spot and chatted gaily together, and Maggie and her subjects could not be induced to say one word of what was to take place on the 15th of October.

"It is wonderful," thought Aneta to herself. "Why does Mrs. Ward come? But, of course, as she comes we must all come."

# CHAPTER XVIII.

## THE TREASURE.

Maggie had by no means forgotten her promise to the Tristram girls to give them a bracelet apiece. It was easy to do this, for they were her very special friends in the school. The fact is that Molly and Belle had a somewhat peculiar position at Aylmer House, for they were not only Maggie's special friends, but also the undoubted friends and allies of Cicely, Merry, and also of Aneta. But they were such good-humored, good-natured, pleasant sort of girls —so lively, so jolly—that they could take up a position with ease which would oppress and distress other people.

When Maggie presented them with their bracelets they were in wild raptures, accepting them gleefully, and on occasions when ornaments were permitted to be worn—which, as a matter of fact, was only in the leisure hours—they invariably had them on their arms.

But other girls noticed them, and one and all admired them immensely.

"Oh, I have others," said Maggie in a careless tone; "many more. My dear father was a great traveler, and these are some of the treasures he brought from the East."

Maggie had by no means forgotten to bring her two boxes of jewellery to Aylmer House. These lay at the bottom of her little trunk, which was, it is true, stowed away in the box-room. But as the girls were at liberty to go there for anything they especially required, she was not troubled on this account.

There came a day, shortly after the great party was arranged, when the rain poured incessantly, and some of the girls were a little restless. Molly and Isabel were wearing their queer Oriental bracelets. Kathleen suddenly caught sight of them, and demanded in an eager tone that Maggie should exhibit her treasures. Maggie, only too pleased to have anything to do which glorified herself, immediately complied. She ran to find Miss Lucy in order to obtain the key of the box-room.

"What do you want it for, dear?" said Miss Johnson in her pleasant voice.

"I have two boxes in the bottom of one of my trunks, Miss Lucy; they are full of curiosities which my father collected from time to time. The girls want to see them. Do you mind my showing them?"

"Of course not, Maggie; but if they are of any value you had better give them to Mrs. Ward to take care of for you."

"Oh, well," said Maggie, "I don't know really whether they are of value or not." She got rather red as she spoke.

"I should like to see them myself," said Miss Johnson. "I know a little bit about gems and curios."

"Certainly, Miss Lucy; do come," said Maggie. "We're in our sitting-room, and I shall be only too delighted to show them to you."

Maggie fetched down her two precious boxes, and soon she was surrounded, not only by her own special satellites, but by every girl in the school. They were all loud in their expressions of rapture at the unique and lovely things which she exhibited to them.

Kathleen, as usual, was quick in suggestion. "Would not Mrs. Ward love to see them?" she said.

"I am sure she would," remarked Miss Johnson.—"I hadn't the least idea, Maggie, that you had such treasures in those old tin boxes. They must be carefully put away in the safe for you. My dear girl, they're worth a great deal of money."

"Oh, I don't suppose they are," said Maggie, trying to speak carelessly, although she by no means wished to part with her treasures.

"I tell you what," said Kathleen. "Can't we make an exhibition of them on *the* day?"

"Yes, why not?" said Molly and Isabel. "That would be quite lovely."

"Oh yes, do!—do, Maggie darling!" said Merry Cardew.

Maggie at once agreed; and Miss Johnson said, "Now, if you will put them all back in their boxes I will take them and lock them into the safe myself. I shouldn't have an easy moment if I thought such valuable things were in one of your school-trunks."

"Oh!" said Maggie, looking up with flushed cheeks and bright eyes, "please —please let me keep them until after our party. Then we will consult Mrs. Ward, and she will tell me what to do."

"If you must keep them, then, Maggie," said Miss Johnson, "you had better have them in your own bedroom. They would be at least safe there. Put them into your locked drawer, dear; I think it will hold both these boxes."

"Thank you very much," said Maggie. She put the ten bracelets into their tin box, and the necklets and other curios into the other, locked each, and took them upstairs. "It would never, never do," she said to herself, "for me to lose control of these precious things. I am almost sorry now that I allowed the girls to tempt me to show them."

After a few minutes she came downstairs. Her stepfather's allowance of pocket-money was certainly not ample, and she knew that at the party which was to be so specially distinguished she must give, if she wished to keep up her prestige in the school, a lion's share towards the expenses. There was a quaint little brooch in one of her boxes containing one large ruby and set with diamonds which she intended to sell in order to provide herself with funds. But what use would any of her treasures be if they were consigned to the safe at Aylmer House?

After a great deal of consultation, it was resolved that the girls were to meet in their own special sitting-room at four o'clock, where tea and light refreshments were to be provided by Queen Maggie and her subjects. Afterwards they were to play games, have recitations, and amuse themselves in different ways until five o'clock; when a curtain which would be put across a portion of the room would be raised, and tableaux vivants, in which Maggie, Kathleen, and both the Tristram girls, who were all adaptable for this purpose, were to take special parts. The tableaux were under the management of Janet Burns, who was exceedingly clever, and had studied the scenes—which she took from different episodes in Scott's novels—with great care. The rehearsing for the tableaux was a little difficult, but this was done each evening after tea, when Maggie and her subjects had the sitting-room to themselves.

Immediately after the tableaux there would be that wonderful supper, at which Mrs. Ward was to be the principal guest, and then the happy evening would end with all sorts of dances and frolics.

Now, all these things would cost money, and it was arranged, after brief consultation, that each girl was to subscribe in an equal ratio towards the proposed entertainment. Janet, who had a head for figures as well as a taste for tableaux vivants, suggested that, to do the entertainment properly, they would have to expend something like fifteen shillings each. This was immediately agreed upon, and even the Tristrams did not feel embarrassed by the amount which was decided upon, for Mr. Tristram was wise in his generation, and would not send his girls to an expensive school if he could not give them a sufficient supply of pocket-money to make them feel independent. The only person who was short of funds on this occasion was Maggie, for her stepfather had arranged that she was to receive her allowance at the end of the term, not at the beginning. He had given her a few shillings to go to school with; but these she had already spent on chocolates, which were considered essential during the leisure hours. It is true that Mrs. Ward would have advanced a little money to Maggie, but Maggie could not bear to ask her. She had a great dislike to the subject of money being mentioned in Mrs. Ward's presence. She was afraid beyond everything else that the fact of her being received at such a select school for forty pounds a year might reach the ears of her fellow-pupils. What more easy than to sell that charming little Oriental brooch, which was one of the treasures in one of those tin boxes? But Maggie could not manage this in Miss Lucy's presence, and it was quite against the rules at Aylmer House for any girl to go shopping or even to leave the house unaccompanied.

On one or two previous occasions Maggie had, however, managed to evade this rule without being found out, and she thought she could do so now. She planned the whole thing rather cleverly. She had a room to herself; which of course made it easier for her, and there were always the leisure hours. She made up her mind to feign headache or some slight indisposition, to go downstairs by the back way, and sell her brooch on a certain afternoon during the leisure hours. She must do it quickly, for the girls had proposed to put the necessary money for the entertainment into a bag on a certain Tuesday. Maggie must, therefore, go out on Monday in order to sell her brooch. Her absence from the little party in the girls' sitting-room was explained by Molly Tristram, who said that Maggie was upstairs lying down. No one troubled to make any comment with regard to this. Any girl might have a headache, and Mrs. Ward did not wish her girls to be catechised as to how they spent their leisure hours. Besides, Janet Burns was occupying all their attention with the tableaux vivants, Queen Aneta's girls most good-naturedly leaving them the sitting-room to themselves for this purpose.

Maggie, in her distant bedroom, felt the quiet in the house. She had been lying down; now she rose noiselessly. This was the time when the servants had their tea, when Mrs. Ward was busy writing letters or resting in her own sitting-room, when Lucy Johnson and the other governesses were either reposing in their bedrooms, or were out, or were reading. There was, of course, the chance that Maggie might meet some one; but, having calculated all possibilities, she thought that she could most likely get out unobserved.

During her expeditions with Miss Lucy Johnson she had noticed a jeweller's shop not far away, and resolved to go to him with her precious brooch. It was a very respectable shop, and she was certain he would give her fair value. She could be back again before she was missed, and, in fact, could join her companions in the girls' sitting-room long before the leisure hours had expired. The days were now getting very short, but this fact was in Maggie's favor rather than otherwise.

She ran downstairs unnoticed by any one, opened a side-door which was used as a tradesmen's entrance, and got into the street. Then, putting wings to her feet, she quickly turned the corner, left the square where Aylmer House was situated, and reached the jeweller's shop. She entered. There were a few people standing by the counter; and the jeweller, a certain Mr. Pearce, was attending to them. Maggie felt impatient. She awaited her turn as best she could. How she disliked those showy-looking people who were purchasing goods of some value, whereas she only wanted to sell! She could scarcely restrain her great impatience, and was relieved when another shopman came forward.

He asked her what he could do for her. She immediately showed him the quaint little brooch set with rubies and diamonds.

"I want to sell this," said Maggie, speaking abruptly and the color flaming into her cheeks. "What will you give me for it?"

"Oh my!" suddenly exclaimed one of the ladies who was purchasing jewels in Pearce's shop, "what a lovely curio! Wherever now did you get it from?"

Maggie turned and said in a low tone, "It belongs to me. It was left to me by my father."

The man who was attending to Maggie took up the brooch and examined it carefully. He took it into another room, where he subjected it to various tests. He then came back to Maggie.

"I will give you five pounds for this, miss, if you can satisfy me that you have come rightly by it."

"Oh my!" said the American lady, drawing near, and her eyes glistening.

"What is your address, miss?"

Maggie by no means wished to give her address. "I haven't, stolen that brooch," she said. "It belongs to me; I have a right to sell it."

"Of course, miss, I shall never trouble you in any way, but I really must have your address. In purchasing secondhand from young ladies like yourself it is essential that everything should be above-board and quite correct."

"Well," said Maggie in a hurried voice, "take the brooch and give me the money. I must get back as quickly as I can. I am one of Mrs. Ward's pupils at Aylmer House."

The man looked at Maggie with all respect. "And your own name?"

"Howland," said Maggie. "Miss Howland."

The man entered name and address in his book, and then handed Maggie five sovereigns. She was hurrying from the shop, when the customer who had been standing near all the time, and listening with great attention, followed her.

"I say, young lady," she exclaimed, "I am from New York, and I like your quaint old English things. That man cheated you, I take it. If you had offered me that brooch I'd have given you fifteen pounds for it, not five. If you have any more curios to sell, my address is Miss H. Annie Lapham, Langham Hotel. I am straight from the States, and would like to take a collection of beautiful things home with me."

"Thank you," said Maggie in a hurried voice.

She ran back to Aylmer House as quickly as she could. As soon as she was quite out of sight the lady re-entered the shop.

"Say," she remarked to the shopman, "I witnessed that little transaction between you and Miss Howland. I want to buy that brooch for ten pounds."

"I am sorry, madam," said the man, "but it is not for sale just at present."

"That means," said Miss Lapham, coloring crimson, "that you have cheated the young lady. You ought to have given her four times as much for the brooch."

The man shrugged his shoulders.

Miss Lapham grew redder than ever, "I happen to know Miss Howland's address," she said. Then she went away without giving' him time to add a word.

When she had left the shop the younger Mr. Pearce turned to his brother, took the little brooch from the drawer into which he had carelessly thrown it, and gave it to the elder Mr. Pearce to examine. "There's a find here," he said; "only, somehow, I feel a bit uncomfortable. How did one of the young ladies from Aylmer House come by a treasure of this sort?"

The other man examined the brooch carefully. "It's worth a good bit," he said. "What did you give her for it?"

"Five pounds; but somehow I think that I ought not to have taken it for that sum."

"It is worth at least two hundred," said the elder Mr. Pearce. "Where did you say she lived?"

"She is one of the young ladies at Aylmer House—Miss Howland."

"What! from Mrs. Ward's school?"

"Yes."

"You had better give me that brooch, Alfred," said his brother. "We'll have to consider what is to be done. We can't rob the young lady of it. We had best consult Mrs. Ward."

"Oh, as to that," said the younger Pearce, "that sounds almost as shabby as giving the schoolgirl too little money."

"Well, lock it up for the present," said the elder Pearce; "but I am an honest tradesman, and I can't see even a schoolgirl robbed."

"She was up to some little lark," said the younger man, "and evidently did not know the value of the brooch. Why, I think she'd have taken a pound for it. But what she did know the value of was her precious time; she was very much annoyed at being kept waiting and at being asked for her address. It is plain she got out without leave; and although the brooch may belong to her—I am sure I hope it does—she has broken a rule, you mark my words. Those schoolgirls are always up to larks. Well, I'd never have thought it of one of Mrs. Ward's girls."

"It is a pity you didn't consult me, Alfred," said his brother. "The best thing to do now is to put the brooch carefully away. We'll consider what is best to be done with it; but as to giving the young lady only five pounds for what we can sell any day at Christie's for a couple of hundred, that is not to be thought of."

# CHAPTER XIX.

## THE LETTER.

Maggie got out and came back again without any apparent adventure. She had five pounds in her pocket, and thought herself rich beyond the dreams of avarice. What a delightful fairy-gift had been handed down to her by her dear dead father! She did not miss the brooch in the least, but she valued the small sum she had obtained for it exceedingly.

But while Maggie thought herself so secure, and while the pleasant jingle of the sovereigns as she touched them with her little hand comforted her inexpressibly, things quite against Maggie Howland's supposed interests were transpiring in another part of the school.

It was a strange fact that on this special afternoon both the queens should be prostrated with headache. It is true that Queen Maggie's headache was only a fiction, but poor Queen Aneta's was real enough. She was lying down in her pretty bedroom, hoping that quiet might still the throbbing of her temples, when the door was very softly opened, and Merry Cardew brought in a letter and laid it by her side.

"May I bring you some tea upstairs, Aneta?" she said. "Is there anything I can do for you?"

"Oh no, darling," said Aneta. "I can't eat or drink; but if I stay very still I shall be better by-and-by. Leave me now, dear; all I want is perfectquiet."

"I am so sorry for you, Aneta," said Merry.

"What are you doing downstairs?" said Aneta as the girl turned away.

"Well, Maggie has a headache too."

"Oh!" said Aneta.

"So we are without our queens," continued Merry; "but Maggie's girls have taken possession of our sitting-room, and we are all in the schoolroom. We're having great fun and are very happy, so don't worry about us at all, Aneta."

"I won't," said Aneta, closing her eyes, while a feeling of drowsy relief stole over her.

Her anxiety with regard to Maggie was really making her ill. Her sense of responsibility with reference to the Cardew girls seemed to oppress her usually calm spirit. She could not conceal the fact from herself that Merry loved Maggie, most passionately. The knowledge, therefore, that Maggie was not downstairs gave her such a sense of comfort that she dropped into a doze, and when she awoke a short time afterwards her headache was gone.

Yes, her headache had departed, but there lay by her pillow what is a great treasure to all schoolgirls—an unopened letter. She looked at the handwriting, and saw that it was from her aunt, Lady Lysle. Aneta was very fond of Lady Lysle; and, sitting up against her pillows, she tore open the letter and began to read. She was surprised to see that it was dated from Meredith Manor.

"MY DEAR ANETA"—it ran—"I have been staying with the dear Cardews for the last week. We have been having a very pleasant time; although, of course, the house is vastly different without Cicely and Merry. But the dear Cardews are so sensible that they never would regret anything that was for the real benefit of their children.

"Your letter assuring me that the children were happy at school gave me great delight, and when I told the Cardews they were equally pleased. Altogether, this school-venture seems likely to turn out most satisfactory, and the dear children will be properly equipped for the brilliant life which lies before them.

"But now I have a curious piece of information for you. You told me about Miss Howland and her mother's second marriage to one of the Martyns of The Meadows. Well, dear, we went there yesterday, and I happened incidentally to speak on the subject; and, whatever may be the position of Miss Howland's stepfather, he certainly is no relation to our dear friends the Martyns. They have no uncles or cousins in England at all. All their people come from Australia, and they assured me that such a marriage as I have described has, in the first place, never reached their ears, and, in the next, is impossible, for they have no marriageable relations in the country. I mention this to show that your friend has made a mistake. At the same time, it is strange of her to say that her mother, has married into such a well-known and distinguished family. I can add no more now.—Yours, with love, and in haste,

LUCIA LYSLE."

Aneta thought over this letter for some time. Her face was very grave as she tried to put two and two together. She rose from her bed, dressed herself with her usual immaculate neatness, and came down to supper, which took place each evening at half-past seven.

All the girls were present, and each and all were in the best of good-humor. Maggie was radiant. Why not? She had performed a difficult task discreetly, and she had five lovely golden sovereigns in her drawer upstairs. She could put the required money into the bag for the school-treat, and she would have plenty over to buy chocolates and little things that she might require for herself. She did not in the least miss that one small brooch which her father had left her; but she thought with a feeling of intense satisfaction of her treasures. She need no longer be a penniless girl. She had but at rare intervals to visit Pearce the jeweler, and her pocket would be well lined. She had no romantic feeling with regard to those beautiful things which her father had collected on his travels. She had been so poor all her life that money to her represented power. She even thought of getting a couple of new dresses made by a fashionable dressmaker. She resolved to consult Lucy on the subject. She was never quite as well dressed as the other girls, although very plain clothes were the order of the hour at school.

Immediately after supper those girls who required to look over their lessons went into the schoolroom and spent a quiet time there; but the others, as a rule, joined Mrs. Ward in the drawing-room. There those who could play were requested to do so, and those who could sing did likewise. Mrs. Ward was very fond of needlework. She could do rare and wonderful embroideries, and knew some of the tapestry stitches which were in vogue hundreds of years ago. The girls who cared to be taught those things she was only too glad to instruct; but she never pressed any one into her working-party. This was always an hour of relaxation for those girls who had all their lessons ready for the following day.

Maggie, who was exceedingly clever and learned with the utmost ease, was generally a member of the drawing-room coterie. She wore a white dress on this evening, with a somewhat crude pink sash round her waist. She hated the crudity of the color, and it occurred to her that she could get some soft and becoming sashes out of part of the money which Pearce had given her for the brooch.

By-and-by she found herself near Aneta. Aneta was working a center-piece which she meant to present to Lady Lysle at Christmas. Maggie was no good whatever at needlework, and seldom joined the band of needlewomen. But Aneta now motioned the girl to come and sit by her side. Maggie did so. Aneta looked full in her face.

"Is your headache better, Maggie?" she asked.

Maggie had to reflect for a time, she had so absolutely forgotten that she had pretended to have a headache that afternoon! Then she said, with a slight flush and a suspicious narrowing of her eyes, "Oh yes; thank you, I am quite all right again." Maggie had not heard of Aneta's headache. She, therefore, did not ask about it.

"I pity people who have headaches," said Aneta. "I suffer from them very badly myself. Nothing cures me but perfect rest. I was lying down all the afternoon. Merry came to see me, and told me that you were also prostrated with headache. I was sorry for you."

"Oh, thank you so much!" said Maggie. "Mine is quite gone; is yours?"

"Yes, thank you."

Aneta sat quiet and very still. When her face was in repose she never moved her body. There was an absolute sense of rest about her which was refreshing to those who really knew her well. But Maggie hated it. She wanted to leave her; she wanted to go and talk to Merry, who was playing a solitary game of patience in a distant part of the drawing-room; she wanted to do anything rather than remain by Aneta's side.

Then Aneta looked up. "I had a letter this afternoon from my aunt, Lady Lysle."

"Oh!" said Maggie. She could not quite understand why her heart beat so fast, but she had undoubtedly a premonition of some sort of trouble ahead.

"Aunt Lucia is staying with the Cardews," continued Aneta.

"Is she?" said Maggie. "Oh, that sweet and beautiful place!" she continued.

"Yes," said Aneta, "Meredith Manor will always be lovely. There is no season of the year when it is not, in my opinion, more charming than any other place I know."

"Is your aunt going to stay there long?" asked Maggie, who felt that she need not say anything further with regard to the delights of Meredith Manor just now.

"I cannot tell you," replied Aneta. "She mentioned something rather curious. It is connected with you."

"With poor little me?" said Maggie.

"With you," said Aneta. "You remember telling me that your stepfather is one of the Martyns of The Meadows?"

Maggie's face grew crimson, then turned pale.

"Well," said Aneta, bringing out her words with great calmness, "it turns out to be a mistake. Your stepfather is no relation whatever to our friends the Martyns. Aunt Lucia and Mrs. Cardew went to call on them the other day, and asked the question. You made a mistake in announcing your stepfather as being a connection of our friends."

"Did I? Perhaps so," said Maggie. "I thought he was, that's all."

"You thought wrong," said Aneta. "I felt I would mention it to you. He may be just as well connected," she added quietly; "but he is *not* related to the Martyns of The Meadows."

"You speak in a very disagreeable tone," said Maggie.

"I don't mean to," replied Aneta; "but I thought I would tell you in order that you should not spread the report any further."

"I am sure I don't want to. My stepfather has just as good connections as any one else."

"No doubt," said Aneta gently; "only, he is not related to our special friends. You might let Merry and Cicely know."

"Why?" asked Maggie in a dogged voice.

"You can please yourself. I shall tell them if you don't."

"Why do you hate me so much, Aneta?" said Maggie then.

"I hate subterfuge and untruth," said Aneta. "I don't hate you. If you would be straight and open and above-board you would find me your best friend."

"Thank you so much!" said Maggie in a sneering tone. "When I require you for my best friend it will be time enough for you to offer me that enviable position." Then she added, speaking in a low tone of intense dislike, "Is it likely that any girl would wish to make a best friend of another girl who accused her of subterfuge and want of truthfulness?"

The delicate pink rose in Aneta's cheeks. She raised her eyes and looked full up at Maggie. Her clear, calm eyes seemed like mirrors. Maggie felt that she could not meet them.

It was just at that moment that Cicely Cardew, in a state of suppressed excitement, came into the room.

"Maggie," she said, coming straight up to Maggie Howland, "there's a very large parcel addressed to you in the hall. It has been paid for; we are all dying with curiosity to know what it is."

Maggie rose abruptly.

"I will go and look at it myself," she said. "A large parcel addressed to me! Who can have sent me anything?"

"It looks like a huge dress-box," said Cicely. "We're all curious about it."

Before any girl could leave the drawing-room it was necessary that she should ask Mrs. Ward's permission. So Maggie now went up to that good lady and asked if she might go and look at her parcel.

"A parcel for you, dear?" said Mrs. Ward. "And you want to see its contents? But bring it in here; we shall all be delighted to look at it—sha'n't we, girls?"

Maggie went away, wondering a good deal. Cicely accompanied her. Miss Johnson also appeared on the scene.

"Why, Maggie," she said, "what can you have got? Such a huge box, and all covered over with brown paper! I don't suppose Mrs. Ward would really like that box to be brought into the drawing-room. I'll just go and ask her."

One of Mrs. Ward's peculiarities, and perhaps one of the reasons why she was such a favorite and led her girls with such gentle, silken cords, was her power of entering into their pleasures. She used to confess with a smile that she was like a child herself over an unopened parcel; and when Miss Johnson appeared with the information that the box was large and cumbersome, Mrs. Ward still gave directions that it was to be brought into the drawing-room.

"You can put some of the brown paper on the floor, if you like, Lucy," she said, "and Maggie can show us its contents."

Now, one glance at the parcel told Maggie Howland who had sent it. She recognized her stepfather's writing. That bold commercial hand was painfully visible on the label. She would have given worlds not to have anything selected for her by Martin exhibited in the drawing-room at Aylmer House. But to refuse to show the contents of the box would but raise strong suspicion against her. She therefore, although very unwillingly, followed Miss Johnson into the drawing-room. The box was laid on the floor. The lid was removed, some tissue-paper was next extricated, and beneath lay a wardrobe such as poor Maggie even in her wildest dreams had never imagined. There was a letter lying on the top which she clutched and put into her pocket. This letter was in her stepfather's writing. She could not read it before the others. Aneta and all the girls of her set, also Kathleen O'Donnell, Rosamond Dacre, Matty and Clara Roache, Janet Barns, the Tristrams, the Cardews, all clustered round the box.

"Oh, what fun!" said Kathleen. "A box of dresses for you! You lucky Queen Maggie! How I wish some one would send me some clothes!"

"Take them out, dear, and let us look at them," said Mrs. Ward.

The first dress to be removed was a magenta cachemire. It was made with a short skirt trimmed with little frills of the same. The bodice had sleeves to the elbows, and long, coarse cream-colored lace sleeves below. The front of the dress was also much bedizened by the same coarse cream lace.

Maggie felt her face nearly purple with rage. "Oh, why must all these things be looked at here?" she said; and there was a piteous note in her voice.

"I don't see the necessity, dear," said Mrs. Ward kindly.

"But, oh! please, please," said Kathleen, "we *must* see the others. Here's a sage-green dress trimmed with bands of black silk: that will be quite useful in the winter, won't it, Mags?"

She tried to speak kindly, for the sage-green dress was as little to her taste as the impossible magenta. Under the two dresses were ribbons of different shades and hues, some strong, coarse stockings, some square-toed shoes, and finally, below everything else, an evening-dress made of voile, and deep blue in tone.

"Some of the things will he very useful," said Miss Johnson. "I will put them all back again now."

"But whom have they come from?" said Mrs. Ward. "I saw you take a note and put it into your pocket, Maggie."

"Yes, these are a present from my stepfather," said Maggie.

"Miss Johnson, you will take them upstairs, won't you?" said Mrs. Ward.
—"It is kind of your stepfather to think of you, Maggie."

Maggie looked up and met Aneta's glance. Was Aneta thinking of the Martyns of The Meadows? The color rushed all over Maggie's face. She clenched her hands. "I hate the horrid, horrid things!" she said. "I won't wear one of them."

"Oh, come, dear," said Mrs. Ward kindly; "your stepfather means very well indeed by you. He has doubtless had very little to do with dressing a lady before.—We can slightly alter those dresses, can we not, Miss Johnson?"

Miss Johnson had now placed all the hideous garments back in the box. She said with a smile, "The sage-green dress can be made quite useful; but I rather despair of the magenta."

"Well," said Mrs. Ward, "it was meant kindly. Perhaps, Maggie, if you gave me your stepfather's address I might write to him and tell him the sort of things that I like my girls to wear."

Maggie turned crimson. That would indeed be the final straw. She murmured something which Mrs. Ward did not choose to hear. To her great relief, the hour for bed had arrived, and all the girls went to their rooms.

Miss Johnson came down again after she had deposited the hideous dresses in Maggie's wardrobe. "I quite pity poor little Maggie," she said. "What frightful taste! There is really nothing in the whole of that box that she can possibly wear."

"I must write to Mr. Martyn," said Mrs. Ward. "Didn't somebody tell me that he was a country gentleman—a relation of the Martyns of The Meadows? Such particularly nice people!"

"I know nothing about that," said Miss Johnson. "I only know that the contents of the box are simply atrocious."

"Well," said Mrs. Ward, "we won't say anything to annoy Maggie to-night; I could see that the poor dear child was greatly mortified. I only regret that I had the box opened here; but you know it is one of our customs to share all our pleasures. Poor little Maggie! The thing was most unlucky."

Up in her room, Maggie had locked her door. She would unlock it again, but she must read that frightful letter without any chance of being disturbed. She opened it, tore it from its envelope, and read the contents:

"DEAR POPSY,—I came across a cheap lot of frocks the other day at a bankrupt's sale, and thought at once of Little-sing and her daughter Popsy-wopsy. I am sending the dresses off to you without saying a word to Little-sing. You will be well off now for some time, and won't require the five pounds from me for dress at Christmas. Hope you're enjoying your fine young ladies and fine life. Neither Little-sing nor me miss you a bit; but, all the same, your room will be ready for you at Christmas. Take care of those good clothes, for I can't often spend as much on you.

"Good-bye for the present.—Your affectionate father,

"BO-PEEP.

"*P.S.*—I have a good mind to call on that fine-lady schoolmistress of yours, Mrs. Ward. There's no saying but that Little-sing and me may come along some afternoon when you least expect us."

Maggie crushed the letter in her hand. Fresh terrors seemed to surround her. Dreadful as the impossible clothes were, they were nothing to what the appearance on the scene would be of the impossible stepfather and her poor mother. Oh, why had she concealed the position of the man whom her mother had married? Already Aneta had detected her little act of deception with regard to the Martyns of The Meadows. But that, Maggie felt, could be got over. It was easy for a girl to make a mistake in a matter of that kind, and surely there were other Martyns in the country high-born and respectable and all that was desirable. But James Martin who kept a grocer's shop at Shepherd's Bush—James Martin, with "grocer" written all over him!—rich, it is true; but, oh, so vulgarly rich! Were he to appear and announce his relationship to her at the school, she felt that, as far as she was concerned, the end of the world would have arrived. What was she to do? There was not a minute to be lost. In one way or another she had seen a good deal of Bo-peep during the last half of those dreadful summer holidays, and she knew that he was, as he expressed it, as good as his word.

Her only chance was in writing to her mother. But then, if, by any chance, Maggie's letter got into the hands of Bo-peep, his wrath would be so great that he would, in all probability, take her from the school at once. What was to be done? Poor Maggie felt herself between two fires. In either direction was danger. On the whole, she resolved to throw herself on her mother's mercy. Mrs. Martin, as she was now, would much prefer Maggie to remain at school, and she might be clever enough to keep Maggie's stepfather from putting in an appearance at Aylmer House.

Maggie wrote a short and frantic letter. She was in the midst of it when there came a tap at her room-door.

"It's I, Maggie," said Miss Johnson's voice from without. "Your light is still burning; you ought to be in bed."

Maggie flew and opened the door. "I am sorry," she said. "I was a good deal upset about those detestable clothes. I am writing to my mother. Please, Lucy, let me finish the letter. When it's done—and I won't be a minute longer—I'll put it in the post-box myself, so that it can go by the first post in the morning."

"Very well, dear," said Lucy, who was too kind not to be good to any girl in the school; "only be quick, Maggie," she said, "for you know you are breaking the rules."

"Yes! oh yes!" said Maggie; "and I will never do it again."

Miss Johnson left her, and Maggie flew back to bend over her paper and continue her writing:

"Darling, you must not let him come here. He threatens to come, but you must keep him away. All will be up with me if he is seen at the school. I beseech of you have a little mercy on me. For the sake of my own father, keep him—do keep him—from Aylmer House.—Your distracted daughter,

"MAGGIE HOWLAND."

This letter was addressed to Mrs. Martin (spelt this time with an "i"), Laburnum Villa, Clapham. Maggie stamped it, and, flying downstairs, popped it into the box which held the letters.

---

# HAPTER XX.

## THE VILLA.

Laburnum Villa, in the suburb of Clapham, was, in the new Mrs. Martin's eyes, quite a delightful place. She had never appreciated her first husband, Professor Howland, but she thoroughly appreciated Bo-peep, and after her own fashion was fond of him. He gave her comforts. She had lived so long without comforts that she appreciated these good things of life to the full. She had never really been much attached to Maggie, who was too like her own father and too unlike herself to allow of the existence of any sympathy between them. Maggie, even before Mrs. Howland met Martin the Shepherd's Bush grocer, had been more or less a thorn in the flesh to her mother.

Laburnum Villa was furnished, as James Martin expressed it, with an eye to comfort. There were solid arm-chairs with deep seats and good springs, and these were covered with maroon-colored leather. There were thick, maroon-colored curtains to the dining-room windows, and all the furniture of the room was of solid oak. There was a rich Turkey carpet on the floor, and prints of different hunting scenes—by no means bad in their way—hanging on the walls. The paint-work of the room was of dull red, and the paper was of the same tone. It was a small room, and the furniture was large and heavy, but it represented in Martin's eyes the very essence of comfort. The fireplace was modern, and when it was piled up with goodly lumps of coal it caused a warmth to pervade the whole room which, as Mrs. Martin expressed it, was very stimulating. The house had electric light, which both Mr. and Mrs. Martin considered distinguished.

They spent most of their time in the dining-room, although Mrs. Martin, with some faint instinct still left of her own life, would have preferred to use the drawing-room in the evenings; but when she suggested this Bo-peep said, "No, no, Little-sing; I can smoke here and sit by the fire, and enjoy the rest which I have rightly earned. I hate rooms full of fal-lals. You can keep your drawing-room for the time when I am out, Little-sing."

Mrs. Martin knew better than to oppose her husband. She recognized her own weakness, and knew that against his fiat she could no more exercise her puny strength than a babbling stream can disturb a great rock. She used her drawing-room when Bo-peep was out, and regarded it with intense satisfaction. It is true that the colors were crude, for James Martin would have screamed at any Liberty tints. But the carpet was good of its kind, the pictures on the walls not too atrocious. Although they were in gilt frames, the large mirrors over the mantelpiece and at one end of the room were first rate; in short, the drawing-room was fairly presentable, and Mrs. Martin had some traces of her old life still lingering about her which gave a look of domesticity and even repose to the place. Her little work-basket, with its embroidery, was home-like and pleasant. She had forgotten how to play, but she always kept the piano open. Bo-peep suggested buying a pianola, and Mrs. Martin thought it would be a good idea.

"We'll have all the comic operas on it," said Bo-peep; "nothing of the classic order for me—nothing over-my-head, but the popular tunes, plenty of them— no stint. What do you say, Little-sing?"

Little-sing replied that it would be charming; but in her heart she somewhat shuddered, and was glad that the pianola was still a thing to be purchased.

Tildy had been turned into a very presentable little parlor-maid. There was also a first-rate cook, for Martin was fond of the pleasures of the table. On the whole, the little household was comfortable, and Mrs. Martin enjoyed her life. She had some cards printed with her new name and address, and the notification that she was "at home" on the third, fourth, and fifth of each month. Tildy was very much excited about these At Home days; but the first month after Mrs. Martin's marriage passed without a single individual calling upon her.

Mrs. Martin had been settled for over six weeks, and the day of Queen Maggie's great reception at the school in Kensington was drawing on apace. Mrs. Martin was in a state of subdued excitement. She was dressed in her best. Her best consisted of a light fawn-colored silk with velvet trimmings of the same. The silk rustled as she walked. On her fingers were many rings of much brilliancy, and she wore a small diamond brooch at her throat. The reason of all this festive attire was a simple one, a good one, a domestic one. James Martin was coming home. He had been in Liverpool, engaged on special business, for the greater part of a week; but he was now returning to his beloved Little-sing, who had missed him, and he was pleased to feel that he would be with her again. She knew his tastes to a nicety, and had desired the cook to prepare a very special dinner for his delectation.

"Beef-steak pudding, cook," she said, "with mutton kidneys, and plenty of oysters; and be sure the crust is very light."

Cook replied that if she did not know how to make beef-steak pudding she ought immediately to leave her "perfession." She was a stout, red-faced woman, and had a way of frightening Mrs. Martin, who generally retreated from the kitchen premises as quickly as possible.

"Very well," said Mrs. Martin; "I am glad you quite understand. You know that my husband is very particular. Then we'll have potatoes and fried mushrooms, and I think afterwards apple-tart and cream."

The cook, whose name was Horniman, condescended to signify her willingness to provide this dinner, and Mrs. Martin went up to the drawing-room.

"You had better light a fire here, Matilda," she said. "It's going to be a very cold day."

"I'd a sight rayther you called me Tildy, mum. It seems like as though a lump o' ice got on my 'eart when you say Mat-tilda."

"'Matilda' is more refined and suitable," said Mrs. Martin with dignity.

"Oh yes, 'um—'course, 'um. When 'ull Miss Maggie be comin' to see us, 'um?"

"Not before Christmas, you silly girl. Miss Maggie is at school."

"So I 'ave 'eard," said Matilda. "You 'aven't give me no 'olidays, 'um, sence I come to yer; and it were understood, sure-*ly*, that I were to 'ave my day out once a month."

"You shall go out to-morrow, Matilda. I haven't the slightest wish to keep you indoors against your will."

"To-morrer's cook's day, 'um."

"Well, then, you shall go the next day."

"Thank you, 'um. I thought I'd go and see Miss Maggie ef you'd give me her address."

"Well, now, that's a very good idea," said Mrs. Martin. "I could write her a little note, and you could take it to her. That's very thoughtful of you, Tilda. Yes, I should like you to go and bring me word how she is."

"It's longin' I am to lay eyes on 'er, mum. She's a bee-utiful way with 'er," said Matilda.

When she was quite alone Mrs. Martin took that letter of Maggie's, which she had received during her husband's absence, from her pocket. She was terrified lest Bo-peep should read it. The letter had offended her. Maggie had written with great fire and distress: "You must not let him come here. All will be up with me if he is seen at the school. For the sake of my own father, keep him from Aylmer House."

Mrs. Martin slipped it back into her pocket, and then sat by her comfortable drawing-room fire waiting for the arrival of the good Bo-peep. He was a very playful creature. His one idea of happiness consisted in endless jokes—

practical jokes or otherwise, just as it suited him at the moment.

He had done a very successful stroke of business in Liverpool, and was returning to Laburnum Villa in the highest spirits. While he was in the train he was planning how he could most effectively announce his return. To ring at his own hall-door, or to open it with a latch-key, or to walk in in the ordinary fashion of the master of the house did not content him at all. He must invent a more novel manner of return than that. He was really fond of Little-sing. She suited him to perfection. What he called her "fine-lady airs," when they were displayed to any one but himself, pleased him mightily. He thought of her as pretty and gracious and sweet. He really loved her after his own fashion, and would do anything in his power to make her happy. But he must, as he expressed it, have his joke.

Mrs. Martin was seated by the fire in the drawing-room. It was getting late—nearly four o'clock; but, according to an expressed wish of Bo-peep, the window-blinds had not yet been drawn down. He liked, as he said, to see his home before he entered it. Mrs. Martin, therefore, with the electric light on, was perfectly visible from the road. Mr. Martin guessed that this would be the case, and he stopped the cab at a little distance from the house, paid the fare, shouldered his bag, and walked softly down the street. He went and stood outside the window. He looked in. The street was a quiet one, and at that moment there were no passers-by. Mrs. Martin was seated in her smart dress which he had given her, with her profile towards him. He thought her very beautiful indeed. His heart swelled with pride. She belonged to him. He hated fine ladies, as a rule; but a fine lady who was his very own was a different matter. He even felt romantic.

She was reading a letter. Who could have been writing to Little-sing? Suddenly it occurred to him to slip down the area steps and stand close under the window. He did so, to the terror of cook and Tildy. Cook was about to scream, "Burglars!" but Tildy recognized her master.

"It's his joke," she said. "'E's a wonderful man for jokes. Don't let on to Mrs. Martin that 'e's 'ere for your life. 'E'll do something so comic in a minute."

The comicality of Martin consisted, in the present instance, of singing in a harsh baritone the song of the Troubadour:

> "Gaily the Troubadour
> Touched his guitar,
> When he was hastening
> Home from the war;
> Singing, 'From Palestine
> Hither I come.

Ladye love! ladye love!
Welcome me home.'"

Mrs. Martin gave a shriek. She had the presence of mind to pop her letter into her pocket. Then she approached the window, trembling and blushing. Bo-peep uttered a huge laugh of delight, let himself in by the back way, and ran up the stairs.

"Little-sing!" he said, and clasped his wife in his arms.

During dinner James Martin was in high good humor, and it was not until dessert was put on the table and he had helped himself liberally to port wine, and was filling his pipe for his evening smoke, that it occurred to him to speak to his wife about Maggie.

"By the way," he said, "I did a right good turn for that girl of yours, Little-sing, before I left for Liverpool. I sent her a box of clothes—two smart everyday dresses, an evening dress, and no end of fal-lals. She wrote to thank me, I suppose?"

"She wrote to me, dear," said Mrs. Martin, trembling a good deal. "She was very much obliged to you."

"And well she ought to be. Did she clearly understand that I sent her the things—that you had nothing to do with them?"

"Oh yes, yes," said Mrs. Martin. "Won't you have some coffee, James? I'll tell Matilda to bring it in."

"Coffee—fiddlestick!" said Martin; "and you know I hate to be called 'James.' Where's Bo-peep?"

"You are Bo-peep," said his wife with a funny smile.

"Well, then, no 'Jamesing' of me. I think it is very queer of your daughter not to reply to me when I send her expensive and handsome things. What did she say in her letter to you?"

"Oh, she was very grateful, of course, Bo-peep."

"Well—but—where's the letter? I may as well see it. There's stuff in that girl. I don't despair of her yet. She has a head for business. I wouldn't have your dear little head muddled with business, but your daughter's a different person. She has nothing whatever to live on except what I allow her, and unless she is to starve she has got to please me."

Mrs. Martin might have said, had she not been afraid, that Maggie was certainly entitled to her own father's money; but it is to be regretted that Little-sing had not much courage.

Matilda came in with the coffee, which caused a slight diversion, more particularly as it was not to Martin's taste, who desired her to take it away again, and request Horniman to send him something fit to drink. When the door was closed behind Matilda he renewed the subject of the letter.

"I saw you reading something as I came along," he said. "When I peeped in at the window you had a letter in your hand. Who has been writing to you?"

"Only Maggie."

"And that is the letter you spoke about?"

"Yes, dear James—I mean Bo-peep—yes. The child is very grateful."

"She ought to be. I'd like to see the letter. Where is it?"

"I will go upstairs and fetch it," said Mrs. Martin, who knew well that it was safe in her pocket all the time.

James Martin roused himself and gave her a studied look.

"Do so," he said. "Bring it back to me at once. If I have to support that girl, and keep her at school, and pay for her clothing, I'll allow her to have no secrets from me. You understand that, don't you, Little-sing?"

"Yes. I will fetch the letter," said Mrs. Martin.

She left the room. Martin was fond of her, but he was no fool. He was certain now that there was something in the letter which his wife did not wish him to see, and his curiosity was instantly aroused. He was determined to read poor Maggie's letter at any cost. He waited impatiently, drumming his large, fat hand on the highly polished oak table the while. Tildy came in with fresh coffee.

"Please, sir," she said, "cook wants to see you for a minute."

"I can't see her now. Tell her so," replied Martin.

"Which is no message for a woman of my class," said Horniman, entering the room and showing a very heated face. "I wishes to give notice that I leave your service this day month."

"You can go to-morrow," said Martin.

"As you please, sir; wages in full."

"You go to-morrow," said Martin; "and if you say another word you go to-night. Leave the room."

Tildy breathed a little quickly, felt inclined to pat master on the back, thought better of it, and left the room.

173

"Whatever is keeping Little-sing?" thought Martin to himself.

He was not going to worry about cook and her whims, but of Little-sing and the letter. He grew a little more suspicious, and consequently a little more angry.

"She has that letter in her pocket; I saw her put it there when I was acting the part of the Troubadour," he said to himself. "She is destroying it now; but she sha'n't—not before I get it."

He softly left the dining-room and crept with catlike steps upstairs. He stopped outside his wife's bedroom. There was a light burning there. He turned the handle of the door. It was locked.

"Open the door at once," he said; and Mrs. Martin flew to do so.

"Oh Bo-peep, you gave me a fright!"

"Where is that letter, Victoria?" "It—

it—I can't find it," she replied.

"What are those papers lying on the floor?"

Mrs. Martin gave a cry. Mr. Martin was too quick for her. He swept up the pieces of torn letter, collected them in his great hand, and, taking Mrs. Martin with the other hand, returned with her to the dining-room.

"Now, you sit there, Little-sing," he said, "while I piece the letter together. There is something in it that you want hidden from me; but you've quite mistook your man. There are to be no secrets between you and me. I'm not the least bit angry with you, but I am not going to have that girl ruling you. You're frightened of that girl. Now, let's see what she has to say."

Poor Mrs. Martin trembled from head to foot. Suddenly she went on her knees, clasped her hands round Bo-peep's arm, and looked into his face. "She was naughty. She was a silly child. Oh, forgive her! I ought to have destroyed the letter. I ought not to have kept it until you came back. Please—please, don't read it!"

"Nonsense, Little-sing," he replied, restored once more to the height of good humor. "You have roused my curiosity; nothing will induce me not to see every word of the letter now."

It took Martin some time to piece together poor Maggie's letter; but at last the greater part of its meaning was made plain to him. Mrs. Martin sat, white as death, looking at her lord and master. What was going to happen? What awful thing lay ahead of her? She felt crushed beyond words. Once again she struggled to get on her knees to implore him, to entreat; but Martin put out his

174

great hand and kept her forcibly in her seat.

When he had quite taken in the meaning of the letter he made no comment whatever, but carefully deposited the torn fragments in his pocket-book. Then he said quietly, "I don't blame you, Little-sing, not one bit. But we've got to punish this girl. To-morrow I shall be busy in town. The day after will be Friday, and I shall be busy then; but on Saturday we'll take a half-holiday and go to visit Miss Margaret Howland at Aylmer House—you and me together, Little-sing—the grocer and his wife together. Not a word, my love; not a word."

# CHAPTER XXI.

## TILDY'S MESSAGE.

Nothing ever kept Mrs. Martin awake; and, notwithstanding her anxiety with regard to Maggie, she slept soundly that night. Bo-peep was his own delightful self. His jokes were really too good for anything! She regarded him as the wittiest man of her acquaintance. She laughed till the tears ran down her cheeks. He told her that he would take her to the theater on the following evening, and further said that he would engage a cook himself in town, send her out in the course of the morning, and that Horniman could go.

Horniman came up to interview her mistress soon after Martin's departure. She was penitent now, and willing to stay; but nothing would induce Martin himself to forgive her, and, in consequence, Mrs. Martin did not dare to do so. The woman was paid her wages in full, and dismissed. Then it occurred to Mrs. Martin that here was her opportunity to send a short note of warning to Maggie. Why she did not send it by post it is hard to ascertain; but she thought that it would go more swiftly and surely if Tildy were the messenger.

Accordingly she sent for Tildy and told her what she expected her to do.

"Matilda," she said, "cook has gone, and I shall be quite content with tea and toast and a lightly boiled egg for my lunch. After lunch you can take the train to London and convey a message from me to Miss Maggie."

"Oh mum, 'ow beauteous!" said Tildy.

"I will have a letter ready which you are, if possible, to put into her own hands."

"Yes, 'um; and don't I long to see 'er, jest!"

"Well, this is the address," said Mrs. Martin. "Get everything cosy and comfortable in the house, and bring me my tea by one o'clock. A train will take you to Victoria at half-past one, which you ought to catch. You can easily be back here between four and five; by that time the new cook will have arrived."

"Things ain't dull a bit to-day'," said Tildy. "They're much more Shepherd's Bushy, and I like 'em a sight better than I did."

"Well, go now, and attend to your business," said Mrs. Martin.

Having secured a messenger, Mrs. Martin next prepared to write to poor Maggie:

"My dear Child,—Most unfortunately your father has discovered the letter you wrote to me. He doesn't say much, but I can see that he is furiously angry. He intends to take me with him to call on you next Saturday—I presume, some time in the afternoon. I will try to make him dress in as gentlemanly a manner as possible, and also will endeavor to prevent his talking about the shop. You must make the very best of things you can, dear; for there's no possible way of keeping him from Aylmer House.—Your affectionate mother,

"Victoria Martin."

When the letter was finished Mrs. Martin put it into an envelope, addressed to Miss Maggie Howland, Aylmer House, Randal Square, South Kensington, and put it into Tildy's care. Tildy caught her train all in good time, arrived at Victoria, and took a bus to South Kensington. A very little inquiry enabled her to find Randal Square, and at about half-past two she was standing on the steps of that most refined and genteel home, Aylmer House. The look of the place impressed her, but did not give her any sense of intimidation. When the door was opened to her modest ring, and the pleasant, bright-looking parlor-maid answered her summons, Tildy gazed at her with great interest but without a scrap of shyness.

"I've come from 'er 'ome to see Miss Maggie 'Owland," said Tildy; "and I've a message for 'er from 'er ma."

The girl, whose name was Agnes, stared for a minute at Tildy. She recognized her "sort" in a moment. Tildy belonged to the lodging-house sort of girl. What she could have to do with one of Agnes's young ladies puzzled that young person considerably. It was the rule, however, at Aylmer House that no one, however poor or humble, should be treated with rudeness, and certainly a person bringing a message to one of the young ladies was entitled to respect. Agnes said, therefore, in a polite and superior tone, "Step in, will you, miss? and I will find out if Miss Howland is in."

Tildy stepped into the hall, feeling, as she expressed it, "dream-like and queer all over." She did not dare to sit down, but stood on the mat, gazing with her bright, inquisitive eyes at the various things in this new world in which she found herself.

"How beauteous!" she kept repeating at intervals. "Why, Laburnum Villa ain't a patch on this. How very beauteous! No wonder Miss Maggie 'ave the hair of a queen."

Now, it so happened that Maggie Howland was out, and would not be back for some time. This was the day when she and the other girls belonging to her kingdom had gone forth to purchase all sorts of good things for the coming feast. Maggie, as queen, had put a whole sovereign into the bag. There would, therefore, be no stint of first-class provisions. Every sort of eatable that was not usually permitted at Aylmer House was to grace the board—jelly, meringues, frosted cake, tipsy cake, as well as chickens garnished in the most exquisite way and prepared specially by a confectioner round the corner; also different dainties in aspic jellies were to be ordered. Then flowers were to be secured in advance, so as to make the table really very beautiful.

Maggie, Kathleen O'Donnell, and Janet were the people selected to arrange about the supper. Not a single thing was to be cooked in the establishment; this would give extra trouble to the servants, and was therefore not to be permitted. The girls would make their own sandwiches; and, oh, what troublesome thoughts they had over these! Maggie was in the highest spirits, and left the house with her companions—Miss Johnson, of course, in close attendance—half-an-hour before Tildy with her ominous letter appeared on the scene.

Now, it so happened that Agnes knew nothing at all of the absence of the young ladies. They usually went out by a side-door which had been specially assigned to their use when the house was turned into a school. As Agnes was going upstairs, however, in order to try to find Maggie, she met Aneta coming down.

"Oh miss," she said, "can you tell me if Miss Howland is in?"

"No," said Aneta, "I happen to know that she is out, and I don't think she will be in for some little time."

"Very well, miss; the young person will be sorry, I expect."

"What young person?" asked Aneta, eager in her turn to find out why Maggie was inquired for.

"A girl, miss, who has called, and has asked very particularly to see Miss Howland. She's rather a common sort of girl, miss, although I dare say she means well."

"I will go and see her myself," said Aneta; "perhaps I can convey a message from her to Miss Howland, for I know she won't be back for some little time."

Agnes, quite relieved in her mind, turned down the back-stairs and went to attend to her numerous duties. A few minutes after, Aneta, in all her slim grace, stood in the hall and confronted Tildy. Aneta was herself going out; she was going out with Mademoiselle Laplage. They had some commissions to execute. The day was a foggy one, and they were both rather in a hurry. Nevertheless, Aneta stopped to say a kind word to Tildy. Tildy gazed at her with open-eyed admiration. Beautiful as the house was, this young lady was indeed a radiant and dazzling vision.

"She made me sort o' choky," said Tildy as she related the circumstance afterwards to Mrs. Martin. "There was a hair about her. Well, much as I loves our Miss Maggie, she ain't got the hair o' that beauteous young lady, with 'er eyes as blue as the sky, and 'er walk so very distinguishified."

"What can I do for you?" said Aneta now, in a kind tone.

Tildy dropped an awkward curtsy. "I've come, miss," she said, "to see our Miss Maggie."

"Miss Howland is out," said Aneta.

"Oh, miss!" replied Tildy, the corners of her mouth beginning to droop, "that's crool 'ard on me. Do you think, miss, if I may make so bold as to inquire, that Miss Maggie 'll be in soon?"

"I do not think so," replied Aneta; "but I can convey any message you like to her, if you will trust me."

"Oh miss," said Tildy, worshipping Aneta on the spot, "who wouldn't trust one like you?"

"Well, what is it? What can I do for you?"

"I was maid, miss—maid-of-all-work—at Shepherd's Bush when Miss Maggie and 'er ma used to live there; and when Mrs. 'Owland married Martin the grocer they was that kind they took me to live at Laburnum Villa. It's a very rich and comfortable 'ouse, miss; and the way they two goes on is most excitin'. It's joke, joke, and play, play, from morn till night—that's the ma and steppa of Miss Maggie. I've brought a letter from Mrs. Martin to be delivered straight to Miss Maggie."

"I can give it to her," said Aneta in her calm voice.

"You'll per'aps mention, miss," said Tildy, taking the letter from her pocket, "as I called, and as I love our dear Miss Maggie as much as I ever did. You'll per'aps say, miss, with my dutiful respects, that my 'eart is 'ers, and always will be."

"I will give her a kind message," said Aneta, "and safely deliver her mother's letter to her. I am afraid there's no use in asking you to stay, as Miss Howland is very much occupied just now."

"Very well, miss, I've delivered my message faithful."

"You have."

As Aneta spoke she herself opened the hall-door.

"Good-day, miss," said Tildy, dropping another curtsy, "and I wishes you well."

"Good-day," replied Aneta.

Tildy's little form was swallowed up in the fog, which was growing thicker each moment, and at that instant Mademoiselle Laplage, profuse in apologies for her brief delay, entered the hall.

"Pardon me, *ma chère*, that I have caused you to wait. I was just ready to descend, when—see! the lace of my shoe was broken. But what will you? You will go out in this dreadful fog?"

Aneta replied in French that she did not think the fog was too thick, and the French governess and the girl went out together into the street. But all the time Aneta Lysle was thinking hard. She was in possession of Maggie's secret. Her stepfather, instead of being related to the Martyns of The Meadows, was a grocer! Aneta belonged to that class of persons who think a great deal of good birth. She did not mind Tildy in the least, for Tildy was so far below her as to be after a fashion quite companionable; but—a grocer! Nevertheless, Aneta had a heart. She thought of Maggie, and the more she thought of her the more pitiful she felt towards her. She did not want to crush or humiliate her schoolfellow. She felt almost glad that the secret of Maggie's unhappiness had been made known to her. She might at last gain a true influence over the girl.

Her walk, therefore, with Mademoiselle Laplage took place almost in silence. They hastily executed their commissions, and presently found themselves in Pearce's shop, where Aneta had taken a brooch a day or two ago to have a pin put on.

The shopman, as he handed her the mended brooch, said at the same time, "If you will excuse me, miss, you are one of the young ladies who live at Aylmer House?"

"Yes," said Aneta, "that is true."

"Then I wonder, miss, if"—He paused a minute, looked hard at the girl, and then continued, "Might my brother speak to you for a minute, miss?"

"But it make so cold!" said mademoiselle, who knew very little of the English tongue, "and behold—zee fog! I have such fear of it. It is not to joke when it fogs in your country, *ma chère. Il faute bien dépêcher.*"

"I shall be quite ready to come back with you in a minute or two," said Aneta.

Just then the man who had bought the brooch from Maggie appeared. "I am

180

very sorry, miss," he said, "but I thought that, instead of writing to Miss Howland, I might send her a message; otherwise I should have to see Mrs. Ward on the matter."

"But what matter is it?" said Aneta. "You want to see Miss Howland, or you want me to take her a message?"

"Well, miss, it's no special secret; only my brother and I cannot afford to buy the brooch which she sold us the other day."

"But I don't understand," said Aneta. "Miss Howland sold you a brooch? Then if she sold it, you did buy it."

"The fact is, miss," said young Pearce, coloring rather deeply, "I was not myself quite aware of its value at the time, and I gave the young lady much too small a sum of money for it. I want her to return me the money, and I will give her back the brooch. My brother and I have been talking it over, and we cannot do an injustice to one of the ladies at Aylmer House—it is quite impossible."

"I will give your message," said Aneta coldly. "Please do not purchase anything else from Miss Howland. She will doubtless call to see you to-morrow."

"Thank you, miss; then that is all right," said the man, looking much relieved.

Aneta hastened home. She felt perplexed and alarmed. She must see Maggie, and as soon as possible. It was a strange fact that while Maggie was in no danger at all, while everything seemed to be going right with her, and as long as she held an undeniable position in the school as one of the queens, Aneta could scarcely endure her; that now that Maggie Howland, was, so to speak, at her mercy, this girl, whose nature was fine and brave and good, felt a strong desire to help her.

There were, however, very strict rules at Aylmer House, and one of them was that no girl on any account whatsoever was to sell any of her possessions in order to make money. This was one of the unwritten rules of the school; but the idea of an Aylmer House girl really requiring to do such a thing was never contemplated for an instant. There were broad lines of conduct, however, which no girl was expected to pass. Liberty was allowed to a great extent at Aylmer House; but it was a liberty which only those who struggle to walk in the right path can fully enjoy. Crooked ways, underhand dealings, could not be permitted in the school.

Maggie had done quite enough to cause her to be expelled. There had been times when Aneta almost wished for this; when she had felt deep down in her heart that Maggie Howland was the one adverse influence in the school; when she had been certain that if Maggie Howland were removed all the other girls would come more or less under her own gentle sway, and she would be queen, not of the greater number of the girls at Aylmer House, but of all the girls, and very gentle, very loving, very sympathetic would be her rule. Her subjects should feel her sympathy, but at the same time they should acknowledge her power. Maggie's was a counter-influence; and now there was a chance of putting a stop to it.

Aneta knew well that, kind as Mrs. Ward was to Maggie, she did not in her heart absolutely trust her. Therefore, if Maggie left it would also be a relief to Mrs. Ward. Miss Johnson might be sorry, and one or two of the girls might be sorry; in particular, dear little Merry. Aneta had a great love for Merry, and was deeply sorry to feel that Merry was under Maggie's spell; that was the case, although she did not openly belong to Maggie's party. So Merry too would be saved if Maggie left the school. Oh! it was most desirable, and Aneta held the key of the position in her hand. She also had in her pocket Mrs. Martin's letter. That did not perhaps so greatly matter, for Maggie's father, whatever her mother had done, was himself a gentleman; but the fact of Maggie's slipping out of doors alone to sell an ornament was a sufficiently grave offense to banish her from such a school as Aylmer House.

Yes, Aneta could send her away, but it might be managed dexterously. Maggie might stay till the end of the present term and then go, knowing herself that she would never return, whereas the girls would know nothing about it until the beginning of the next term, when they would no longer see her familiar face or hear her pleasant voice. A few of them might be sorry, but they would quickly forget. The school would be the better for her absence. The thing could be done, and it would be done, if Aneta used that knowledge which she now possessed.

The girls all met at tea, and Maggie was in the highest spirits. She knew nothing whatever of all the information which Aneta had gathered in her absence. She knew nothing of Tildy's arrival, of Tildy's departure, nor of the letter which Aneta had put into one of her drawers. Still less did she know anything of Pearce and his betrayal of her. She and her companions had had a very pleasant time, and immediately after tea, in the "leisure hours," they were to meet in the girl's private sitting-room to discuss matters officially.

The Aneta girls had, by common consent, given up the room to them during these last important days. There were plenty of nooks and corners all over the cheerful house where they could amuse themselves and talk secrets, and have that sort of confidence which schoolgirls delight in.

As soon as tea was over Maggie jumped up and said, "Now, Kitty"—she turned to Kathleen O'Donnell as she spoke—"you and I, and Rosamond and

Jane, and Matty and Clara, and the Tristrams will get through our work as quickly as possible.—I suppose, girls"—here she glanced at Aneta in particular—"you will let us have the sitting-room as usual during the leisure hours?"

"Of course we will," said Sylvia St. John in her gentle tone; but she had scarcely uttered the words before Aneta rose.

"Of course you can have the sitting-room," she said; "but I want to talk to you, Maggie."

"You can't, I am afraid, just now," said Maggie. "I am much too busy.—We have to go into accounts, girls," she added. "There are no end of things to be done, besides, at the rehearsal." Here she dropped her voice slightly.

"The rest of you can go to the sitting-room and do what is necessary," continued Aneta. "I want you, Maggie, and you had better come with me." She spoke very firmly.

A dogged look came into Maggie's face. She threw back her head and glanced full at Aneta. "I go with you," she said, "just because you ask me, forsooth! You forget yourself, Queen Aneta. I also am a queen and have a kingdom."

"My business with you has something to do with a person who calls herself Tildy," said Aneta in her gravest voice; and Maggie suddenly felt as though a cold douche had been thrown over her. She colored a vivid red. Then she turned eagerly to Kathleen.

"I won't be a minute," she said. "You all go into the sitting-room and get the accounts in order. You might also go over that tableaux with Diana Vernon.— Kathleen, you know that you must put a little more life into your face than you did the other day; and—and—oh dear, how annoying this is!—Yes, of course I will go with you, Aneta. You won't keep me a minute?"

Maggie and Aneta left the room.

Merry turned to her sister and said in a troubled voice, "I can't imagine why it is that Aneta doesn't care for poor Maggie. I love Aneta, of course, for she is our very own cousin; but I cannot understand her want of sympathy for dearest Maggie."

"I am not altogether quite so fond of Maggie as you are, Merry; and you know that," said Cicely.

"I know it," said Merry. "You are altogether taken up with Aneta."

"Oh, and with school generally," said Cicely, "it is all so splendid. But come, we are alone in the room, and losing some of our delightful leisure hours."

The Maggie-girls had meanwhile retired into the sitting-room, where they stood together in groups, talking about the excitement which was to take place on the following Saturday (it was now Thursday), and paying very little heed to Maggie's injunctions to put the accounts in order.

"Don't bother about accounts," said Kitty; "there's heaps of money left in the bag. Wasn't it scrumptious of old Mags to put a whole sovereign in? And I know she is not rich, the dear old precious!"

"She is exactly the sort of girl who would do a generous thing," said Clara Roache, "and of course, as queen, she felt that she must put a little more money into the bag than the rest of us."

"Well, she needn't," said Kathleen. "I'd have loved her just as much if she hadn't put a penny in. She is a duck, though! I can't think why I care so much about her, for she's not beautiful."

"Strictly speaking, she is plain," said Janet Burns; "but in a case like Maggie's plain face doesn't matter in the least."

"She has got something inside," said Matty, "which makes up for her plain features. It's her soul shining out of her eyes."

"Yes, of course," said Kathleen O'Donnell; "and it fills her voice too. She has got power and—what you call charm. She is meant to rule people."

"I admire her myself more than Aneta Lysle," said Janet Burns, "although of course all the world would call Aneta beautiful."

"Yes, that is quite true," said Kathleen; "but I call Aneta a little stiff, and she is very determined too, and she doesn't like poor old Mags one single bit. Wasn't it jolly of Mags to get up this glorious day for us? Won't we have fun? Aneta may look to her laurels, for it's my opinion that the Gibsons and the Cardews will both come over to our side after Saturday."

While this conversation was going on, and Maggie's absence was deplored, and no business whatever was being done towards the entertainment of Saturday, Maggie found herself seated opposite to Aneta in Aneta's own bedroom. Maggie felt queer and shaken. She did not quite know what was the matter. Aneta's face was very quiet.

After a time she drew a letter from her pocket and put it into Maggie's hand.

"Who brought this?" asked Maggie.

"A person who called herself Tildy."

Maggie held the letter unopened in her lap.

"Why don't you read it?" said Aneta.

Maggie took it up and glanced at the handwriting. Then she put it down again. "It's from my mother," she said. "It can keep."

"I cannot imagine," said Aneta, "anybody waiting even for one moment to read a letter which one's own mother has written. My mother is dead, you know."

She spoke in a low tone, and her pretty eyelashes rested on her softly rounded cheeks.

Maggie looked at her. "Why did you bring me up here, Aneta, away from all the others, away from our important business, to give me this letter?"

"I thought you would rather have it in private," said Aneta.

"You thought more than that, Aneta."

"Yes, I thought more than that," said Aneta in her gentlest tone.

Maggie's queer, narrow, eyes flashed fire. Suddenly she stood up. "You have something to say. Say it, and be quick, for I must go."

"I don't think you must go just yet, Maggie; for what I have to say cannot be said in a minute. You will have to give up your leisure hours to-day."

"I cannot. Our entertainment is on Saturday."

"The entertainment must wait," said Aneta. "It is of no consequence compared to what I have to say to you."

"Oh, have it out!" said Maggie. "You were always spying and prying on me. You always hated me. I don't know what I have done to you. I'd have left you alone if you had left me alone; but you have interfered with me and made my life miserable. God knows, I am not too happy"—Maggie struggled with her emotion—"but you have made things twice as bad."

"Do you really, really think that, Maggie? Please don't say any more, then, until you hear me out to the end. I will tell you as quickly as possible; I will put you out of suspense. I could have made things very different for you, but at least I will put you out of suspense."

"Well, go on; I am willing to listen. I hope you will be brief."

"It is this, Maggie. I will say nothing about your past; I simply tell you what, through no fault of mine, I found out to-day. You gave the girls of this school to understand that your mother's husband—your stepfather—was a gentleman of old family. The person called Tildy told me about Mr. Martin. He may be a gentleman by nature, but he is not one by profession."

Maggie clutched one of her hands so tightly that the nails almost pierced her flesh.

"I won't hurt you, Maggie, by saying much on that subject. Your own father was a gentleman, and you cannot help your mother having married beneath her."

Maggie gasped. Such words as these from the proud Aneta!

"But there is worse to follow," continued Aneta. "I happened to go to Pearce's to-day."

Maggie, who had half-risen, sank back again in her seat.

"And Pearce wants to see you in order to return a brooch which you sold him. He says that he cannot afford the right price for the brooch. He wants you to give him back the money which he lent you on it, and he wants you to have the brooch again in your possession. You, of course, know, Maggie, that in selling one of your belongings and in going out without leave you broke one of the fundamental rules of Aylmer House. You know that, therefore—Why, what is the matter?"

Maggie's queer face was working convulsively. After a time slow, big tears gathered in her eyes. Her complexion changed from its usual dull ugliness to a vivid red; it then went white, so ghastly white that the girl might have been going to faint. All this took place in less than a minute. At the end of that time Maggie was her old disdainful, angry self once more.

"You must be very glad," she said. "You have me in your power at last. My stepfather is a grocer. He keeps a shop at Shepherd's Bush. He is one of the most horribly vulgar men that ever lived. Had I been at home my mother would not have consented to marry him. But my mother, although pretty and refined-looking, and in herself a lady, has little force of character, and she was quite alone and very poor indeed. You, who don't know the meaning of the word 'poor,' cannot conceive what it meant to her. Little Merry guessed— dear, dear little Merry; but as to you, you think when you subscribe to this charity and the other, you think when you adopt an East End child and write letters to her, and give of your superabundance to benefit her, that you understand the poor. I tell you you *don't*! Your wealth is a curse to you, not a blessing. You no more understand what people like mother and like myself have lived through than you understand what the inhabitants of Mars do—the petty shifts, the smallnesses, the queer efforts to make two ends meet! You in your lovely home, and surrounded by lovely things, and your aunt so proud of you—how *can* you understand what lodgings in the hot weather in Shepherd's Bush are like? Mother understood—never any fresh air, never any tempting food; Tildy, that poor little faithful girl as servant—slavey was her right name; Tildy at every one's beck and call, always with a smut on her cheek, and her hair so untidy, and her little person so disreputable; and mother alone, wondering how she could make two ends meet. Talk of your knowing what the poor people in my class go through!"

"I don't pretend that I do know, Maggie," said Aneta, who was impressed by the passion and strength of Maggie's words. "I don't pretend it for a moment. The poverty of such lives is to me a sealed book. But—forgive me—if you are so poor, how could you come here?"

"I don't mind your knowing everything now," said Maggie. "I am disgraced, and nothing will ever get me out of my trouble. I am up to my neck, and I may as well drown at once; but Mrs. Ward—she understood what a poor girl whose father was a gentleman could feel, and she—oh, she was good!—she took me for so little that mother could afford it. She made no difference between you and me, Aneta, who are so rich, and your cousins the Cardews, who are so rich too. She said, 'Maggie Howland, your father was a gentleman and a man of honor, a man of whom his country was proud; and I will educate you, and give you your chance.' And, oh, I was happy here! And I—and I should be happy now but for you and your prying ways."

"You are unkind to me, Maggie. The knowledge that your stepfather was a grocer was brought to me in a most unexpected way. I was not to blame for the little person who called herself Tildy coming here to-day. Tildy felt no shame in the fact that your mother had married a grocer. She was far more lady-like about it than you are, Maggie. No one could have blamed you because your mother chose to marry beneath her. But you were to blame, Maggie, when you gave us to understand that her husband was in quite a different position from what he is."

"And you think," said Maggie, stamping her foot, "that the girls of this house —Kathleen O'Donnell, Sylvia St. John, Henrietta and Mary Gibson, the Cardews, the Tristrams, you yourself—would put up with me for a single moment if it was known what my mother has done?"

"I think you underrate us all," said Aneta. Then she came close to Maggie and took one of her hands. "I want to tell you something," she added.

Maggie had never before allowed her hand to remain for a second in Aneta's grasp. But there was something at this moment about the young girl, a look in her eyes, which absolutely puzzled Maggie and caused her to remain mute. She had struggled for a minute, but now her hand lay still in Aneta's clasp.

"I want to help you," said Aneta.

"To—help me! How? I thought you hated me."

"Well, as a matter of fact," said Aneta, "I did not love you until"—

"Until?" said Maggie, her eyes shining and her little face becoming transformed in a minute.

"Until I knew what you must have suffered."

"You do not mean to say that you love me now?"

"I believe," said Aneta, looking fixedly at Maggie, "that I could love you."

"Oh!" said Maggie. She snatched her hand away, and, walking to the window, looked out. The fog was thicker than ever, and she could see nothing. But that did not matter. She wanted to keep her back turned to Aneta. Presently her shoulders began to heave, and, taking her handkerchief from her pocket, she pressed it to her eyes. Then she turned round. "Go on," she said.

"What do you mean by that?" asked Aneta.

"Say what you want to say. I am the stepdaughter of a grocer, and I have broken one of the strictest rules in the school. When will you tell Mrs. Ward? I had better leave at once."

"You needn't leave at all."

"What do you mean?"

"I mean," said Aneta, "that if you will tell Mrs. Ward everything—all about your stepfather, and all about your selling that jewel and going out without leave—I am positively sure that dear Mrs. Ward will not expel you from the school. I am also sure, Maggie, that there will not be one girl at Aylmer House who will ever reproach you. As to your stepfather being what he is, no girl in her senses would blame you for that. You are the daughter of Professor Howland, one of the greatest explorers of his time—a man who has had a book written about him, and has largely contributed to the world's knowledge. Don't forget that, please; none of us are likely to forget it. As to the other thing—well, there is always the road of confession, and I am quite certain that if you will see Mrs. Ward she will be kind to you and forgive you; for her heart is very big and her sympathies very wide; and then, afterwards, I myself will, for your sake, try to understand your position, and I myself will be your true friend."

"Oh Aneta!" said Maggie.

She ran up to Aneta; she took her hand; she raised it to her lips and kissed it.

"Give me till to-morrow," she said. "Promise that you won't say anything till to-morrow."

Aneta promised. Maggie went to her room.

# CHAPTER XXII.

## ANETA'S PLAN.

The girls downstairs wondered why Maggie Howland did not appear. After an hour of waiting Kathleen O'Donnell took the lead. The accounts were left alone, but the tableaux vivants were diligently rehearsed, the Tristrams and Jane Burns being the three critics; Rosamond Dacre, Kathleen O'Donnell, and Matty and Clara Roache the performers. But, somehow, there was no life in the acting, for the moving spirit was not there; the bright, quick eye was missed, the eager words were lacking, with the pointed and telling criticism. Then there was the scene where Maggie herself was to take a part. It was from *The Talisman*, and a night-scene, which she was able to render with great precision and even beauty, and the dun light would be in her favor. It was to be the crowning one, and the last of the tableaux. It was expected to bring down the house. But Maggie was not there, and the girls could not help feeling a little disconsolate and a little surprised.

At supper that evening there were eager inquiries with regard to Maggie Howland. All the girls came up to ask Aneta where the other queen was.

"She is not quite well, and has gone to bed," said Aneta. "She does not wish to be disturbed until the morning."

Aneta's words had a curious effect upon every one who heard her speak. It was as though she had, for the first time in her life, absolutely taken Maggie's part. Her eyes, when she spoke of Maggie, were full of affection. The girls were puzzled; but Merry, as they turned away, suddenly ran back to Aneta, swept her arm round the girl's neck, and said, "Oh Neta, I do love you!"

Aneta pressed Merry's hand. For the first time these two understood each other.

Meanwhile poor Maggie was living through one of the most dreadful periods of her life. Her mother's intimation that she and her stepfather were coming without fail to Aylmer House on Saturday—*the* day, the glorious day when Maggie and her friends were to entertain Mrs. Ward and the rest of the school —drove the girl nearly wild. Aneta had discovered her secret, and Aneta had urged, as the one way out, the painful but salutary road of confession. Maggie writhed at the thought, but she writhed far more terribly at the news which her mother's letter contained.

The girl said to herself, "I cannot stand it! I will run away! He has destroyed my last chance. I will run away and hide. I will go to-night. There is no use in waiting. Aneta is kind; she is far kinder than I could ever have given her credit for. She would, I believe, help me; and dear Mrs. Ward would help me —I am sure of that. And I don't really mind now that it comes to the point of losing my position in the school as queen; but for all the school—for the Tristrams, for Merry Cardew, for Kathleen—to see that man is beyond my power of endurance. He will call here, and he will bring poor mother, but as I won't be here I won't feel anything. I will go to-night. I'll slip downstairs and let myself out. I have some money—thank goodness for that!—and I have my father's treasures. I can take them out of the tin box and wear them on my person, and I can sell them one by one. Yes, I will run away. There's no help for it."

Maggie, at Aneta's suggestion, had got into bed, but even to think of sleep was beyond her power. She got up again presently, dressed, and sat by the foggy window. The fog was worse; it was so thick now that you could not see your way even as far as the trees in the middle of the square. There were fog-signals sounding from time to time, and cabs going very slowly, and boys carrying torches to light belated and lost passengers.

Maggie was safe enough in her room, which had, like all the other bedrooms at Aylmer House, a small fire burning in the grate. By-and-by some one tapped at the door. Maggie said, "Don't come in"; but her words were unheeded. The door was opened an inch or two, and Merry Cardew entered.

"Oh Merry, you—of all people!" said Maggie.

"And why not?" said Merry. "I am your friend—your own very, very great friend. What is the matter, Mags? You were so jolly at tea; what can have happened since?"

"Something most dreadful," said Maggie; "but you will know on Saturday."

"Oh!" said Merry, coming up to Maggie and dropping on her knees and fondling one of the girl's cold hands, "why should I wait till Saturday? Why should I not know now?"

"I can't talk of it, Merry. I am glad you—you—*loved* me. You won't love me in the future. But kiss me just this once."

"I am not going to leave you like this," said Merry.

"You must, dear; yes, you must. Please, please go! And—please, be quick. Some one will see us together. Lucy Johnson will come in. Oh! don't make matters worse for me. Good-night, Merry, good-night."

Maggie seemed so anxious that Merry should go that the girl felt hurt and rose to her feet.

"Good-night, Merry dear," said Maggie as Merry was walking towards the door. Then she added, in a semi-whisper which Merry did not catch, "And good-bye, Merry dear; we shall never meet again."

Merry left the room, feeling full of apprehension. She thought for a minute as she stood outside. Then she went and knocked at Aneta's door.

"Aneta, may I come in?"

"Of course, dear. What is the matter?" said her cousin.

Merry entered at once.

"I have been to see Maggie. She is awfully queer. Oh, I know I broke the rules. I must tell Miss Johnson in the morning."

"I did beg of you, Merry, not to go to her," said Aneta.

"Yes, I know you did; but I could not help thinking and thinking about her. She is very queer. Her eyes look so strange."

"I hoped she was in bed and asleep," said Aneta.

"In bed!" said Merry. "Not a bit of it. She was up and sitting by the window gazing at the fog."

"I will go and see her myself," said Aneta.

"Will you, Neta? And you will be kind to her?"

"Yes, darling, of course."

"Somehow, she used to think that—that you didn't love her," said Merry.

"Nor did I," said Aneta. "But I will be kind to her; don't be afraid. I think I can guess what is the matter."

"It is all very queer," said Merry. "She was in such splendid spirits to-day; all the girls said so when they were out preparing for our party, and now she looks years older and utterly miserable."

"Go to bed, Merry, and leave your friend in my care."

"Then you don't think it wrong of me to be very fond of her?"

"I do not, Merry. There was a time when I hoped you would not care for her; now I earnestly want you to be her true friend. There is a very great deal of good in her, and she has had many sorrows. Pray for her to-night. Don't be anxious. Everything will come as right as possible."

"Oh Neta," said Merry, "you are a darling! And when you talk like that I love you more than I ever did before. You see, dear, I could not help caring for

Maggie from the very first, and nothing nor anybody can alter my love."

Aneta kissed Merry, who left the room. Then Aneta herself, taking up her candle, went out. She was wearing a long white wrapper, and her clouds of golden hair were falling far below her waist. She looked almost like an angel as she went down the corridor as far as Miss Johnson's room.

Lucy Johnson was just getting into bed when Aneta knocked.

"What is it, Neta?" said the governess in a tone almost of alarm.

"I want to break a rule, Lucy," said Aneta; "so put me down for punishment to-morrow."

"Oh, but why? What are you going to do?"

"I am going to do something which I shall be punished for. I am going to spend to-night, if necessary, with Maggie Howland."

"Is she ill, Neta? Ought we to send for the doctor?"

"Oh no, she is not a bit ill in that way. Good-night, Lucy; I felt I ought to tell you."

Aneta continued her way until she reached Maggie's room. It was now past midnight. The quiet and regular household had all retired to bed, and Maggie had feverishly begun to prepare for departure. She knew how to let herself out. Once out of the house, she would be, so she felt, through the worst part of her trouble. She was not unacquainted with the ways of this cruel world, and thought that she might be taken in at some hotel, not too far away, for the night. Early in the morning she would go by train to some seaside place. From there she would embark for the Continent. Beyond that she had made no plans.

Maggie was in the act of removing her father's treasures from the tin boxes when, without any warning, the room-door was opened, and Aneta, in her pure white dress, with her golden hair surrounding her very fair face, entered the room.

"Oh!" said Maggie, dropping a curiously made cross in her confusion and turning a dull brick-red. "Whatever have you come about?"

Aneta closed the door calmly, and placed her lighted candle on the top of Maggie's chest of drawers.

"I hoped you were in bed and asleep," she said; "but instead of that you are up. I have made arrangements to spend the night with you. It is bitterly cold. We must build up the fire."

Maggie felt wild.

Aneta did not take the slightest notice. She knelt down and put knobs of fresh coal on the fire. Soon it was blazing up merrily. "That's better," she said. "Now, don't you think a cup of cocoa each would be advisable?"

"I don't want to eat," said Maggie.

"I should like the cocoa," said Aneta; "and I have brought it with me. I thought your supply might be out. Here's your glass of milk which you never drank, and here's a little saucepan, and there are cups and saucers in your cupboard, and a box of biscuits. Just sit down, won't you? while I make the cocoa."

Maggie felt very strange. Her dislike of Aneta was growing less and less moment by moment. Nevertheless, she by no means gave up her primary idea of running away. She felt that she must hoodwink Aneta. Surely she was clever enough for that. The best plan would be to acquiesce in the cocoa scheme, afterwards to pretend that she was sleepy, and go to bed. Then Aneta would, of course, leave her, and there would still be plenty of time to get out of the house and disappear into the foggy world of London. The glowing fire, the beautiful young girl kneeling by it, the preparation for the little meal which she made with such swiftness and dexterity, caused Maggie to gaze at her in speechless amazement.

Maggie drank her delicious cocoa and munched her biscuits with appetite, and afterwards she felt better. The world was not quite so black and desolate, and Aneta looked lovely with her soft eyes glowing and the rose-color in her cheeks.

"Why are you doing all this for me?" said Maggie then.

"Why?" said Aneta. "I think the reason is very simple." Then she paused for a minute and her eyes filled with sudden tears. "I think it is, Maggie, because quite unexpectedly I have learned to love you."

"You—to love me—me?" said Maggie.

"Yes."

Maggie felt herself trembling. She could not reply. She did not understand that she returned the love so suddenly given to her—given to her, too, in her moment of deepest degradation, of her most utter misery. Once again the feeling that she must go, that she could not face confession and the scorn of the school, and the awful words of Bo-peep, and her poor mother as Bo-peep's wife, overpowered her.

"You are—very kind," she said in a broken voice; "and the cocoa was good; and, if you don't mind—I will—go to bed now, and perhaps—sleep a little."

"What have you been doing with all those lovely curios?" said Aneta.

"I?" said Maggie. "I—oh, I like to look at them."

"Do pick up that cross which is lying on the floor, and let me examine it."

Maggie did so rather unwillingly.

"Please bring over all the other things, and let me look at them," said Aneta then.

Maggie obeyed, but grudgingly, as though she did not care that Aneta should handle them.

"Why have you taken them out of their boxes and put them all in a muddle like this?" said Aneta.

"I—I wanted something to do," said Maggie. "I couldn't sleep."

"Was that the only reason—honor bright?" said Aneta.

Maggie dropped her eyes.

Aneta did not question her any further, but she drew her down to a low chair by the fire, and put a hand on her lap, and kept on looking at the treasures: the bracelets, the crosses, the brooches, the quaint designs belonging to a bygone period. After a time she said, "I am not at all sure—I am not a real judge of treasures; but I have an uncle, Sir Charles Lysle, who knows more about these things than any one else in London; and if he thinks what I am inclined to think with regard to the contents of these two boxes, you will be"—She stopped abruptly.

Maggie's eyes were shining. "Aneta," she said, "don't talk of these any more; and don't talk either of wealth or poverty any more. There is something I want to say. When you came into my room just now I was packing up to run away."

"Oh yes, I know that," said Aneta. "I saw that you had that intention the moment I entered the room."

"And you said nothing!"

"Why should I? I didn't want to force your confidence. But you're not going to run away now, Mags?" She bent towards her and kissed her on the forehead.

"Yes," said Maggie, trembling. "I want you to let me go."

"I cannot possibly do that, dear. If you go, I go too."

"I must go," said Maggie. "You don't understand. You found things out about me to-day, and you have behaved—well, splendidly. I didn't give you credit for it. I didn't know you. Now I do know you, and I see that no girl in the school can be compared to you for nobleness and courage, and just for being downright splendid. But, Aneta, I cannot bear that which is before me."

"The fact is," said Aneta, "you are in the midst of a terrible battle, and you mean to give in and turn tail, and let the enemy walk over the field. That is not a bit what I should have expected at one time from Maggie Howland."

"I will tell you," said Maggie. "I am not really a bit brave; there is nothing good in me."

"We won't talk about that," said Aneta. "What we have to think about now is what lies straight ahead of you; not of your past any more, but your immediate future. You have a tough time before you; in fact, you have a very great battle to fight, but I do not think you will turn tail."

"You want me," said Maggie, "to go to Mrs. Ward and tell her everything?"

"You must do that, Maggie. There is no second course to pursue. There is no way out. But I have been thinking since I saw you that perhaps you might have your day on Saturday. I think it would be best for you to tell Mrs. Ward to-morrow; and I think she would not prevent you having your day on Saturday. Perhaps it will be necessary—but she is the one to decide—that some of your schoolfellows should be told; and of course your little brooch which you sold to Pearce must be got back. Even Pearce is far too honest to keep it for the price he paid you."

"He gave me five pounds, and I have spent one. There are still four pounds left," said Maggie. "I meant to run away with the help of these."

"I will lend you a pound," said Aneta, "and we'll get the brooch back to-morrow."

"But, Aneta, I have not yet told you—it is too fearful—you cannot conceive what my stepfather is like. It isn't only his being a grocer—for I have no doubt there are lots of grocers who are quite, quite tolerable; but you cannot imagine what he is. I had a letter from him a little time ago—that time, you remember, when he sent me those perfectly awful dresses—and he said then that he and my mother were coming to see me, as he wanted to interview Mrs. Ward and to look at the school for himself. Well, that poor Tildy brought me a letter to-day from mother. I had written to mother to beg of her not to let him come; but he got hold of the letter, and he was nearly mad about it. The end of it is that he and she are coming on *Saturday*, and, somehow, I can't bear it. I must run away; I *cannot* endure it!"

"I don't wonder," said Aneta. "Let me think. Lay your head on my shoulder,

Maggie. Oh, how tired you are!"

"Aneta, you seem to me quite new—just as though I had never seen you before."

"I think you and your story have opened my eyes and done me good," said Aneta. "Then what you said about the sufferings of the poor—I mean your sort of poor—gave me great pain. Will you take off your things and lie down, and let me lie by your side? Do, Maggie darling!"

Maggie darling! Such words to come from Aneta Lysle's lips! Maggie felt subjugated. She allowed her rival queen to undress her, and presently the two girls were lying side by side in the little bed. Maggie dropped off into heavy slumber. Aneta lay awake.

It was early morning when Aneta touched her companion.

"Maggie, I have been thinking hard all night, and I am going to do something."

"You! What can you do? Oh, I remember everything now. Oh, the horror! Oh, how can I endure it? Why didn't I run away?"

"Maggie, you must promise me faithfully that you will never run away. Say it now, this minute. I believe in your word; I believe in your fine nature. I will help you with all my might and main through school-life, and afterwards. Give me your word now. You will stay at Aylmer House?"

"I will stay," said poor Maggie.

"I don't ask any more. Thank you, dear. Maggie, do nothing to-day, but leave matters in my hands. You are not well; your head aches, your forehead is so hot."

"Yes, I have a headache," owned Maggie.

"I shall be away for the greater part of the day, but I will ask Miss Johnson to look after you. Don't say anything until I return."

"But what are you going to do?"

"I am going to see your mother and your stepfather."

"Aneta!"

"Yes."

"Oh Aneta, you must not see him!"

"It is probable that I shall seem him, dear; I am not easily alarmed. I will take Aunt Lucia with me. I am going downstairs now to ask Mrs. Ward's permission."

"And you will say nothing about me?"

"Something, but nothing of your story. When you feel well enough you can get up and go on with the preparations for to-morrow. I believe we shall have our happy day."

# CHAPTER XXIII.

## AT LABURNUM VILLA.

Aneta went back to her room, where she dressed with her usual expedition and extreme neatness. When she had finished her toilet she ran downstairs. It was not yet eight o'clock; but most of the girls were assembled in the large hall waiting for prayers, which always took place before breakfast. Mrs. Ward was seen passing to the library, where prayers were held. Aneta went up to her.

"Prayers first, of course," said Aneta, "and afterwards may I talk to you?"

Mrs. Ward looked at Aneta. "What is the matter, dear?"

"Something very important indeed. I must see you."

"Well, breakfast follows prayers; come to me the minute breakfast is over."

"Thank you, dear Mrs. Ward," said Aneta.

At breakfast Merry asked Aneta how Maggie was. Aneta said that Maggie had a headache, and would not be in school during the morning.

"Then what are we to do about our day?" said Molly Tristram, who overheard this remark. "We have absolutely more to get through than we can possibly manage."

"Oh, to-morrow will be quite all right," said Aneta; "and Maggie will join you presently."

Aneta was so respected in the school, so little given to exaggeration, so absolutely to be relied on, that these words of hers had a most calming effect. The girls continued their breakfast, those who were in the secret of to-morrow occasionally alluding to the subject in French, which was the only language allowed to be spoken. The others talked about their different occupations.

As soon as ever breakfast was over, Aneta went to Mrs. Ward's private room.

"Now, dear, what is it?" said the head-mistress. "I have to take the class for literature at half-past nine, and have very little time to spare."

"I won't keep you," said Aneta; "but what I wanted was to beg for a day's holiday."

"My dear girl! What do you mean? In the middle of term—a day's holiday! Can you not take it to-morrow?—oh, I forgot, to-morrow Maggie is having her grand carnival, as I call it. But what is the matter, Aneta? Have you any trouble?"

"Yes," said Aneta; "and I cannot tell you, dear Mrs. Ward."

"I trust you, of course, Aneta."

"I know you do; and I want you to trust me more than ever. It has something to do with Maggie."

Mrs. Ward slightly frowned. "I am never sure"—she began.

But Aneta stopped her impulsively. "If you give me that holiday to-day," she said, "and if you trust me, and if you will also give me Mrs. Martin's address, which, of course, you must have on your books"—

"Mrs. Martin's address?" said Mrs. Ward.

"Yes. You know Maggie's mother has married again; she is Mrs. Martin."

"Of course, of course; I had forgotten for the moment. Yes, I have her address."

"Well, if you will do all that," continued Aneta, "I think that you will find a new Maggie in the future, one whom you—will trust, and—and love, as I love her."

"My dear girl! as you love Maggie Howland?"

Aneta lowered her head for a minute. "It is true I did not love her," she said, "in the past, but I have changed my views. I have been narrow-minded, and small, and silly. She herself has opened my eyes. I cannot tell you more now. Maggie will come down, and will be able to go on with her lessons just as usual this afternoon; but I want a day off, and I want it at once."

"But where are you going, dear?"

"I am going to Aunt Lucia. You will let me have a cab, and I will drive to Aunt Lucia's house in Eaton Square at once?"

Mrs. Ward looked doubtful. "You have a very grave reason for this?" she said.

"Very, very grave; and I will tell you all presently."

"I have never had reason to doubt you," said Mrs. Ward, "and I won't doubt you now. Does Maggie know of this?"

"Yes—oh yes; but please don't question her until I return."

"Very well, dear; you shall have your way. Oh, you want Mrs. Martin's address. It is Laburnum Villa, Clapham."

Aneta entered the address in a little tablet bound in gold which she always wore at her waist.

"Thank you ever so much," she said, and then left the room.

A minute or two later she met Miss Johnson. "Give me something stiff to learn—something that I don't like—to-night, dear Lucy," she said. "I am off for a whole day's holiday, but I shall be back in the evening."

"That is very queer," said Miss Johnson. "What does it mean?"

"I cannot explain, but Mrs. Ward knows. Be specially kind to dear Maggie, and give me something that I don't like to do when I return."

Miss Johnson smiled. "You shall hem some dusters," she said.

Aneta made a wry face. "Thanks ever so much," she replied; then she ran upstairs to get ready for her visit.

Just before leaving the house she looked in at Maggie. "I'm off, Mags. It's all right. I shall probably see you about tea-time."

Before Maggie had time even to expostulate Aneta closed the door, and a minute or two later had stepped into the cab which Agnes had called for her. The cabman was desired to drive Miss Lysle to Lady Lysle's house in Eaton Square. This was accordingly done, and soon after ten o'clock Lady Lysle, who had not yet completed her morning toilet, was most amazed at being informed by her maid that Miss Lysle was waiting for her downstairs.

"Aneta! You don't mean Aneta, Purcell?"

"Yes, my lady; and she wants to see you in a very great hurry."

"Then send her up to me."

Purcell disappeared. Lady Lysle wondered what was wrong. Presently Aneta burst into the room.

"My dear child," said her aunt, "what can be wrong? Why have you left school? I do hope no illness has broken out there. It would be very inconvenient for me to have you here at present."

"There is no illness whatever at the school, Aunt Lucia," said Aneta, going up to her aunt and kissing her; "only there is a girl there, one of my schoolfellows, in a good bit of trouble, and I want to help her, and I have got a day off from Mrs. Ward, who doesn't know why she is giving it to me, but trusts me all the same. And now, auntie, I want you to come with me at once."

"Oh my dear child, where?"

"To Clapham, auntie."

"Clapham! I never stopped at Clapham in my life. I have driven through the place, it is true."

"Well, we'll stop there to-day," said Aneta, "at Laburnum Villa, Clapham. I want to see Mrs. Martin, Maggie's mother."

"Oh, dear child," said Lady Lysle, "you mean Miss Howland when you speak of Maggie? Now, you know I told you that her stepfather is no relation whatever to the Martyns of The Meadows. I cannot make out why she should have given you to understand that he was. A man who lives at Clapham! Dear Aneta, I would rather be excused."

"There is no excuse, auntie, that I can listen to for a single moment. I know all about Maggie's stepfather, and I will tell you as we are driving out to Clapham. You have always let me have my own way, and I have—yes, I have tried to be a good girl; but there is something before me to-day more important and more difficult than I ever tackled yet, and if I can't come to my own aunt—I, who am a motherless girl—for help at this crisis I shall think the world is coming to an end."

"What a strange, earnest way you do speak in, Aneta!"

"I am very sorry, darling; but I assure you the case is most urgent. You are quite well, aren't you?"

"Oh yes, my love; I am never an ailing sort of person."

"Well, then, I will send Purcell back to you, and please order the carriage, and please be as quick as possible. We have to go somewhere else after we have done with Mrs. Martin."

"Well, Aneta, I always was wax in your hands, and I suppose I must do what you wish. But remember your promise that you will tell me the meaning of this extraordinary thing during our drive to Clapham."

"I promise faithfully to tell you what is necessary, for the fact is I want your help. Darling auntie! you are doing about the best work of your life to-day. I knew you would stand by me; I felt certain of it, and I told Maggie so."

"That girl!" said Lady Lysle. "I don't care for that girl."

"You will change your mind about her presently," said Aneta, and she ran downstairs to request Davidson, the butler, to bring her something to eat, for her breakfast had been slight, and she was quite hungry enough to enjoy some of her aunt's nice food.

By-and-by Lady Lysle, looking slim and beautiful, wearing her becoming sables and her toque with its long black ostrich plume, appeared on the scene, and a minute later Davidson announced that the carriage was at the door.

The two ladies stepped in, Aneta giving very careful directions to the driver.

He expressed some astonishment at the address. "Laburnum Villa, Clapham!" he said. "Martin, Laburnum Villa, Clapham! Clapham's a big place, miss."

"I know that," said Aneta; "but that is all the address I can obtain. We must call at the post-office, if necessary, to get the name of the street."

The footman sprang into his place, and Aneta and her aunt drove off in the comfortable brougham towards that suburb known as Clapham.

"Now, Aneta, I suppose you will tell me what is the meaning of this?"

"Yes, I will," said Aneta. "I made a mistake about Maggie, and I am willing to own it. She has been placed in a difficult position. I do not mean for a minute to imply that she has acted in a straight way, for she has not. But there is that in her which will make her the best of girls in the future, as she is one of the cleverest and one of the most charming. Yes, auntie, she has got a great power about her. She is a sort of magnet—she attracts people to her."

"She has never attracted me," said Lady Lysle. "I have always thought her a singularly plain girl."

"Ugliness like hers is really attractive," said Aneta. "But, now, the thing is this: if we don't help her she will be absolutely lost, all her chance taken from her, and her character ruined for ever. We do a lot at our school for those poor slum-girls, but we never do anything for girls in our class. Now, I mean my girl in future to be Maggie Howland."

"Aneta, you are absurd!"

"I mean it, auntie; her father's daughter deserves help. Her father was as good a man as ever lived, and for his sake something ought to be done for his only child. As to her mother"—

"Yes, the woman who has married a person of the name of Martin, and to whose house I presume we are going"—

"Auntie, I have rather a shock to give you. Poor Maggie did mean to imply that her stepfather was in a different class of life from what he is. He is a— grocer!"

Lady Lysle put up her hand to pull the check-string.

"Pray, auntie, don't do that. Maggie isn't the daughter of a grocer, and she can't help her mother having married this dreadful man. I want Maggie to have nothing to do with her stepfather in the future, and I mean to carry out my ideas, and you have got to help me."

202

"Indeed, I will do nothing of the kind. What a disgraceful girl! She must leave Aylmer House at once."

"Then I will go too," said Aneta.

"Aneta, I never knew you behave in such a way before."

"Come, auntie darling, you know you are the sweetest and the most loving and sympathetic person in the world; and why should you turn away from a poor little girl who quite against her own will finds herself the stepdaughter of a grocer? Maggie has given me to understand that he is a dreadful man. She is horrified with him, and what I am going now to Laburnum Villa about is to try to prevent his visiting the school with his wife on Saturday. I will do the talking, dear, and you have only to sit by and look dignified."

"I never was put in such a dreadful position before," said Lady Lysle, "and really even you, Aneta, go too far when you expect me to do this."

"But you would visit a poor woman in East London without the smallest compunction," said Aneta.

"That is different," replied Lady Lysle with dignity.

"It is different," replied Aneta; "but the difference lies in the fact that the grocer's wife is very much higher up in the social scale than the East End woman."

"Oh my dear child, this is really appalling! I have always distrusted that Miss Howland. Does Mrs. Ward know of your project?"

"Not yet, but she will to-night."

"And what am I to do when I visit this person?"

"Just look your dear, sweet, dignified self, and allow me to do the talking."

"I think you have taken leave of your senses."

"I haven't taken leave of my senses, and I would do more than I am now doing to help a fine girl round a nasty corner. So cheer up, auntie! After we have seen Mrs. Martin we have to go on and visit the grocer."

"Aneta, that I do decline!"

"I am sure you won't decline. But let us think of Mrs. Martin herself first, and try to remember that by birth she is a lady."

Just at this moment the carriage drew up outside a post-office. There was a short delay while Laburnum Villa was being inquired for by the footman. At last the street in which this small suburban dwelling was situated was discovered, and a few minutes later the carriage, with its splendid horses and two servants on the box, drew up before the green-painted door.

The villa was small, but it was exceedingly neat. The little brass knocker shone, even though yesterday was a day of such fog. The footman came to the carriage-door to make inquiries.

"I will get out," said Aneta.

"Hadn't James best inquire if the woman is in?" said Lady Lysle.

"No, I think I will," said Aneta.

She went up the narrow path and rang the front-door bell. Tildy opened the door. The new cook had been peeping above the blinds in the kitchen. Tildy had hastily put on a white apron, but it is to be regretted that a smut was once more on her cheek. Somehow, Aneta liked her all the better for that smut.

"I want to see your mistress, Tildy," she said. "It is something about Miss Maggie, and I am, as you know, one of her schoolfellows."

"Lor', miss! yes, for certain, miss. Mrs. Martin 'll be that proud, miss."

"I have brought my aunt with me," said Aneta. "She would like to come in too in order to see Mrs. Martin."

"Yes, miss; in course, miss. There's no fire lit in the drawin'-room. But there's the dinin'-room; it do smell a bit smoky, for master 'e loves 'is pipe. 'E smokes a lot in the dinin'-room, miss."

"Show us into the dining-room," said Aneta. She ran back to fetch Lady Lysle, and conducted that amazed and indignant woman into the house.

Tildy rushed upstairs to fetch her mistress. "You get into your best gown in no time, mum. There's visitors downstairs—that most beauteous young lady who spoke to me yesterday at Aylmer House, and a lady alongside of 'er as 'u'd make yer 'eart quake. Ef Queen Victoria was alive I'd say yes, it was 'erself. Never did I mark such a sweepin' and 'aughty manner. They're fine folks, both of 'em, and no mistake."

"Did they give their names?" asked Mrs. Martin.

"I didn't even arsk, mum. They want to see you about our Miss Maggie."

"Well, I will go down. What a queer, early hour for visitors! What dress shall I wear, Tildy?"

"I'd say the amber satin, mum, ef I'd a voice in the choice. You look elegant in it, mum, and you might 'ave your black lace shawl."

"I don't think I will wear satin in the morning," said Mrs. Martin.

Tildy helped her into a dark-brown merino dress, one of her extensive trousseau. Mrs. Martin then went downstairs, prepared to show these visitors that she was "as good as them, if not better." But the glimpse of the carriage and horses which she got through the lobby-window very nearly bowled her over.

"Go in, mum, now; you've kept them waitin' long enough. I can serve up an elegant lunch if you want it."

Tildy felt almost inclined to poke at her mistress in order to hurry her movements. Mrs. Martin opened the dining-room door and stood just for a minute on the threshold. She looked at that moment a perfect lady. Her gentle, faded face and extreme slimness gave her a grace of demeanor which Lady Lysle was quick to acknowledge. She bowed, and looked at Aneta to speak for her.

"How do you do, Mrs. Martin," said that young lady. "I am Aneta Lysle, one of your daughter's schoolfellows. My aunt, Lady Lysle"—Mrs. Martin bowed —"has kindly come with me to see you. We want to have a little confidential talk with you."

"Oh, indeed!" said Mrs. Martin. "Has Maggie done anything wrong? She always was a particularly troublesome girl."

"I quite agree with you," said Lady Lysle. At that moment she had an idea of Maggie in disgrace and banished from Aylmer House, which pleased her.

Mrs. Martin stopped speaking when Lady Lysle said this.

"Doubtless you agree with me, Mrs. Martin," continued the lady, "that your daughter would do better at another school."

"Oh no," said Mrs. Martin; "we wish her—Bo-peep and I—I mean James and I—to stay where she is."

"And so do I wish her to stay where she is," said Aneta.—"Auntie darling, you don't quite understand; but Mrs. Martin and I understand.—Don't we, Mrs. Martin?"

"Well, I am sure," said Mrs. Martin, "I haven't the faintest idea what you are driving at, Miss—Miss Lysle."

"Well, it is just this," said Aneta. "You sent a letter yesterday to Maggie."

"I did," said Mrs. Martin; "and great need I had to send it."

"In that letter you informed Maggie that you and your husband were coming to see her to-morrow."

"Bo-peep wishes—I mean, James wishes—to."

"Really, Aneta, had not we better go?" said Lady Lysle.

"Not yet, auntie, please.—Mrs. Martin, I begged for a holiday to-day on purpose to come and see you."

"If it's because you think I'll keep James—Bo-peep—I mean James—from having his heart's wish, I am sorry you have wasted your time," said Mrs. Martin. "The fact is, he is very angry indeed with Maggie. He considers her his own child now, which of course is true, seeing that he has married me, and I really can't go into particulars; but he is determined to see her and to see Mrs. Ward, and he's not a bit ashamed of being—being—well, what he is—an honorable tradesman—a grocer."

"But perhaps you are aware," said Lady Lysle, "that the daughters of grocers —I mean tradesmen—are not admitted to Aylmer House."

Mrs. Martin turned her frightened eyes on the lady. "Maggie isn't the real daughter of a tradesman," she said then. "She is only the stepdaughter. Her own father was"—

"Yes," said Aneta, "we all know what her own father was—a splendid man, one of the makers of our Empire. We are all proud of her own father, and we do not see for a moment why Maggie should not live up to the true circumstances of her birth, and I have come here to-day, Mrs. Martin, to ask you to help me. If you and your husband come to Aylmer House there will be no help, for Maggie will certainly have to leave the school."

"Of course, and the sooner the better," said Lady Lysle.

"But if you will help us, and prevent your husband from coming to our school to-morrow, there is no reason whatever why she shouldn't stay at the school. Even her expenses can be paid from quite another source."

Mrs. Martin looked intensely nervous. A bright spot of color came into her left cheek. Her right cheek was deadly pale.

"I—I cannot help it," she said. "I never meant Bo-peep to go; I never wished him to go. But he said, 'Little-sing, I will go'—I—I forgot myself—of course you don't understand. He is a very good husband to me, but he and Maggie never get on."

"I am sure they don't," said Aneta with fervor.

"Never," continued Mrs. Martin. "I got on with her only with difficulty before I married my present dear husband. I am not at all ashamed of his being a grocer. He gives me comforts, and is fond of me, and I have a much better time with him than I had in shabby, dirty lodgings at Shepherd's Bush. I don't want him to go to that school to-morrow; but I thought it right to let Maggie know he was coming, for, all the same, go he will. When James puts his foot down he is a very determined man."

"This is altogether a most unpleasant interview," said Lady Lysle, "and I have only come here at my niece's request.—Perhaps, Aneta, we can go now."

"Not yet, auntie darling.—Mrs. Martin, Maggie and I had a long talk yesterday, and will you put this matter into my hands?"

"Good heavens! what next?" murmured Lady Lysle to herself.

"Will you give me your husband's address, and may I go to see him?"

"You mean the—the—shop?" said Mrs. Martin.

"I don't go into that shop!" said Lady Lysle.

"Yes, I mean the shop," said Aneta. "I want to go and see him there."

"Oh, he will be so angry, and I am really terrified of him when he is angry."

"But think how much more angry he will be if you don't give me that address, and things happen to-morrow which you little expect. Oh! please trust me."

Aneta said a few more words, and in the end she was in possession of that address at Shepherd's Bush where Martin the grocer's flourishing shop was to be found.

"Thank you so very much, Mrs. Martin. I don't think you will ever regret this," said the girl.

Lady Lysle bowed to the wife of the grocer as she went out, but Aneta took her hand.

"Perhaps you never quite understood Maggie," she said; "and perhaps, in the future, you won't have a great deal to say to her."

"I don't want to; she never suited me a bit," said the mother, "and I am very happy with Bo-peep."

"Well, at least you may feel," said Aneta, "that I am going to be Maggie's special friend."

Mrs. Martin stood silent while Lady Lysle and her niece walked down the little path and got into the carriage. When the carriage rolled away she burst into a flood of tears. She did not know whether she was glad or sorry; but, somehow, she had faith in Aneta. Was she never going to see Maggie again? She was not quite without maternal love for her only child, but she cared very much more for Bo-peep, and quite felt that Maggie would be a most troublesome inmate of Laburnum Villa.

"Now, Aneta," said her aunt as the carriage rolled away, "I have gone through enough in your service for one day."

"You haven't been at all nice, auntie," said Aneta; "but perhaps you will be better when you get to the shop."

"I will not go to the shop."

"Auntie, just think, once and for all, that you are doing a very philanthropic act, and that you are helping me, whom you love so dearly."

"Of course I love you, Aneta. Are you not as my own precious child?"

"Well, now, I want you to buy no end of things at Martin's shop."

"Buy things! Good gracious, child, at a grocer's shop! But I get all my groceries at the Stores, and the housekeeper attends to my orders."

"Well, anyhow, spend from five to ten pounds at Martin's to-day. You can get tea made up in half-pound packets and give it away wholesale to your poor women. Christmas is coming on, and they will appreciate good tea, no matter where it has been bought from."

"Well, you may go in and give the order," said Lady Lysle; "but I won't see that grocer. I will sit in the carriage and wait for you."

Aneta considered for a few minutes, and then said in a sad voice, "Very well."

Lady Lysle looked at her once or twice during the long drive which followed. Aneta's little face was rather pale, but her eyes were full of subdued fire. She was determined to carry the day at any cost.

---

# CHAPTER XXIV.

## A VISIT TO THE GROCER.

James Martin abhorred the aristocracy—so he said. Nevertheless, he greatly admired his elegant wife in her faded beauty. He liked to hear her speak, and he made some effort to copy her "genteel pronunciation." He also, in his inmost heart, admired Maggie as a girl of spirit, although not a beautiful one. He had his own ideas with regard to female loveliness, and, like all men, was impressed and attracted by it.

On this special foggy day, as he was standing behind his counter busily engaged attending to a customer who was only requiring a small order to be made up, he gave a visible start, raised his eyes, dropped his account-book, let his pencil roll on to the floor, and stared straight before him. For somebody was coming into the shop—somebody so very beautiful that his eyes were dazzled and, as he said afterwards, his heart melted within him. A radiant-looking girl, with wonderful blue eyes and hair of the color of pure gold, a girl with a refined face—most beautifully dressed—although Martin could not quite make out in what fashion she was apparelled—came quickly up to the counter and then stood still, waiting for some one to attend to her. The other men in the shop also saw this lovely vision, and an attendant of the name of Turtle sprang forward to ask what he could do.

"I want to see Mr. Martin," said the silvery voice.

Martin felt pleased, and said *sotto voce*, "Chuck it, Turtle; you're out of it, old boy." A minute later he was standing before Aneta, inquiring in a trembling voice what he could do for her.

"I want to order fifty pounds of tea to be made up in half-pound packets and sent to my aunt, Lady Lysle, 16B Eaton Square," said Aneta. "The tea will be paid for on delivery, and please let it be the very best. I also want a hundred pound-packets of the best currants, and a hundred pound-packets of the best sugar."

"Demerara, miss, or loaf?" inquired Martin, tremblingly putting down the order.

"Loaf, I think," said Aneta. "Will you kindly send everything within the next day or two to Eaton Square, 16B, to Lady Lysle?"

"I will enter her ladyship's name in my book. Yes, it shall be done," said Martin.

He looked at Aneta, and Aneta looked straight back at him.

"Mr. Martin," she said suddenly, "I am the school-friend of your stepdaughter, Maggie Howland. May I have a little conversation with you in your private room?"

"Ah, I thought there was something!" said Martin. "To be sure, miss," he added.—"Turtle, you see that this order is *h*executed. It's for her ladyship, Lady Lysle, 16B Eaton Square.—Come this way, my lady."

"I am only Miss Lysle," said Aneta.

All the attendants in the shop gazed in wonder as the beautiful girl and the excited Martin went into the little parlor at the back of the business establishment. There Martin stood with his hands behind him; but Aneta sank into a low chair.

"I want to ask you a great favor, Mr. Martin," said the girl. She looked full up at him as she spoke.

Martin thought that he had never in his life seen such melting and lovely blue eyes before. "She bowls me over," he kept saying to himself. "I hate the aristocrats, but somehow she bowls me over."—"Anything in my power, miss," he said aloud, and he made a low bow, pressing his hand to his chest.

"I think," said Aneta—"indeed, I am sure—to judge from your most flourishing shop—that you are a good business man."

"Well, now, there's no doubt on that point, Miss—Miss Lysle."

"But you would like to extend your custom?" said Aneta.

"Business is always business to me," replied Martin.

"Well, the fact is, it lies in my power to induce my aunt, Lady Lysle, to get her groceries from you. She has a large establishment and sees a great deal of company. She gets them now at the Army and Navy Stores, but I haven't the slightest doubt that she would not object to have them from you."

"You are exceedingly good, Miss Lysle, and I am sure anything that her ladyship ordered should have my very best attention; in fact, I should make it my business to get in specially good things for her. If I might let you into a business secret, miss, the people round here don't want the very best things; they don't, so to speak, appreciate them."

"I quite understand that," said Aneta. "Of course Lady Lysle would require the very best."

"She should have the best, miss; I'd be proud of her custom. Things should be punctually delivered; just an order overnight, and my cart would convey them to her ladyship's door at an early hour on the following day."

"Yes, it could be arranged," said Aneta.

"Then, perhaps, miss," said Mr. Martin, who saw brilliant prospects opening before him, and the possibility of a West End shop, a genuine West End shop, being his, as well as the profitable establishment at Shepherd's Bush, "her ladyship might be so kind as to recommend me to others."

"It is possible," said Aneta coldly; "but of course I can only speak for my aunt herself." Then she added, "And even for her I cannot quite speak, although I believe the matter can be arranged. I have given you a large order to-day."

"You have, Miss Lysle, and most faithfully will it be attended to."

Martin took out his red silk handkerchief and mopped his forehead.

"Now," said Aneta gently, "I haven't come here all the way from Aylmer House, and practically given up a day of my school-life, for nothing. I have come on behalf of another."

"Ho, ho!" said Martin, "so the cat's going to be let out of the bag."

Aneta colored.

Martin saw he had gone too far, and immediately apologized. "You will forgive my coarse way of expressing myself, miss. I know it isn't done in your circle."

"It doesn't matter," said Aneta. "I will come to the point at once. I am interested in Miss Howland."

"Ah! my little stepdaughter. I keep her at a fine, smart school, don't I? I do the knowing by her, don't I?"

"Well, all I want you to do in future—and I believe her mother will consent, for I have seen Mrs. Martin this morning"—

"You went to Laburnum Villa this morning? Tasty place, that, eh?"

"Yes, a very comfortable sort of house. My aunt, Lady Lysle, and I went together."

"Her ladyship and you?"

"We drove there."

"I hope the neighbors saw," said Martin. "They'll come in shoals to see Little-sing after they've peeped at her ladyship's carriage."

Aneta could scarcely keep back a smile.

"Mr. Martin," she said, "if I do what I intend for you—and it lies in my power—will you please not come to Aylmer House to-morrow?"

"Ho, hi! And why not? Ashamed of me, eh?"

"Not at all," said Aneta. "I am not ashamed of you in your walk in life; but I think it would be best for Maggie if you did not come; therefore I ask you not to do so."

"But the girl's my girl."

"No, she is her mother's daughter; and, to tell the truth, we all want—I mean, my aunt and I, and others—to have her to ourselves, at least until she is educated."

"But, come now, miss, that's all very fine. Who pays for her education?"

"Her father's money."

"So she let that out?" said Martin.

"I know about it," said Aneta. "That is sufficient. Now, Mr. Martin, I ask you to become grocer to my aunt, Lady Lysle, of Eaton Square, and to any friends who she may recommend, on the sole condition that you do not come to Aylmer House, and that you allow Maggie Howland to spend the holidays with us."

"Oh, my word, I am sure I don't care," said Martin,

"You promise, then?"

"Yes, I promise fast enough. If you're going to take Maggie and bring her up a fine lady she'll never suit me. All I beg is that she doesn't come back to me like a bad penny some day."

"That I can absolutely assure you she will never do. I am exceedingly obliged to you. Will you come with me now and let me say a few words to my aunt; for as you have made your definite promise to leave Maggie alone, my aunt must make a definite promise to you."

Lady Lysle was much astonished, as she sat wearily in her carriage, when a red-faced, bald-looking, stout grocer accompanied her elegant young niece to the carriage-door.

"Aunt Lucia," said Aneta, "this is Mr. Martin."

Lady Lysle gave the faintest inclination of her head.

"Proud to see your ladyship," said Martin.

"I have been making arrangements with Mr. Martin," said Aneta, "and on certain conditions he will do what I want. Will you please, in future, get your groceries from him?"

"I will faithfully attend to you, my lady, if agreeable to you. I will come weekly for *h*orders. I will do anything to oblige your ladyship."

"Please, auntie, you've got to do it," said Aneta.

"My dear, it depends on Watson, my housekeeper."

"Oh, I'll manage Watson," said Aneta, springing lightly into the carriage, her face all beams and smiles.—"It is quite right, Mr. Martin; and you will get your second order this evening. You won't forget about the tea and currants and sugar for the poor people.—Now, auntie, will you drive me back to Aylmer House, or shall we go straight to Eaton Square?"

"Eaton Square, I think."

"Good-day, Mr. Martin."

The carriage rolled out of sight. Martin stood bareheaded in the doorway of his shop. There was not a prouder man than he in the whole of Christendom. When he returned to the sacred precincts of the shop itself he said to Turtle, "Fresh customer, Turtle—West End, Turtle. That's a fine young lady—eh, Turtle?"

"The most beautiful young female I ever saw," returned Turtle.

"When I ask you what you think of her personal appearance you can tell me, Turtle. Now, go and attend to the shop."

Meanwhile Aneta, her heart full of thankfulness, accompanied her aunt to Eaton Square.

"I have got what I want," she said, "and dear Maggie is practically saved; and you have done it, auntie. You will feel happier for this to your dying day."

Lady Lysle said that at the present moment she did not feel specially elated at the thought of getting her tea and numerous groceries at a shop in Shepherd's Bush; but Aneta assured her that that was a very tiny sacrifice to make for so great an end as she had in view.

"It will help Mr. Martin," she said. "He is not a gentleman, and doesn't pretend to be, but he's a good, honest tradesman; and perhaps Mrs. Ward, too, will give him some of her custom."

"Well, my dear Aneta, if you're happy, I have nothing to say," responded her aunt. "But you must tackle Watson, for I really cannot attempt it."

Aneta did tackle the old housekeeper to some purpose. At first there were objections, protests, exclamations; but Aneta was sure of her ground. Did not Mrs. Watson idolize the girl, having known her from her earliest days?

About tea-time a tired and triumphant girl returned to Aylmer House. She had had her way. The great difficulty was overcome. Maggie, looking pale and tired, was having tea with the others. Aneta sat down by her side. Maggie turned anxious eyes towards the queen of the school whom she used to fear and almost hate. But there was no hatred now in Maggie's eyes. Far, far from that, she looked upon Aneta as a refuge in the storm. If Aneta could not get her out of her present trouble no one could.

"You will be very busy during the leisure hours this afternoon," said Aneta when the meal was coming to an end. "But, first of all, I want to speak to you just for a minute or two."

"Yes," said Maggie.

"We have done tea now. May Maggie and I go away by ourselves, please, Miss Johnson, for a few minutes?" said Aneta.

Miss Johnson signified her consent, and the two queens left the room together. The other girls looked after them, wondering vaguely what was up.

"Maggie," said Aneta, "I have managed everything."

"Aneta—you haven't"—

"Yes; he isn't coming to-morrow, nor is your mother; and Aunt Lucia has invited you to spend the Christmas holidays with us. You can see your mother occasionally; but, somehow or other, Maggie dear, you are to be my friend in future; and—oh, Maggie!"

"Oh Aneta! how can I ever, ever thank you?"

"Well, the beginning of the way is a little hard," said Aneta. "Come now, at once, straight to Mrs. Ward, and tell her every single thing."

"She will expel me if I do," said Maggie.

"That I know she will not. She is too true and dear and kind. Besides, I will stay with you all the time while you are telling her. Come, quick. You can get your confession over in a very few minutes."

"Oh Aneta! for you I would do anything. But how did you manage to get my dreadful stepfather to give up his plan."

"That matters little. He has given it up. Now, come. There's much to do to prepare for to-morrow; but you must get your confession over first."

Mrs. Ward always had her tea alone, and she was just finishing it on this special evening when there came a tap at her door, and, to her great amazement, Aneta and Maggie entered, holding each other's hands.

"Mrs. Ward, Maggie has something to say to you."

"Yes," said Maggie; and then in a few broken words, choked by tears of true repentance, she told her story. She had been ashamed of her stepfather. She had been deceitful. She had been afraid to confess that she was taken at a lower fee than the other girls at the school. She had gone out, without leave, to sell one of her own father's treasures. Everything was told. Mrs. Ward looked very grave as the girl, with bent head, related the story of her deceit and wrong-doing.

"I know you can expel me," said Maggie.

"But you will not," said Aneta. "I feel sure of that, for I, who never cared for Maggie until now, love her with all my heart. There will be no rivalry in the school any more, and dear Maggie must not go."

"Oh, if you would keep me! If you would keep me," said Maggie, "and give me one more chance!"

"Have you asked God to forgive you, Maggie?" said Mrs. Ward.

"I cannot, somehow; my heart is so cold. But if—if you would"—

"We will ask Him together," said Mrs. Ward.

There and then she knelt down, and Aneta and Maggie knelt at each side of her, and she said a few words of prayer which touched Maggie's heart as no words had ever touched it before. "Keep from her all hurtful things, and give her those things which are necessary for her salvation," pleaded the mistress.

Suddenly Mrs. Ward's hand was taken by Maggie and covered with kisses. "Oh, I will try!" she said; "I will try hard to be really good! And," she added, "I will take any punishment you give me."

Mrs. Ward looked at her with sparkling eyes. She was a very keen observer of character. She put her hand under the girl's chin and looked into her downcast face.

"My dear," she said, "full and absolute forgiveness means the doing away with punishment. You have suffered sorely; I will not add to your suffering in any way. Now, go and prepare for to-morrow's entertainment.—Aneta, you will stay with me for a few minutes."

Maggie left the room, but in a short time she returned. She carried in her arms the two tin boxes which contained her father's treasures.

"I want you to keep these for me, or to sell them, or to do what you like with them," said Maggie. She then immediately left the room.

Mrs. Ward and Aneta bent over the treasures. Mrs. Ward gave a start of great surprise when she saw them.

"Why, these," she said, "are a fortune in themselves."

"I thought so," said Aneta, her eyes sparkling. "I felt sure of it. We must get that brooch back from Pearce."

"Yes, Aneta; I will send Miss Johnson round for it at once. What did you say he gave Maggie for it?"

"Five pounds, Mrs. Ward."

"It is very honest of him to offer to restore it to her. Ring the bell, dear, and Lucy Johnson will come."

Miss Johnson was very much interested when she saw the sparkling treasures.

"Maggie's!" she exclaimed. "I am glad she has given them to you to take care of for her. I was always terrified at her keeping such priceless things in her drawer."

Mrs. Ward gave the girl some directions and the necessary money; she went off to fulfill her errand in considerable amazement. Lucy returned in less than half-an-hour with the lovely little brooch, which was immediately added to the collection.

"The best person to see these, as you suggested, Aneta," said Mrs. Ward, "is Sir Charles Lysle. They are really no good to Maggie, but ought to be sold for their utmost value for her benefit. She has many fine points, and considerable strength of character; and if you take her up, dear, I feel certain that she will be saved from all those things which would ruin a nature like hers."

"I mean to take her up," said Aneta with spirit.

"Well," said Mrs. Ward, "the first thing to do is to get to-morrow over. I have no doubt it will be a success. Meanwhile, will you write a line to your uncle, Sir Charles, and ask him if he can call here to see these treasures?"

"Yes, I will write to him at once," said Aneta. "He spends most of his time at the British Museum. Couldn't I send him a wire, Mrs. Ward, and then he would come to-night?"

"Yes, that is a very good idea. Do so, my love."

The girls had a very spirited rehearsal, and Maggie was her old vivacious, daring, clever self once more. That inward change which no doubt had taken place brought an added charm to her always expressive face.

Between seven and eight that evening Aneta's uncle, Sir Charles, arrived. He and Mrs. Ward had a long consultation. His opinion was that the bracelets and other curios were worth at least seven thousand pounds, and that such a sum could easily be obtained for them.

"In fact, I myself would buy them for that figure," said Sir Charles. "It is not only that there are in this collection some unique and valuable stones; but the history, the setting, and the make of these ancient relics would induce the British Museum to buy many of them. Doubtless, however, Miss Howland will get the biggest price of all for them if they are auctioned at Christie's."

Before she went to bed that night Aneta told Maggie that she was by no means a penniless girl, and that if she would consent to having her father's treasures sold she would have sufficient money to be well educated, and have a nice nest-egg in the future to start in any profession she fancied.

"Oh Aneta, it is all too wonderful!" said poor Maggie—"to think of me as I am to-night, and of me as I felt last night when I wanted to lose myself in the London fog. Aneta, I can never love you enough!"

"You want a good long sleep," she said. "Think of to-morrow and all the excitement which lies before us!"

Maggie did sleep soundly that night, for she was quite worn out, and when Saturday arrived she awoke without a fear and with a wonderful lightness of heart. The day of the festival and rejoining passed without a hitch. The supper was delightful. The tableaux vivants were the best the school had ever seen. The games, the fun, made the Cardews at least think that they had entered into a new world.

But perhaps the best scene of all came at the end when Aneta went up to Maggie and took her hand, and, still holding it, turned and faced the assembled school.

"Maggie and I don't mean to be rival queens any longer," she said. "We are joint-queens. All Maggie's subjects are my subjects and all my subjects are Maggie's. Any girl who disapproves of this, will she hold down her hand? Any girl who approves, will she hold her hand up in the air?"

Instantly all the pairs of hands were raised, and there was such a clapping and so many cheers for the queens who were no longer rival queens that mademoiselle was heard to exclaim, "But it is charming. It makes the heart to bound. I do love the English manner, and Mademoiselle Aneta, *si jolie, si élégante*; and Mademoiselle Maggie, who has a large charm. I do make homage to them as the two queens. I would," she continued, turning and clasping Miss Johnson's hands, "be a schoolgirl myself to be a subject of them."

A few words will suffice to end this story. Lady Lysle might be proud and perhaps somewhat disdainful, but she was at least as good as her word, and in a very short time Martin the grocer thought it worth his while to open a very smart-looking shop in the West End. This shop Lady Lysle took a curious interest in and recommended to her friends, so that Martin began to do as sound a business in the neighborhood of Eaton Square as he did in Shepherd's Bush. Of all things in the world, he liked best to make money, and he was quite glad to be rid of Maggie when his own prospects became golden owing to her absence from his premises.

As to Mrs. Martin, she was content to see her daughter occasionally.

Maggie's curios were all sold, except the little brooch (which she kept for herself in memory of her father), for a sufficiently large sum to pay for her education and to leave her enough money to do well for herself by-and-by. Having no longer anything to conceal, and under the beautiful, brave influence of Aneta, she became quite a different girl. That strength of character and that strange fascination which were her special powers were now turned into useful channels. Maggie could never be beautiful, but her talents were above the average, and her moral nature now received every stimulus in the right direction. Merry Cardew could love her, and gain good, not harm, from her influence. But, strange to say—although perhaps not strange—Aneta was her special friend. It was with Aneta that Maggie mostly spent her holidays. It was Aneta's least word that Maggie obeyed. It was for Aneta's approval that Maggie lived.

Queens of the school they still remain, each exercising her influence in her own way, and yet both working in perfect harmony.

"Have they not both the characters beautiful?" said mademoiselle. "I think there is no girl like the English girl."

Doubtless she is right.

THE END

Lightning Source UK Ltd.
Milton Keynes UK
UKHW010634240820
368739UK00001B/290